Also, by Michael P Brawn
Pangur Ban
Flaming Margarita
TENSE
The Wollemi
Wollemi Dreaming
Killara

FLAMING MARGARITA

MARGARITA

THE STORY OF PATERSON CURSE

MICHAEL BRAWN

Published 2018

First Printing 2018

2nd Edition 2023

ISBN 978-0-6480912-9-5

Published by Louise Brawn

ashbourne.publishing1@gmail.com

DEDICATION

To my soul mate, wife and publisher, Louise.

Thank you. Without your support and patience, this little book would never have seen the light of day.

This book is dedicated to Louise, who has had to read, edit and comment on every last page. Thank you, my love.

CONTENTS

ACKNOWLEDGEMENTS

I would like to thank Ivana Milosavljević and Jelena Telečki without whose helpful comments and advice, this book would never have been completed.

UNDERSTANDING

I was born the second son of an Irish Aristocrat and a British spy. Many peculiar incidents and odd coincidences sprinkle themselves throughout my young life. And so, I come to understand the value of ambiguity at an early age. It is just as well as things turned out. But more of that later.

I learned the Bemba language as a child in Zambia and Afrikaans when we moved to Swaziland. Bemba and Afrikaans were the languages of play – one for use with the Afrikaner kids who lived near us and the other with the African kids who lived on our farm. Being at least a little bilingual was helpful as my family hosted anti-colonial African political events in our garden as well as BBQs with the settler neighbours, quite a social mix. I learned to be equivocal at all times. My entire worldview became relativistic and vague.

Later I lost my innocence, my tolerance for ambiguity and my wife, all in one gut-wrenching moment - more on that later too.

Right at this instant, as I stand here now, I have lost my mind. I firmly believe I am going mad. In any case, I am now behaving rashly, incoherently and with apparent indifference to the truth.

If I'm honest, I have no way of knowing the actual state of affairs, if there is one, and I am long past caring if there is.

I have several millimetres of grey stubble on my face, my hair is lank and uncombed, I don't smell particularly good, and I haven't brushed my teeth in days. I am in desperate need of a long hot shower. However, at this juncture, none of these matters to me at all.

What matters is what I am throwing away. My marriage and most of my friendships. Why, after a quarter of a century, am I chucking it all away? I have no truly convincing answer. Not yet.

I am able to fumble towards the beginnings of an answer with the blessed peace on the line after she hangs up - before some automated nanny system starts beeping at me to hang up too.

I don't know if I am in love with the woman who now shares my bed or if I am merely infatuated, as my wife says. I wonder if it will all come crashing down on my head one day. Will I go crawling back?

Now that it really matters, now that it is absolutely of the essence, I find that I do not know, or perhaps no longer know, what love is anyway, exactly. I thought I was in love before, but I realise our marriage was mainly just convenient. My life was comfortable. Work was ok, home life was ok, and sex was acceptable if perfunctory.

Suppose I went back home now. If I threw myself on her mercy and begged to be taken back. If I said she was right all along, it was just an infatuation, a middle-life crisis or a nervous breakdown. Would that actually fix things? Would it solve our problems? Is going back a solution at all to anything, ever?

I do know this, though. I have glimpsed blue sky and sunshine. I have been provided with an image of another life, an afterlife in a way, perhaps a better life. It may be a lie, or a mirage, but so what?

I wonder if she is real, my lover. Is she as I see her, or is she, in fact, a perfectly pleasant woman in early middle age who, like me, is just not quite ready to give up? Is she the angel she appears to me to be or is that an illusion that will also fade, revealing just another woman fighting the effects of gravity and disappointment?

I'm not sure if this is really relevant, but I'll tell you anyway. I met a mad man once. A man whom I now recognise could easily have been myself or who might as well have been for all the difference it would make. He told me he had walked with angels and talked with demons. He explained how, in the plain light of day, in an ordinary English pub, he would often meet them. A demon, leaning his saturnine bulk against the bar, nursing a pint of bitter, glaring around at the unseeing humans clumped here and there around the room, and an angel, smoking a pipe by the fire, reading the sports pages of the London Times. The man would nod politely at each and make his way to the bar. Sometimes, occasionally, they would engage him in conversation. Nothing earth-shattering. Who did he fancy for the upcoming Grand National? Did he agree that the referee of last night's match was plainly either blind or stupid? Just idle chit-chat.

Who else could say that he asked me? Why would he give up an existence that included angels and devils for the drab, mundane greys of everyday life?

"No, son, give me my madness any day, and I'll take the transcendental joy and despair that come with it."

In the end, I think it is better to have suffered, every moment of every day, of a long and extraordinary life than to have lived comfortably in mediocrity. I can afford to think that now, from the safety of distance, but there is absolutely nothing in my history to suggest I could actually stick it out.

If nothing else, I do feel that I have won the freedom to experience a little joy in my life alongside the pain.

And I know this, there is no going back, ever, for anyone.

DOH!

I am drawn out of the demanding swirl of memory into my haphazard reality by insistent banging on my hotel room door accompanied by the wheedling tones of a drunk.

"Charlene, honey, let me in. I lost the damned key card".

I re-orient myself in time and space, New Orleans, again. I glance at the clock. It is two in the morning. I have been sitting at the window staring into space for hours. I am covered in a slick of sweat. My head is pounding. A rank smell pervades my hotel room, and there is a bitter taste on my tongue. Daggers of pain shoot through my head with each imbecilic bang on the door. I have a high fever. I am delirious.

I do not open the door, but through it, I explain that he has the wrong room. There is no Charlene here. This requires several iterations and variations until I hear him stumble off along the corridor.

I return to the window and stare out over New Orleans, still heaving with people, the sidewalks far below still crowded. A few moments later, I hear loud knocking on another door, followed by an altercation. I turn on the TV, CNN (something has happened somewhere).

Gazing out over the party city of New Orleans, remembering its various incarnations in movies and on TV, the Big Easy, home of the blues, I start to piece things together. I am a little late in doing this, decades late, but better late than never.

I am dimly aware that I have already set in motion a series of events that are likely to result in the ending of my marriage.

- Firstly, I have started a hopeless, wonderfully romantic, and entirely passionate, impossible long-distance affair with my wife's supposed best friend.

- Secondly, and this is a biggie, following on from the above, I have fallen madly in love – for the first time.
- Thirdly, I know now that I will never return to live in Ireland, or England for that matter.
- Finally, I am beginning to recognise that my wife's mental processes are not really compatible with mine and may not, in truth, be compatible with reality.

This all comes as something of a surprise, which, on reflection, is surprising in itself.

I am Paterson Curse. Everyone calls me Pat. This is my statement. Always an approximation, partial, aspectual and incomplete. The boy I once was, is gone. His memory remains.

I have woken from a twenty-year coma. There is a name on a crumpled scrap of paper clasped tight in my closed fist. It is *her* name. From a state of 'innocence', I have re-entered Karma. I am responsible. I take responsibility. I am no longer innocent. I am … Pinocchio.

Maybe I should back up a bit.

I am ten years old. Happy, though tending always to solitude and my own thoughts. We live, my family and I, above the tree-line almost at the summit of the Drakensberg Mountains in Swaziland, in a cluster of round, conjoining huts known as 'rondavels'. The view is breathtaking. We are on top of the world. Seas of wattle forest heave and sway off and away, blue in the distance. The thatched roofs of the rondavels ensure cosy warmth in winter and coolness in summer. In the huge open fireplace, green logs have been arranged, waiting for winter. Amber sap oozes, sticky to the touch. The hand-woven grass mats on the floor have a familiar, slightly sickly, sweet smell.

Next to our home, there is a fold in the hills through which runs a stream of pure spring water from its source two hundred metres above. The water tastes good. I lean over a flat dry rock, bringing my lips down to the crystal flow, sipping directly from the source.

In the many waterfalls and pools scattered across the mountains live the shy, mercurial platannas, a rare species of amphibian, a kind of cross between a frog and a newt, of extraordinary antiquity, said to be contemporaneous with the dinosaurs. While on the grassy mountainsides live what is, to almost all intents and purposes, a species of rabbit, differing from rabbits only insofar as they are entirely unrelated. These we know by the Afrikaans word 'dassies' (Hyrax to a zoologist). I am told that, morphologically, their nearest living relative is the hippopotamus or maybe a horse, but I am only ten and cannot vouch for the accuracy of that.

To me, at this time, life is idyllic. I am completely happy.

I have awakened sexually but am still innocent. I am ten. So is she. We walk together across the barren heath to a secret place, a dell hidden from prying eyes, surrounded by stunted cork trees. The yellow-brown grass is soft and warm and smells of summer. We regard each other, frankly, as children, unaware that all this will change. Each on our several missions of discovery, unknowing, almost oblivious of the other, but set, nevertheless, on the same path.

The sounds, almost the very existence, of the world outside our hiding place are muffled and dampened by twisted, fire-blackened trees. We talk briefly for appearances and then set to our platonic, scientific courtship. Stuttering, we manage to convey the same meaning, each to the other – or similar enough. Let us nonchalantly remove our clothes, let us undress. No ostensible end in mind, offhand. Let us, as if by chance, see the other, naked, insipient.

Lovely, beautiful golden hairs, almost invisible to the eye, adorn her. Fascinating, wonderful, of unknown, perhaps unknowable, significance. Transfixed, mesmerised, seduced, we watch each other disrobe. Mine is the most remarkable response, rigid, hard. Eager for that which is yet unknown.

"Is it usually like that?" A simple question.

"Well, sometimes. No, not usually" Absolute innocence.

"Why is it like that now, then?"

Honestly perplexed, I search for some explanation, some rationale. I fail.

"I have no idea. Can I touch you? You have lots of little golden hairs".

"No. I don't think it's allowed, but you can look if you like."

I look, I stare, I examine, amazed.

We both, without a signal, get dressed again.

I have learned perhaps the fundamental lesson of my life. The female is simultaneously worldly, mysterious and divine.

. . .

We live at the school, Waterford-Kamkhlaba, protected, for a little while, from the political, ideological and magical forces sweeping Africa.

The school, set in a wattle forest a few hundred metres below our home, is structured after the manner of, or, more accurately, apes, a British public school. The curriculum is designed to prepare children for the Oxford and Cambridge examination boards – an antipodean Hogwarts, alien in both culture and ethos to the societies from which its inmates are drawn, offering a similarly bewildering introduction to a world hitherto at best suspected – manufacturing the Magi of modern Africa.

I am wandering across the high heath with a friend, a boy of startling physical ugliness whose name, fortunately, I have forgotten. I am engaged in a reverie on the absolute beauty of the wilderness. I am, as always, aware of myself taking in the innocence of nature and of watching myself doing it. The scene stays with me as one of those perfect childhood moments when one's intellect has become capable of seeing the adult world but has neither entered into it fully nor yet succumbed.

BOURBON STREET

I have been living. We have been living in Sydney for nine months, the first several of which have been much like a holiday. We tour the harbour by boat, visit the Opera House, eat seafood in Darling Harbour and sunbathe on Manly and Bondi beaches. Peter, our eldest boy (thirteen), takes to Australia with gusto – wet suit, board shorts, shark tooth pendant etc.

Over the last three months, things have begun to unravel. Miniscule fissures begin to appear in our marriage, or I begin to notice them. I am exhausted at work, and at home, I feel alone.

My wife is still beautiful at forty-five, still smart, sassy, and funny. Companion of over twenty years and the mother of our two glorious boys.

Things have not been great in our relationship for many years, but through custom and habit, we soldier on, for my part, scarcely noticing. It is not until Australia that the cracks, so carefully papered over, become plain. Thrown back on our own resources, no friends, no family, and our support network missing, I begin to see through the illusion so cunningly co-constructed over many years in Dublin. We are obviously no longer 'in love' though love is present.

We have not slept in the same bed for thirteen years (my snoring, she says), and we scarcely make love. We are sharing a home and co-parenting our children. She is intensely homesick and cannot bring herself to find work or really engage with Australia. She is rootless, a tumble weed, likely to blow away into the desert at the slightest breeze. I, on the other hand, love Australia. It has been my dream to move here for fifteen years. Indeed, the entire reason I got into the computer industry in the first place, even why I joined 'the company that powers the internet', was to get to Australia.

When I first look into moving, the preferred jobs are.

- Teacher of Mathematics
- Teacher of Japanese
- Silver Service Waiter
- Systems Analyst

Even though I have no idea what a Systems Analyst is, the choice is clearly a no-brainer.

I am now in New Orleans again, at another conference, staying in another huge, soulless hotel, slightly feverish from a chest infection picked up on the flight from Sydney to Dublin via London (round-the-world ticket), seriously jet lagged, inevitably drunk, disorientated and alone. I am beginning to realise that all is not well with me mentally. In short, I am seriously losing it.

I am brooding, of course. New Orleans is sweating and heaving outside. I am sitting on the edge of the bed, dozens of floors up, overlooking a lazy bend in the Mississippi River, watching CNN (something else has happened somewhere else) and brooding. I do not feel loved and have not felt loved for many years. She does not feel loved and has not felt loved for many years. My head is pounding gently, and there is heat behind my eyes. I suspect that I have drunk a little too much beer on an empty stomach. Brooding becomes reverie. Reverie becomes waking dream. Memories flood back. This is all getting a bit too heavy. I decide to leave my hotel room and face the music of New Orleans.

Late night, Bourbon Street, steamy heat, blues blaring from somewhere, from everywhere. Men on balconies shouting, "Get yer tits out for the boys!" or some American equivalent thereof. Girls promenading the street below, occasionally obliging in return for strings of tacky, brightly coloured beads. Roars of appreciation from the balconies, seductive giggles from the street. That's better.

WHOEVER SAID LIFE WAS FAIR?

We are leaving Swaziland today. I can't believe it! Why are we going? What's the point? I am dejected, utterly bereft.

My sister Minnie is saying her last goodbyes to Jenny. Jenny is heading off to school. She stops to give me a big hug.

"I won't see you again. Have a lovely time in England".

"That's it!?" I think to myself, impotent, furious.

Out of the corner of my eye, I see Minnie heading up the mountainside towards 'her rock', the flat rock we all call Elangeni (a Swazi word meaning sun or sunlight) because it catches the morning sun. Minnie will lay there basking like a lizard and thinking her thoughts until it's time to leave. A warm breeze brings with it the susurration and trace of the wattle forest.

My sister Ingrid is only three years old, born in Zambia just before we moved south. She barely understands what's going on. I think she thinks we are going on holiday somewhere. My older brother Sam is eager to go. He can't wait to explore a whole new country!

Most of our stuff, what survived the trip from London to Zambia, and from Zambia to Swaziland, has already been shipped. I am wearing a pair of shorts and a stripy T-shirt. The sun is warm on the mountain side. The air is clear, the world is clean, and I am leaving.

"What's it like in London?" I ask my Dad.

"It's wonderful. A huge city, marvellous museums, you can get anything you want in London".

"Do they have dassies?"

"Well, no, probably not dassies exactly, but rabbits – same thing, really."

"What about platannas?"

"No platannas either, old son, but plenty of frogs and toads."

I begin to ask something else, but he wanders off, distracted.

"Mum." I tug at her sleeve, demanding her attention, "Mum. It's just not fair!"

She looks down at me, neither angry nor empathetic if anything slightly surprised.

"Fair?" She rolls the word around silently for a moment or two, considering it.

"Whoever told you life was fair?"

Her delivery takes my breath away, so matter-of-fact, as though it were so blindingly obvious she couldn't understand how I had not figured it out for myself. I am being dragged away from the lovely, lonely mountains to some stinking frozen city of substitutes, where life is not only not fair, but fairness is not even to be looked for.

The journey to the ship in Cape Town (one way, one-time family visa from the apartheid government) takes several days by coach, train, car and taxi.

My brother and sisters are sitting with mum and dad at the front of the coach. Minnie has her nose stuck in a book as usual, and Ingrid is making eyes at the bus driver. Sam is staring resolutely out of the window, stifling any show of emotion. I am sitting at the back of the coach, chatting with a friend as the bus approaches the South African border. The driver pulls the bus over and looks back at me meaningfully. My friend's mother catches the driver's eye and explains to me that we are approaching the border and I have to go sit up front with my parents.

"That's ok", I say. "They know where I am".

She looks uncomfortable and tries to explain again. My mum, realising what is going on, walks back down the bus to get me.

"Why do I have to move?" I ask.

"In South Africa, white people sit at the front of the bus, and black people sit at the back."

I smile, enjoying the joke.

"No, really darling, black people and white people are not allowed to sit together in South Africa."

I realise she is serious and follow her up the bus. I am about halfway up when it hits me.

"That's the most ridiculous thing I've ever heard." I proceed to fits of giggles.

The other passengers stare at me, amazed, aghast. Then slowly, they, too, break into fits of giggles. It is hilariously, *insanely* funny. Even the driver smiles a little as he re-starts the bus, and we trundle off towards the border.

At the border, on the South African side, two or three paramilitary policemen board the bus and demand, in Afrikaans, to see all passports. They pass through the Whites with perfunctory courtesy and proceed to the back of the bus, where they examine all documents minutely and, apparently out of habit rather than for any real purpose, cross-examine each individual at some length. The process concludes without incident. The bus moves on.

I experience the journey from then on as a series of disconnected, possibly random, impressions. We are in the diamond capital, Kimberley, at midnight, about to board a steam train to take us through the Karoo dessert to Cape Town. Many people move around the floodlit station, striding purposefully. The shouting of railmen, the clanging of gates and the clashing of steel blend with the pervasive smell of diesel and coal. The fluttering moths in the baleful, bitter lights, and the warmth of the night air to combine to create a frightening alien wonderland, full of promise.

I wander off from my family to a French-style pissoir to relieve myself. While I am in there, two enormous, black, diamond mine security guards enter carrying metre-long nightsticks and stand on either side of me, attending to their business. I stare up at them in awe. They are two of the tallest, blackest people I have ever seen. They must be twice my height, stern, aloof, and in some archetypal way, incredibly beautiful. The men prepare to leave, hardly having deigned to notice the tiny little white boy in the wrong toilet. I hear three loud hoots from the steam engine. My father strides in, looking for me and bumps into one of the men. He looks up at the man's face and, with his perfect, patrician manners, apologises. There is a momentary stand-off as the men absorb the apology. With graceful nods, they acknowledge my father's right to exist. Both men look down at me and shuffle past without a word.

"Where do they come from?" I ask my dad.

"They're Ashanti. The mines use them as security guards because everyone is terrified of them".

"I bet you're not afraid of them."

"I wouldn't be too sure of that old son."

A blue-white flood-light buzzes overhead in a swarm of insects. The engine hoots twice, and we hurry back to my mother, brother and sisters.

The next day, by the time I awake, we are already well out into a scrubby desert. I run up and down the train annoying all the other passengers and getting in everyone's way. Ingrid and Minnie are doing a jigsaw puzzle of an elephant. Mum and Dad are reading, and Sam has disappeared.

I stick my head out of the window as far as I can. There is a small, worn notice on the sill, written in English and Afrikaans, saying, "Do not put your head out of the window!"

As the train rounds a lazy bend, I see, way, way off in the distance, across the flat, featureless plain, a tiny settlement. Smoke from the engine and tiny cinders swirl back along the train. I pull my head back in and slam the window shut as the guard appears at the opposite end of the carriage. He gives me a stern look.

Hours pass as the town separates by infinitesimal degrees into individual structures. I can make out the water tower, the station itself and a couple of other buildings - tiny specs on the horizon. Hours after that, we approach the town, near enough now to distinguish people, trucks, and horses.

On the station platform, three or four men sit on straight-backed chairs leaning against the wall. They appear to be asleep, wide-brimmed leather hats pulled down over their faces, long straight rifles or shotguns leaned against the wall next to them. They have impressively bushy sideburns and moustaches, long straggly beards. They look for all the world like a little row of Rip Van Winkles. I watch, fascinated, as the train thunders into the station. The wagon I am in pulls up alongside the men. They do not wake up or so much as stir. I imagine that the arrival of the train is probably the only single thing that has happened in this remote settlement for weeks. The engine hisses at length and falls silent. There is some desultory moving about. Someone jumps down from the train for a minute to stretch their legs.

All is quiet until the shouts of the driver and mate to the station master cut across the stillness as arrangements are made to refill the water compartment and load on more coal. Still, the Rip Van Winkles snooze, insensible, inert.

Perhaps twenty minutes pass before the engine coughs back into life, and the train chugs breathily out towards the desert evening. As I look back, I see that the men on the station platform still have not moved.

In the distance, towards the back of the train, I can hear one of the stewards (double-breasted 1930s Bell Hop uniform, pill box hat with a strap under chin) playing the 'dinner' tune on a small xylophone as he walks the length of the train. My mother wanders up. She is looking for me. Families with children attend the first sitting for dinner. I point at the men, now all but invisible against the receding station wall.

"They stayed asleep the whole time."

My mother looks back at the settlement for a few moments before replying.

"There are no steam trains in the Old Testament".

She takes my hand, and we head back down the train towards the dining car. I have absolutely no idea what she means.

I experience the most peculiar effect as I step down from the train in Cape Town two days later. The concrete platform sways slightly, and passengers totter this way and that. In the matter-of-fact way of children, I note the phenomenon as just one more oddity pertaining to South Africa.

"Don't worry, old son. You'll get your land legs back in a minute or two".

I am not worried, but by the same token, I am not at all sure what 'land legs' are.

"Three days on a moving train is like three days at sea. It makes you feel wobbly when the movement stops". A moment later, my father continues, "What's the Afrikaans word for 'Taxi'?" he asks me. (In Swaziland, we were taught in English, Zulu and Afrikaans, so he assumes I am fluent in each). I look around and see a sign saying "Taxi".

"Taxi?" I suggest.

All our stuff is loaded into the taxi, and we head off like The Clampets into the bustling metropolis. As far as I can recall, I have never seen such a huge city. The noise of car horns and traffic is deafening, and there are people everywhere, charging this way and that as though their lives depended on it.

We drive for some considerable time until it becomes plain that the driver cannot, among the maze of tiny streets in the port area, find the specific berth we need. The car pulls to a stop by the side of the road, and a brief conversation starts up (unaccountably, in a combination of French and German) between my father and the hapless driver. It emerges that the driver (who speaks perfectly good English or would, if he were allowed to) is standing-in for his brother who is sick, using his brother's dompass (internal passport – bizarre country) for the day in order to protect his brother's job. Assurances are sought and given that no mention will be made to the authorities of this infringement. My father turns to my elder brother, Samuel, and explains that in a moment or two, a car will come around the bend a few hundred metres behind us and stop a little way back. When it does, my brother is to walk back to the car and ask the occupants if they know the way to the berth we want.

We all wait silently for the predicted vehicle and are suitably impressed when, sure enough, a few moments later, a car does appear and stop, exactly as foretold. All of us children look curiously at my father from the back seat of the taxi, hoping for some explanation.

"Quick now, Sam" My father is wearing his "I am the All-Seeing-All-Knowing-One" expression, "Pop back and ask them the way".

We all squint through the grubby back window of the taxi at my brother's receding back. Even Minnie sets down her book for a moment to watch. In the distant car, we can make out a flurry of shuffling newspapers and window closing.

My brother approaches the car in which two men, now with their windows tightly shut against the cooling breeze, are sitting nonchalantly, reading the day's news. My brother taps on the driver's window. He peers over the edge of his newspaper, apparently startled at the unexpected appearance and reluctantly lets his window down an inch or two. There follows a short interchange between my brother and the driver. The window is wound back up as the driver confers with his passenger. Several minutes pass. My brother looks back towards our taxi holding his arms in the air with a "What do I do now?" expression on his face.

The driver lets down his window an inch and speaks to my brother, who nods and jogs back to the taxi. He gets in and tells my father that, as a matter of fact, the two men do know the whereabouts of our ship and have offered to lead us to it. My father is laughing quietly to himself. He turns to the taxi driver and, with obvious relish, declaims, "Follow that car" – in English.

We follow that car back through most of the little streets we have just traversed and turn right into the passenger terminal area. The berths are numbered, and in a few minutes, we have arrived at the ship. It is a very large P&O passenger liner with many decks. I do not like the look of it at all.

Our escorts drive away, my mother and father watching them surreptitiously.

"Just making absolutely sure we leave." I hear my father whisper.

"You know it's the strangest thing," my brother pipes up, "They read their newspapers upside down in South Africa." Another datum to be stored and pondered.

The ship is full of Australians, picked up earlier in Melbourne, heading back to Britain to visit 'the rellies'. Until then, I hadn't realised that England was part of something bigger. We board slowly and awkwardly, a straggling line of suitcases and bags stumbling up the gang plank. Once on board, I notice different accents. My siblings and I have the Afrikaans accents of white settlers, my father has a refined BBC English accent, and my mother has the endearingly plummy accent of the British aristocracy in Ireland. By the time we arrive at Tilbury docks on the Thames outside London six weeks later, I have an Australian accent. This need to change myself to fit my environment, which still characterises my adult life, has been present since my earliest youth. I resist for a bit out of sheer bloody-mindedness, then adapt, eventually.

Despite my doubts the trip to England is fantastic. There are hundreds of kids to play with and virtually no supervision. My mother and father share a cabin with my sisters, but my brother and I have our own cabin. We strike the obvious mutual non-interference pact the first night. Thereafter, I am unfettered and free for six whole weeks, no questions asked.

We stop off in the Canary Islands to buy sombreros, wicker donkeys and metre-long cigars, and in Lisbon to be dunked, briefly, in baroque culture.

After that comes the Bay of Biscay and the flying fish. We are warned by the crew that the Bay is often very rough, and they are right, it is. Within a few hours of leaving port, the wind comes up, and the sea swells. Within a few more hours, a powerful gale is blowing, and the ship is pitching and yawing alarmingly. The wind is wailing like a banshee. All very exciting.

From the top deck, I can make out the flying fish emerging like silver-green darts from the top of the swells and hurtling through the air, apparently for the sheer joy of it, only to crash back into the troughs. The smell of ozone and sea water is strong, and there is a constant fine shower of froth blown from the tops of the waves.

Suddenly the most brilliant idea occurs to me. I am on 'A' deck, way above the water, but I remember the tiny 'F' deck, five levels below. Naturally, there is nothing for it but to scamper down the stairs to see if I can get a closer look. The bulkhead door to 'F' deck has not been locked! I slip through and close it behind me. The sea is absolutely wild. The waves crash against the outer bulkhead, and, glory of glories, flying fish leap in some inexplicable fishy frenzy and collide in their dozens against the back wall of the narrow observation deck. Fish are swirling around my feet as I hang on to the outer rail. The sea heaves the ship this way and that. The noise is deafening. A couple of times, I lose my footing. Suddenly I feel myself being lifted bodily by the scruff of the neck. My feet leave the ground, and I am deposited unceremoniously inside the ship. The bosun is short and massively square. He is covered in tattoos, sweat and stains and stinks of diesel. Sweat drips from his fat red nose onto his dirty, faded blue shirt. I am at peace. I have temporarily lost the faculty of fear, thank God. He stares at me for a moment in bewilderment and fury before explaining.

"You are a stupid, stupid little cunt! What are you?!" He locks the 'F' deck door and stamps off without waiting for an answer. I am soaked to the skin, chilled to the bone and utterly elated – I have a flying fish in my pocket!

SOME KIND OF SPEECH DEFECT

England is unremittingly dreary. The ugly little houses tend to infinity in every direction. The landscape is flat and grey. The people I glimpse hurrying around the terminal are fat and grey. Even the sky is grey. The air smells stale, and the colours, even of familiar things, seem drab and lifeless. This is not going well, this 'England' thing. We take a Taxi (English word 'Taxi') to Clapham South in London, where my Auntie Alice lives. The journey lasts forever. In comparison with London, Cape Town seems like a village. We are all cramped together in a black London cab, jumpers, coats, and cases piled up on top of us.

"Best taxis in the world, the London taxis!" My father pronounces ingratiatingly. Loud enough for the taxi driver to hear through the sliding glass partition. As expected, the taxi driver engages my father in conversation.

"Just back from the colonies, are you?"

"Yes, eight years in Zambia and Swaziland."

"Expect you're glad to get away from all those blacks, aren't you?" Warming to his subject, he continues.

"Mind you. It's just as bad here now. Blacks all over the place!" My mother shoots my father an inscrutable look for which he clearly has no answer. However, before he can introduce a new line of conversation, the driver continues.

"Still, they're not all bad." This is evidently something of a new thought for him which he ponders for a moment or two before continuing.

"There's one of 'em works down the garage, a mechanic that can fix anything."

The taxi driver swerves, rolling down his window, and enquires.

"You, considering getting' a licence, are you love?" An harassed-looking woman throws him a venomous look and sticks up two fingers before turning down a side road. The taxi driver carries on, chuckling at his own enormous wit. My father seizes the opportunity to shift the conversation to a more amenable track.

"How much longer to Clapham South now, do you think?"

"About half an hour, mate. Sit back and enjoy the ride."

London slips by outside the taxi window under a slate grey sky. Conversation ceases. We are all preoccupied with our own thoughts.

Suddenly I see a huge ancient stone castle and a bridge with two tall towers at either end. I recognise these from the lid of Mum's biscuit tin.

"That's the Tower of London. Where they lock up traitors before beheading them". I am not sure if Dad's snippet is of merely historic relevance or not.

We fly over Tower Bridge in a few moments, catching a glimpse of a wide greasy river and a few barges laden with rubbish. My father calls out place names, familiar and new, as we go. Old Kent Road (familiar), Elephant and Castle (new). We know we are closing in as we pass a sign saying Clapham North almost immediately followed by Clapham Common and soon, in the near distance, a large round blue and red sign saying 'Clapham South'.

The taxi pulls into a tiny circular driveway in front of a block of flats. We begin to decant as Sam is sent upstairs to the third floor to announce our arrival. A minute or two later, a pretty dark-haired woman and two girls come racing out into the courtyard. There is much jumping around and cries of "You're finally here!" and "Yes, we're finally here!"

Auntie Alice has the exact same accent my mum has! Until that moment, I think I had subconsciously always assumed it was some kind of speech defect. I meet my two cousins, Finula and Aisling, girls, and my uncle Hamish. They live in a tiny flat above the tube station and have folding wooden chairs with red seats.

They are clearly all very nice, but I am damned if I am going to admit it. Alice is a flurry of hospitality. We are given strong Irish

Breakfast tea in good china cups, tea cakes, large slices of the Barn Brack (Irish fruit cake, also made with tea) and endless crumpets.

Minnie, Ingrid, Aisling and Finula are sitting on the carpet playing nicely. They have tipped out the enormous button box and are now peacefully sorting the contents, each according to their own arbitrary taxonomy. This appears to be a family thing, as we used to sort the button box in Swaziland during the winters when the snow was too thick to venture out.

I zone out. I stare out of the window at Clapham Common, green, featureless other than a number of threadbare trees devoid of dassies or, for that matter, even rabbits.

We move into a flat nearby on Cavendish Road. My brother and I are enrolled in an apparently 'good' school, Nathaniel College, in Battersea. The school uniform is to be purchased at Harrods. My mother finds Minnie a place in 'well thought of' Grammar School for girls in Tooting. Schooling for girls is not a priority for my father. Ingrid goes to the local primary school round the corner. Mum and Dad get jobs.

We are finally here. I hate it. I shut down. I make a secret vow with myself never to like it here, never to give in to it.

The entry requirement for Nathaniel College is a successful pass mark in the 'Eleven Plus' exam. However, my father thinks this is unnecessary. He visits the College Principal bringing with him my brother and myself (cleaned and scrubbed) and a briefcase containing a bottle of very good malt Scotch and two glasses. His meeting with the principal goes on and on. We are sent out to explore the ancient grounds. The college itself is made of Redbrick with castellations covered in red and gold Virginia Creeper. There is a Coat of Arms barely visible on one gable wall. After an hour or so, we are called back.

Father is vindicated. The Eleven Plus exam is superfluous. We are in.

My first day at Nathaniel College was a bit mixed. My mother and father can only afford for one of us to have the Harrods uniform, so I turn up in my Waterford burgundy blazer, a gold phoenix on the pocket, and grey flannel shorts. It is England in late autumn, I am at secondary school, and no one would be seen dead in shorts. Great start. I get a blue blazer from the school's second-hand shop and some grey flannel trousers. Better. I am eleven years old, and against my better judgement, I make friends. Things are ok. Time passes.

Nathaniel College is, formally, similar to Waterford, however, as it is located within the English state education system and situated within the historical and cultural traditions of a now decrepit colonial power, imbued with the class consciousness and supposed ethos of the British ruling elite. It is a hell hole.

SEX!

I am thirteen and desperate to lose my virginity, which I sort of do as follows. I meet one of Minnie's school friends, a mature girl of sixteen, known to be 'experienced'. She is blonde and big boned with exemplary breasts. Something about my upbringing in Africa has given me a small head start over my comrades in terms of self-confidence and emotional maturity. I am not in the least concerned that she is three years older than me. I am, indeed, quite delighted.

We go back to her house to listen to records and talk about the meaning of life. We are sitting on her bed, chatting. I am attempting to be engaging and funny and much, much more mature than thirteen. It seems to be working, somehow. She intervenes with some peculiar sleight-of-hand that girls must be taught secretly by older girls (like that weird thing they do when they take their bras off without taking their tops off first – apropos of which, I would just like to put on record what a despicable and mean trick it is!) and we are suddenly in a slightly awkward embrace.

She kisses me wetly on the lips. It is not my first time. It is not entirely unpleasant. I am not sure what to do next. I stroke a wisp of blonde hair from her forehead. It seems to be the right thing to do. She leans closer and strokes my cheek. She has a pleasant face. She is comfortably round and warm. I stroke her neck, allowing my hand, accidentally, to slip slowly down across her breast. She smiles - thank God. I decide to kiss her. I am not certain how one negotiates noses. They seem to be strategically placed to get in the way. I tilt my head and lean forward. It is an awkward, inept movement. She comes to my rescue. Slipping her hand behind my head, she pulls me towards her. This is more like it!

We kiss again, this time allowing a momentary conjunction of tongues, also not entirely unpleasant. I go for the breasts, sliding my hand under her t-shirt and up over her bra. I halt, wondering what to do with them now that I have them. I am simultaneously aware that I have an uncomfortably eager erection.

Sophisticated woman that she is, she removes her bra (by the underhand method alluded to above), and I cup her breast in my hand, allowing my fingertips gently to explore her hardening nipple.

Raw instinct kicks in - encouraged by lashings of hormones. I take her t-shirt by the hem and remove it in one upward sweeping movement. She is lying on the bed beneath me, face slightly flushed, hair tousled by the unceremonious divestment, her breasts glorious, full, heaving slightly. I straddle her, leaning forward slowly until my lips are mere millimetres from her ample bosom. She is expectant, waiting. The discomfort in my crotch area is extreme. I brush my lips against her warm silky skin. I kiss her breasts, her neck, her lips. We are both flushed and breathing hard. We kiss again, this time as lovers, our lips tender, our tongues gentle. Fired with raging new desire, having only the sketchiest notion of sex, we kiss with raw instinctual craving. Ripping off her remaining clothing, I touch her clumsily, innocently. I find her thigh – so smooth! So warm and inviting. My fingers seek out her pubic area (if 'area' is quite the right word. My friend Alison says it can only really be used bureaucratically, in partnership with words like 'picnic').

I explore a woman intimately for the first time. She lets out a little squeak of pleasure as my fingers enter her. She is hot and wet. I stroke her swiftly, my fingers seeming to know what is required. The discomfort in my jeans is too great to bear. Fumbling, I undo my belt and the top button of my jeans. She comes to my aid again, pulling down the zip and, in the same movement pulling my jeans and underpants down to my knees. Her soft, warm hand closes around me. I am ready to explode. I have never experienced such a glorious sensation. She strokes me with the tips of her fingers. I know it will not be long now. I continue the same strong rhythm of my fingers. She throws her head back, her lips parted, panting.

She lets out a slow, shuddering sigh, grasps my shaft firmly and finally, thankfully, I do explode. We share long, lingering kisses. We snuggle, we caress.

"Wow!" I think, "That was fantastic."

LIVING IN A PARALLEL UNIVERSE

Madrid in March. Icy winds rattle down from the high sierras. The window, open a few inches to let out cigarette smoke, is coated on both sides with a thin glossing of ice. Sounds from the nearby airport filter into the chilly room, edging past the smoke. The place reeks of tobacco and room service. I am alone again in a hotel-come-convention-centre, next to the motorway, across from the airport. I have seen my lover off at the airport. This is the third time we have been able to be together away from our respective spouses. It will probably be many months until we meet again. Sleet has turned once more to snow, hushing the world outside.

I revel in a warm bath of yearning and loss, self-indulgent, gothic and comforting. I cannot use her name, cannot demean her, define or encapsulate her with a label. She is my GODDESS, uppercase, capitalised. Her scent lingers on my clothes, spicy Spanish jasmine with a hint of flamenco, clinging to me, cloying, sweet. I recall the warmth of Her body next to mine, Her breath on my cheek. In my solitude, I make my affirmation, a prayer to the feminine divine, my Goddess. A part of me, the Observer, laughs spitefully just out of earshot. I trace complex desperate figures of adoration, scratching them in ice on the window with my fingernail, wishing for numbness and pain, invoking the Goddess through silly, futile sacrifice. I am desperate to erase the tactile memory of her skin etched upon my fingertips. I imagine my fingerprints on her body, revealed under ultraviolet light. The memory of her breast remains warm, cupped in my palm. I worship Her.

"Fuckwit!" I hear a snide voice in the back of my mind. Incipient schizophrenia or the Observer? I am past caring.

Her flight will be taking off any moment now. I stand by the window. With listless hatred, I watch each plane launch into the thin cold air. Time passes. I sit. I work through many hundreds of digital images on my lap-top computer. Photographs of friends, family, places, cataloguing and naming. I burn her a CD of these images, a mute taxonomy of broken relationships, a token. There is a light taint of ozone in the air. Somewhere an electrical fault buzzes.

I am ambushed by a photograph of her. My breath catches in my throat. I *want* her. Taunting memory floods back of the previous morning. I taste again the slight saltiness of her skin. My tongue caresses the softness of her thigh. With slow deliberation, I kiss, savouring her, ascending, penitent. Impertinent desire hooded but unashamed. Her hair, coiled, deep red, tickles my brow, my nose, my lips. I have arrived. At first, timidly, my tongue tries the warm softness of her, my lips caress. I am accepted. She shifts forward on the sheets, tilting her hips to accommodate my desire. I probe her more deeply, my tongue tingling with her taste, my senses combining, blurring. She moans, and my heart soars. I want to please her, to feel her rhythm, her mounting joy. She caresses my shoulders, and my neck, her strong hands pulling me firmly to her. Soft moans beat time. Her hips buck against me. My hands hold her fast now, containing, controlling. Tables turned. I have her. She is mine completely! I tease her deliberately, changing rhythm, slowing. I relish her frustration. She pleads silently, rocking her pelvis. I wait, establishing my gift, mastering her. I pull her to me, her body strung tight like a musical instrument. I play an allegro. Ravishing, I am ravished. She cries aloud, rigid, taut. She subsides. I lie next to her, holding her so tenderly, so close. She wraps herself around me, kissing me, stroking my back, murmuring, sensuous, almost wanton. I am complete. She completes me - and I, her. She is my saviour. At long last, I have been awakened by her kiss.

BROKEN

I have been avoiding discussion of my wife, my supposed life partner, mother of my children, knowing that the time shall come, preparing myself for it. Perhaps this is a good time to tell you about her. Not as she is now, but as she was when we first kissed at sixteen.

Her name is Miriam. The only daughter among three brothers of a Russian Jewish immigrant family. Short spiky hair, jet black! Cut somewhere between sassy and saucy. An innocent, other worldly. Lovely to behold. Slim, coltish, beautiful, the sort of girl you would marry. Again, not now, but in a few years, when she becomes a woman.

It is so easy. We have pretty much been betrothed since we were babies. We are, by all metrics, so right for each other. The critical success factors are right. The key performance indicators augur well. It is easier to continue than to discontinue.

We are already 'an item' at seventeen. She looks me up in hospital after a motorbike crash which crippled me and almost took my life.

I am in hospital for six months, being put back together. For six months, I watch young men being stretchered in with horrible injuries. Some surviving permanently mutilated, some dying. A few walking out ok.

Six months in which, at sixteen, though still technically a child, I forego any remaining childhood. I leave hospital precocious in the ways of the world. I have seen too much for my years.

I remember the stir that went through the ward when she arrives at visiting time. A testosterone-enriched murmur of admiration and generalised envy goes up, which I join in until suddenly I recognize her and am able, smugly, to say, "Sorry, lads, she's coming to see me."

I think I know right here, right now (Bright spring morning, Ward 23, St Mary's Hospital), that I will marry her. It is fated, pre-ordained – it is inevitable, inescapable.

My memory is damaged in the accident. I can remember everything clearly from about the age of four (3rd-On-The-Left, Jacopy Road, Luanshya, Zambia) up to arriving in London (82 Cavendish Road, Clapham South) at around the age of eleven. But the period from some time in the first year after our return to London to the moment of impact is jumbled, blurred.

I am by all accounts (well, by my brother's account, and I have no reason to doubt him) a pompous, arrogant, feckless swine (a teenager) as I am stretchered into hospital with an extravagantly expensive Japanese silk scarf tourniquet around my shattered right leg. A Japanese nurse witnessed the hit-and-run and saved my life.

My father comes to see me moments before I am wheeled into the operating theatre. He is grey within grey, sunken, having been told what my chances are. I realise. "He thinks I'm going to die", and at the same time, I know with absolute certainty that I am not. I feel so sorry for him. I want to comfort him. I am all he has left at home. Mother, brother, and sisters all gone. Elsewhere.

The muted voices, clangs and clatter and the smell of disinfectant stretch between us. I smile and tell him I will be fine, but the greyness lies too deep within him, his shadow impenetrable. "Once more unto the breach, dear friends, once more!" I declaim as they wheel me off, the pre-med having finally kicked in.

Let me explain how it is that a sixteen-year-old boy can know with certainty that he is not about to die. Despite having lost, they estimate, around eight pints of blood and having his right leg shattered from hip to ankle, compressed to half its length, his knee torn off by the impact of the oncoming car. Despite all that, knowing he will survive.

The moment of impact. I do not see it coming. *Absolute* pain - one moment elated, laughing, riding pillion (illegally) on Richard's motorbike, the next a world of pain. I lie in a growing pool of blood, a screaming, bewildered animal. No thought, no cognition, just the extended instant, screaming going on and on. Probably it is no more than seconds until I notice the *other*, at some distance, dispassionate, observing. With a sickening lurch of perception, I am the other, dissociated. I regard myself from some 'vantage point'. I notice the cold night air and the whiff of petrol. For a moment, I toy with the ridiculous image of myself clinging to the top of a nearby lamppost, somehow jettisoned, looking down. I am two distinct entities, the screaming animal on the ground trapped in the eternal instant and the intelligent, detached Observer, regarding.

Time slows for me (the Observer). I can see the crowd gathering. I can see beyond the immediate locale – I see people coming out of the tube station, hearing the screaming, looking over, shrugging, and walking on. I see the police car pulling over. I hear the wheeze of its brakes. I survey the scene. Time slowing, not slow-motion like in a movie, just 'slowing', the flow teetering on the edge of inertia, seeking out a suitable parking spot, searching for an appropriate instant in which to stop. I feel the chill tarmac. Time stops.

I continue to observe, from the banks, on the edge of the river of time, now halted, between one instant and the next, outside of time.

I am fascinated. I view the scene from many angles. Infinite points of perception are open to me. Surprised, I realise that time has stopped for them but not for me. Psychological time for me continues. From somewhere, I grasp, or I am told, that I must choose. To re-enter time, to go back, or not.

The prospect of returning to the screaming, broken animal is, to say the least, unappetising. Many moments pass, perhaps weeks of psychological time, perhaps more. I choose at last. Again, the sickening lurch of perception, there is an almost audible pop, a feeling of enormous suction. I am being dragged back into the whirlpool of life. I am screaming on the ground. I take control, soothing the animal with gentle words. The screaming subsides. I, we, merge – almost completely. I know I will not die, at least not now or in the next few hours and days. I know this not because of any physical, objective factors but existentially because I have *chosen,* I have accepted responsibility.

"Pat!" Someone is saying my name, "Pat, can you hear me?"

"No", I think to myself, "No, I cannot. I'm too bloody tired and in too much bloody pain!" Thank God, I pass out.

I call her up when I am released from hospital, my right leg permanently straightened, my body heavier, and my waist-length hair cut, respectably, to my shoulders. We court while she finishes her exams at school. I go to college to see if I can't pass something. We slip into the habit of one another. I become her guide through the adult world, her helper. She, dazzlingly lovely and smart, becomes my proof that, though crippled and without qualifications, I may amount to something. I am grateful, well aware that I am by no means a great catch. Slowly, it seems to me, not in a mad fizz, but by degrees, we come to love each other.

I am deeply affected by the accident, by the breaking of my body, and the loss of my last remaining moments of childhood. She offers me a retreat, a sanctuary. Her family becomes my family.

MOONLIGHT

Moonlight calls to moonlight. My lover's silhouette in the doorway, bright light behind. The little cottage in the Wicklow Hills, the tiny kitchen, those first oh-so-tender kisses – with her. This is another beginning, in a way, our first time alone together. Guilt set aside, repressed. We are so shy of one another. We cast bashful glances beneath hooded eyes. Timid caresses, lightness of touch, so tentative, so uncertain.

The feeling of absolute bliss, of *connection*. The eternity of gentle kissing, the closeness, the feeling of ultimate homecoming. Her warmth, her soft capable hands undoing the buckle of my belt, slowly unbuttoning my jeans, one by one, a ritual, intense. The unexpected heat as, quietly, she slips her hands inside to hold and caress.

She is taller than me, a little, not enough to matter. She has long wavy, deep red-auburn hair, thick and luxurious. Her face is almost symmetrical. Her generous mouth perhaps a little too full, her piercing blue eyes perhaps a little too large. She is stunningly lovely, and I would gladly butcher anyone who says otherwise.

We have not yet declared our love. We are checking, silently cross-referencing our feelings and calibrating. I love her scent! To my eyes, she is lovely. To my heart, utterly beguiling. I know and do not know what I feel. I am out of my depth, tugged by emotional currents for which I am quite unprepared. This is the first time in over two decades that I have dipped a toe in these treacherous waters. I know, and do not know, why I am doing it.

Inevitably, I am jet-lagged, it is one in the morning, and I have been awake for maybe thirty-six hours straight. It is a warm night. Peaceful sounds carry across the darkness from the surrounding woods. The moon is huge and full.

She shakes with adrenalin, fear and expectation. This is new for her too. We wander outside to rest in the moonlight and smoke cigarettes. The gravel path crunches underfoot. To my exhausted eyes, it appears to ripple like water, lapping against our feet.

We speak little, content with closeness. Occasional secret glances cast back and forth between us, like children who have strayed too far from our parents, checking, seeking reassurance. It is real. It seems unreal.

She strokes the soft dark hair of my forearms. She kisses my hands. I am found. I am lost.

It is time to go to bed. I am ready to keel over. I have been travelling from Sydney to Dublin via Heathrow for 36 hours straight. I have not washed in two days. I smell of long travel and unchanged clothes, acrid, a little rank. We wander back inside, and I say I must take a shower. I am momentarily flummoxed as to the etiquette of the situation. Should I simply strip off and hop in the shower? Should I make some improbable gesture of modesty and close the bathroom door? We have never seen each other naked, never been intimate. I am acutely aware that I am a short, fat, middle-aged man with a receding hairline – and I smell like a sweaty dog.

She watches as I strip off and step into the shower. I am deeply uncomfortable – she cannot possibly find me attractive. She must be repelled. I turn on the shower, a little too hot, and stand under the drenching spray, reviving. Across the room, I see her smile. I do not know how to interpret it – self-doubt smashes into me again. I must look ridiculous. I am ridiculous!

She catches my eye. I am halted in mid paroxysm. She is not repelled. She begins to undress for me. She is calm and leisurely. I am ten years old again, transfixed. She is lovely! One by one, she undoes the hooks at the back of her dress. She holds me with her gaze, unashamed. With a delicate shrug, the dress slips from her shoulders and slides in graceful folds to her feet. She is magnificent! She reaches behind her back, undoes her bra and, with her right hand, removes it in one easy gesture. My eyes are drawn immediately to her breasts. I fight the impulse to stare. I lose. Her breasts are small, perfect, upturned and fabulously, unfathomably perky.

I am still held by her gaze. I cannot look away even if I want to – I do not want to. She hooks her thumbs into the top of her panties, bends forward slightly, offering the promise of those exquisite breasts, wiggles her hips and bottom, and in a single feline motion, whisks away the last vestige of clothing.

Blinding embarrassment washes over me. I blush deeply from the crown of my head to my chest. I cannot look away. I have a fine throbbing erection, quivering with eagerness like a Kelpie. She smiles with such warmth, so careful of my feelings. She meets my eye. I am reassured. A smile of rueful amusement steals over my face. I am deeply grateful.

She walks across the room towards me, her hips swaying unselfconsciously, hypnotically. I realise how defenceless men are, how defenceless I am, and I am glad.

She steps into the shower with me. I make awkward movements. She pours shampoo into her hand and begins to wash my hair. I pick up the soap and, with barely hidden desperation, scrub away the grime and sweat of two days as quickly as I can.

She washes my body with slow deliberation. She enjoys the intimacy. She has a natural appreciation of ritual. I am being anointed and prepared. I allow the water to wash away the suds. I begin to shampoo her hair, deep red against the whiteness of her neck. I notice every movement, every droplet of spray, every bubble. I am lost in a meditative spell, entirely in the moment, beyond thought.

She turns towards me, our bodies dripping wet, almost touching. She wraps her arms around my neck and pulls me gently to her. I hold her glorious, slippery, clean, wet body close. We share again those sweet, sweet kisses. We are completely in tune with one another. We are one.

MEMORY AND MADNESS

New Orleans again! I realise I am unbelievably thirsty. My throat is dry, caked in something foul and very sore. I look around. I am in a familiar hotel room, alone, twenty floors up. Four in the morning, I am freezing and covered in drying sweat. The air-con is set to maximum and going full blast. I get up, lurch over to the mini-bar and pull out a bottle of water. The mini-bar is filled with beer and spirits, a few tasteless wafer biscuits and a tiny slab of unnamed cheese in shrink-wrapped plastic. I drink half the bottle in a single go. The ice water works its way inside me, progressing like an iron bar through my innards. I rip open a pack of dry biscuits and take a bite. I gag and swig some more water. I realise that I am seriously sick. I wrench the air-con dial up to thirty degrees C and collapse back onto the queen size bed. The room swims around me. I am now beyond delirious.

Shards of memory torment me. Indiscriminate, insanely brief, hard as diamond. Clean and absolutely real. I am six years old, eating Baked Alaska in the tower of Fitzpatrick Castle in Dublin, my mother's ancestral home. I am five. Minnie is daring my brother to jump fifteen feet into the dry moat of a derelict castle. I am nine, wandering wide-eyed through the Museum of Abnormalidades in Lorenzo Marques, Mozambique, before the revolution. All around me, sad two-headed calves and four-legged chickens peer out of their glass cases. Five again, Minnie shames my brother Sam by jumping off the draw bridge. Nine, I am swimming out to the coral reef at the resort north of Lorenzo Marques. I have a knife in my teeth and a lemon stuffed inside my swimming trunks. I am sitting on the reef with an Afrikaner boy cutting open oysters and eating them raw with a squeeze of lemon. I am about four years old (one of my earliest memories), attempting to pedal a toy ambulance around the drive at Framlington Grange in Suffolk, England. - I am six, in the orchard at my grandparent's house in Foxrock, County Dublin. A fox suddenly rushes past. I ask my grandfather if he is going to jump on it and bite it in the neck (which he declines to do). I am staring into the eyes of the ancient Burmese Buddha brought back to Ireland by my Burmese great, or great-great, grandmother (family myth, possibly true, probably not). I am seventeen in the red-light district of Amsterdam. Eighteen in Barcelona at the top of the Sagrada Familia, nauseous with vertigo. Thirty-one on a tram in Munich. Ingrid is two years old, wracked by whooping cough and gasping for breath. Enough!

I am overcome by nausea. The precursor taste of salt suffuses my mouth. I want to vomit. I am going to vomit imminently. I stagger to the lavatory and kneel over the toilet bowl. I retch, but there is little or nothing in my stomach. I retch again, my head pounding, vision blurred, swirling lights and patterns. There is some relief when finally I manage to throw up – ice cold water (I am, in a detached way, interested that it is still ice cold) and a few flecks of wafer biscuit. I am completely wrung out, at the end of my strength.

I collapse. There is no peace in sleep. The process now started, will grind to its end with or without me. I am tormented by memory. Erotic, nightmarish, sacred and banal, instances, evidence. Everything is present. Everything is now. My madness is in full spate. The law of causality is reversed. The future, as it seems to me, reaches back to the beginning arranging things just so, creating itself, this arbitrary moment. The future, this now, self-caused, demanding, as if by right, that precise ordering of events that leads to itself – perfection, the perfect tense. 'Now' exists simultaneously as an infinitesimal instant, as a continuous flow, and as eternity. There is nothing else. There is some method to this madness. Broken memories, out of sequence for twenty-odd years since the motorbike accident, are being re-ordered and corrected. At long last, there is nothing. I sleep.

CREOLE BREAKFAST SPECIAL

I am beginning to surface. The clock on the bedside table reads six a.m. The room is stifling, the air con droning continuously. I swing my legs off the bed and stand to turn down the air con. I buckle, grabbing hold of the dial and twisting it down to eighteen degrees before folding back onto the bed. The fever has broken. I am completely washed out. I reach out shakily for the bottle and swig tepid water.

Time passes. From my bed, I can make out blue sky and sunshine reflected in the windows of another towering hotel a block or two away. I doze off.

I wake up starving. I have eaten almost nothing for days. I make my way unsteadily to the shower and drench myself for an age in stinging hot water. I begin to revive. I wash my hair. The water runs cold. I step, shivering from the shower and dress quickly. Loneliness settles like frostbite. I am alone. She is thousands of miles away.

I head down to the lobby to get coffee and a croissant from Starbucks. It's Seven a.m. Starbucks is closed. I am irrationally enraged by this and bang my fist hard on the glass, startling the cleaners inside. The concierge hears the bang and looks over. "Sorry, lost my balance." He looks away, the queue of early morning check-outs demanding his attention.

I glance around the lobby. Small groups of revellers lounge around chatting or silent, too wasted to move. I recognise a few faces from the conference. Someone calls out to me to join them. The last thing I want is to make small talk with a bunch of drunken computer nerds.

"Just off for my morning jog." I put on my "Trust me, I'm a consultant" face and limp ostentatiously out into the street. The heat and humidity hit me. Even at that hour, New Orleans in midsummer is unbearable. I cross Canal Street and cut down Bourbon Street, looking for a café. The French Quarter is almost silent, a complete contrast to the nighttime debauchery. I light a cigarette and head randomly along side streets, enjoying the relative peace. There are a few people about, street cleaners, commercial vans making deliveries, and a few kids in groups, heading towards the river. I pass a school a few moments later, a small primary school painted a dull brick red, with pretty large arched windows in a simplified gothic style, chipped paint, wooden shutters coming off their hinges and a sign saying.

WARNING!
ANYONE WHO COMMITS THE CRIME OF CARRYING A FIREARM ON A SCHOOL CAMPUS OR SCHOOL BUS SHALL BE IMPRISONED AT HARD LABOR FOR NOT MORE THAN 5 YEARS.

The morning smells fresh and new. I watch the kids walking past, overwhelmingly black, or Hispanic, happy, laughing, nice kids.

I turn a corner into a narrow alley next to a small private car park enclosed by a high chain link fence. One or two large trucks are parked at the back of the lot. In the space between them, I see a prostitute on her knees giving a blow job to a dishevelled man in an expensive suit. He is holding himself up against the dirty truck. His back is smeared with oily brown dust. She sees me and gives me a wink before returning to her work. I think I recognise the man. I walk on. A rickety old red taxi wheezes past from Westbank Marrero Cab Co. 'Red Fleet Inc.'

I find a small café, a few chairs outside, a blackboard with today's specials and a small sunny black woman with no teeth. She is the proprietor. There is something immediately engaging about her. I like her at once and sit down at one of the tables.

"No smokin' honey", she gives me an enormous gummy grin as she sets down a small stainless-steel ashtray next to me.

"What you havin'?"

"Large skinny Latté and the Creole Breakfast Special, please."

She looks me up and down. A small, polite, foreign male with no discernible waistline.

"You want sweetener in the coffee?" she asks. I laugh.

"Yes, please. I need to maintain my greyhound physique".

"Greyhound bus", I hear her mutter as she heads back inside.

The Creole Breakfast Special is kill or cure. An enormous plate of pan-fried chicken, blackened catfish, some kind of spicy Louisiana sausage, sautéed potatoes and a little bowl of chilli oil. I eat as much as I can face and order another coffee. The man from the parking lot in the grimy suit wanders up and sits down across from me. There is a stain on his trouser leg.

"How's the breakfast? He asks?" with forced heartiness.

"Indescribable." I light another cigarette and gaze down the riverwalk to where a gaily painted paddle steamer is moored. There is a small crowd collecting around it. Nicely dressed, Sunday best. It finally sinks in - Sunday morning – no conference today. I pay, leaving the man negotiating pointlessly for a discount. The proprietor, who is by no means amused, favours me with a little wave.

I wander down to the river to take a closer look. A sign says, "Sunday Brunch and Gospel Cruise!"

Who could resist a gospel choir on a boat? I buy a ticket on the Cajun Queen of New Orleans, Louisiana, and amble on board. There is a seat in the open at the back of the boat, away from the gospel choir. I light another cigarette and look out over the slow-moving water. I am feeling much better. The fever is definitely gone, as is the hollowness in my stomach, replaced by the feeling one would have if one had just gorged on a moderately sized cauldron of pan-fried chicken, blackened catfish, some kind of spicy Louisiana sausage, sautéed potatoes, and a little bowl of chilli oil.

A couple of loud hoots announce our imminent departure. I am alone on my seat at the stern of the boat. The paddles begin to turn sedately. We move off.

New Orleans slips slowly away as we head upstream. It is only a short while until we have left the urban centre behind and are passing light industrial areas (a huge sign says 'Dixie Machine Welding and Metal Works Inc'), wharves, and eventually, scattered homes and dense swamp.

I listen to the choir singing from the bow of the boat. I smoke cigarettes and stare into the middle distance. The countryside glides by. We come to a nature reserve of open meadows and tall grasses. A narrow tributary flows between tall trees. There is no one about except a courting couple on a picnic blanket. In the distance, upon a small hill, only a metre or two above the water, stands an old wooden church, once painted white, with a tall bell tower. My mind wanders where it will. I relive another hot and humid day, half the world and several summers removed. I am with her, in Wicklow, Ireland, walking by a river. Ours is a brand-new love, urgent, extravagant. We can walk for only a few yards without stopping for long minutes to kiss and caress. We come to a nature reserve. A narrow, little-used track leads away from the river and disappears behind a stand of alders. The sun is high and bright. There is no one about.

We lie down in the shade in deep grass and share lingering kisses. She has lovely shoulders. I kiss her tenderly from the tips of her fingers to her shoulders. I push back her mane of hair and kiss her neck. I slip her shoulder straps off and kiss her throat, working my way down to her breasts. I stroke her nipples with my tongue, enjoying the sensation as they harden between my lips. I push her gently down onto the grass and begin to kiss her toes. I take my time, progressing slowly up one leg and then the other, kissing all the way to the embroidered edge of her panties. I begin again, from the knee this time, enjoying the soft skin first of one thigh, then the other. I lift her dress, exposing the smooth plane of her stomach. I kiss my way across her waist. I pull her panties down a little way, revealing demure, enticing red curls. I kiss again, luxuriating in the warm, sweet smell of my woman. I undress her completely. I am fully clothed, she is naked, like the French painting 'Le déjeuner sur l'herbe'. Her nakedness emphasised, made more explicit by comparison. She is lying on the grass, in the shade, her arms thrown carelessly above her head, one knee slightly raised. She is smiling. I am leaning over her. I undo my belt and pull down my jeans. I am rock hard, straining against the fabric. She raises herself on one elbow, reaching forward with the other hand and lifts the waistband of my shorts up and over my erection, setting me free. She cups me in her hand and holds me firmly. I push her back down. I am in charge, commanding. I lie on top of her, allowing most of my weight to rest on her. She strokes my back and wraps her legs around my waist. We kiss again, not with gentleness now but with hot passion. We are on fire. Her fingers dig into my back, leaving angry red welts. Aphrodisiac pain spurs me to greater passion. I take her wrists in my hands and force her back down, wild red hair against the green. She digs her heels into my buttocks, urging me on, demanding satisfaction. I lift away from her for a second. She reaches down and grasps me, guiding me home, brooking no refusal. I am delirious with pleasure. I focus on her rhythm, away from my own urgency. I dare not finish until she is fulfilled. Our bodies develop a powerful sympathetic rhythm, a single heartbeat, hypnotic, primeval. Awareness closes in. Focus narrows. We are oblivious of the meadow, of families out walking by the river on the other side of the alder trees, of everything but our single self and our mounting bliss. We hear only the deafening thud of our one pounding heart, smell only the exotic tang of our merged body, see only ourselves, each reflected in the other, feel only the raging of our union, and taste only the rapture of completion. A noise escapes her throat, deep, ancient and visceral. Her body closes tightly around me, entrapping and containing. I am elated and relieved. I have not committed the unpardonable discourtesy of leaving my woman unsatisfied. I am still erect. It doesn't matter. My lover loves me! I shift my weight as if to move.

"No," She wraps her arms around my neck. "Lie on me. I want to feel your weight".

I lower my body gently over her. We kiss again, with a deeper tenderness than before. I want to cry. I am emotionally full. There is nowhere for it to go.

"Thank you", she strokes my lower back with one lazy finger. I rest my head on her chest. She kisses my ear lobe.

We both, at more or less the same instant, become aware of life all around us, insects, lovely butterflies, birds singing unreasonably loudly, a web of being, a cocoon.

We hear high-pitched, happy, laughing voices – a family out for a Sunday walk. We flatten ourselves against the earth in our little patch of heaven. We are so alive! We fall into fits of giggles. She grabs her pants, desperately trying to pull them up while lying hidden in the long grass. I pretend to help, passing her a shoe. She takes it without thinking, then realising what she is holding, whacks me on the head with it in mock outrage. The voices are getting closer. We are all but debilitated by laughter, our bodies wracked by irrepressible fits of giggling. She manages to pull her dress on over her head and attempts to straighten her hair. I haven't the heart to mention the dress is on back-to-front. She looks like a woman who has just made rampant, passionate love in a clump of flattened grass. She looks lovely! I am, I realise, hopelessly, absolutely, irretrievably, head-over-heels in love.

"There is something I must tell you," I say, "something I swore I would never say, never burden you with." Her smile is open and encouraging, yet I detect an edge of doubt around the eyes.

"I love you." The male panacea, yet at that precise moment, those are the only words I know.

A galumphing Cocker Spaniel chooses that precise moment to leap between us. The spell is broken. We both sit bolt upright. Two young children come running up, contrition wrestling with mischievous enjoyment.

"Sorry, so sorry, he's just a puppy, really", the dog bounds off, enjoying the chase.

"Jasper, come back!"

The parents roll up a moment or two later. The husband rushes after errant children and hound, leaving the wife to apologise further.

"Lovely afternoon for a snooze." She eyes our dishevelled appearance. "Sorry to have disturbed you".

She catches up with her husband a moment or two later. The children have managed to put a lead on the dog. I watch as she leans close to the man and whispers something in his ear. His arm drops from her waist, and then, gently, he squeezes her bottom. They lean together as they walk away.

● ● ●

Ireland gives way, as it has done so many times before for so many emigrants. The Mississippi River glides past. My mind returns to the Cajun Queen of New Orleans. The open glades and water-meadows of the nature reserve give way to the swamp and forest that surround New Orleans. I spot an absurdly emphatic sign, random, crudely hand painted.

NO ONE IS ALLOWED BEYOND HERE

I wonder if perhaps alienation and fear are the foundations of American culture. I stroll up front to get a look at the choir and listen some more. I am weary of the loneliness of international conferences. I want to go home. I am not really sure where home is any more. Not Zambia, not Swaziland, not London or Dublin. I hope it will be Sydney.

I am quite enjoying the choir. I yearn for the closeness of walking with her. I feel like shit.

As I sleepwalk through the following weeks, the emotional crisis or breakdown, or whatever it is, slowly resolves. My damaged memory is fixed. Sequence is restored. Chaos abates. I am awake and more myself than I have been for a quarter of a century. If I am not yet whole, I am at least healing.

THIS IS THE WAY WE MAKE A BROKEN HEART

Intercontinental romance is a severe strain on the nerves. Dublin and Sydney are at opposite ends of the clock. I am ashamed that I still have not told Miriam about it. I am consumed with doubts that a relationship carried out from half a world away can possibly succeed. The difficulties sometimes seem insurmountable. The odds against, too great. I say her name out loud, a little mantra bringing her closer to me, at least in thought. Amelie, Amelie, Amelie. The sound of her name on my lips sounds hollow and desperate. I begin again to reflect on my lover, this strange, unlikely, magical woman, and the deep love I feel for her. I realise that there has always been a very strong attraction between us, even when we hardly knew each other. We flirt shamelessly, but somehow it always seems safe. For my part, I flirt shamelessly with all my wife's friends, so my flirtations with Amelie seem merely par for the course. She is not one of Miriam's close friends, but she is in the broader circle, and her partner Fausto is one of my closest and dearest friends. Fausto and I are of similar height, but Fausto is wiry and slim with black eyes, black hair, and the soul of a poet. We drink together often, setting the world to rights. His father is from Italy or somewhere, and his mother is Scottish. Fausto is a book binder and illustrator by trade.

For years, as our children grow together, attend the same little local primary school, go to the same birthday parties, and become in a way like brothers and sisters, there is never more than an unstated, for my part barely noticed, attraction. I struggle to remember what happened. How did things change? When? I recall tiny moments, fleeting fragments of our lovers' discourse, almost beyond memory.

I recall a party at the home of mutual friends, just across the street from both of us. She is wearing a red velvet dress. She looks stunning! This is perhaps the first moment I can recall when I think of her as a woman, attractive, downright desirable, rather than simply as my best friend's wife. We seek each other out. I compliment her on her outfit. Her eyes shine. She practically purrs. I tell her she looks lovely. For a moment, our eyes lock.

"You know I think you're lovely too".

We are both a little startled by this sudden shift in intimacy. I tell her I need a refill. We drift off in opposite directions. Later, she squeezes past me, rubbing close against me though there is plenty of room.

There is the Salsa Evening in the church hall at the top of the hill. It is very noisy, crowded and hot. The place smells of wood polish and dust. I am attempting to learn to salsa with Miriam. She is a capable dancer. I, with my crippled leg and unfortunate lack of rhythm, am not. Miriam becomes increasingly frustrated with my ineptitude. Almost at boiling point, she grabs my face between her two sweaty palms and shouts, "For God's sake, pay attention, follow me, actually watch what I am doing, will you?".

"This is pointless", I say, "you know I can't dance like you, Miriam, I never have been able to."

Miriam chooses a different partner, a male friend of ours and swirls away. I feel humiliated and angry. I shuffle off in the direction of the bar. I see Amelie sitting with her closest friend, Siobhan. I approach the pair. She looks up. She has a full bottle of beer.

"Hello, sex kitten", addressing Amelie, "can I get either of you ladies a drink?"

She is embarrassed but not displeased. She is deep in conversation with Siobhan.

"I'm fine for now."

"How about you, Siobhan?"

"I'm fine too, thanks."

I trudge off to the bar to get myself a beer.

When I get back, Amelie is dancing with Siobhan. I can't take my eyes off her. Siobhan notices and momentarily catches my eye. She knows.

Miriam is throwing out a Spanish dress, black with white polka dots, frilly, figure-hugging. Miriam offers it to Amelie. She is delighted. It's just her sort of thing. She dashes home to try it on and is back a few moments later to show us how it looks on. She twirls and spins, a mock Flamenco. The dynamic of the occasion is strange. Something is different. And then it dawns on me. She is showing *me* the dress as much as Miriam. She is looking for my approval, too. Perhaps she is really seeking only my approval. I approve, oh I approve very much indeed. She looks bloody fantastic.

I am becoming increasingly aware of the attraction I feel for her. We talk more often, more deeply. She is at something of a crossroads in her life. Things with Fausto are not going well. He is full of unmet potential, energy and self-doubt, and so, in a way, is she. We talk about Fausto and Miriam, counselling each other. I try to explain how things may seem from a man's point of view. I suggest things she might say or do. I tell her to talk to him, tell him how she feels. She tells me Miriam loves me very much and that we seem so happy together. That there must be deep foundations to our relationship for it to have lasted so long. We are thrown together like children seeking comfort and reassurance.

I am smoking again. Miriam hates it. Whenever she finds out, she issues an ultimatum, "Quit or I'm leaving". I quit often. I hide the fact that I am smoking. I live on peppermints and mouthwash. Occasionally, I pop round to Amelie's place for a cigarette and a chat. There is nothing in it, just friends sharing a few moments of idle banter. I bang on the door and shout "Burglar, Burglar, Madam!" something from Monty Python, I think. She appears with her gentle smile and lets me in. We go through to the back garden and smoke, just for a few minutes. It is a haven for me, somewhere where I can be myself, where I do not have to misdirect and deceive.

We grow closer, still friends, our mutual attraction still suppressed. She needs to go shopping in Grafton Street, a few miles away from where we live. Fausto has taken the car and won't be back for hours. I offer to drive her. Miriam encourages me. She consents. We chat as I drive. The traffic is bad even for Dublin. Someone cuts-in in front of me. I am suddenly, incomprehensibly, enraged. I lean over and bellow abuse at the driver through the passenger window. She covers her ears and cringes. I have screamed obscenities right into her ear. I blush crimson. I am hideously embarrassed. I apologise. She has never seen this side of me. I curse silently under my breath.

I drop her off and offer to wait. She says she'll take a bus back. I head home alone, humiliated again.

She wants to take a holiday in Spain with Fausto and the kids. I speak a little Spanish. We sit together in my study and call various hotels on the Costa Del Sol, looking for an affordable family room. My Spanish is not good, but eventually, we find a room in a hotel south of Almeria. I hang up the phone. We are sitting next to each other, very close. We sit for a little while in silence, neither of us wishing to break the spell. We hear noises coming from downstairs. The spell is broken. We get up. She goes downstairs to talk to Miriam.

We begin, with shy glances and secret looks, to acknowledge our growing closeness. Nothing overt, demure. I love to look at her as she passes my study window in the spring. The cherry tree outside is full of blossom. She is wearing a light, cotton 'fifties' dress. She is entrancing.

At no time do I stop to question the trajectory of this sly dance, nor do I consider, even for a moment, the likely outcome? I am, in my way, a little happy. I am, in a small way, content to be the object of someone else's desire. If there is an assumption underlying my conscious thoughts at all, it is that this will all come to nothing anyway. Guys like me don't end up with gals like that.

I begin to delay walking the boys to school by a few minutes so I can watch her walking ahead with her children. I love the way she walks, so graceful, her bottom swaying beguilingly a few metres ahead. I begin to desire her, Miriam and Fausto notwithstanding.

Amelie and Miriam, plus a tag-along-friend, Sharon (known in our close-knit community as 'The Nose' due to her peculiar love of gossip), go for a girl's night out. I know the three of them will be back late, merry, singing. I watch a film on TV and drink brandy. I know I am waiting up for them, matching their drinking, synchronising.

Shortly after midnight, they come bumbling back. They are in high spirits, giggling. They stumble down the stairs into the back sitting room. I get glasses and pour brandies for everyone. We all talk and laugh together. We play loud music. We are all quite drunk.

After perhaps an hour, Miriam goes upstairs to bed. I seize my chance. Amelie is dancing to the music, 'Let's Get It On', some slow soul song from yester year. I walk over and begin to dance with her. I drift closer. I put my arm around her and draw her body next to mine. She does not resist. We dance on, closer and closer. I allow my hand to slide down over her bottom. She reacts immediately, genuinely outraged.

"That's my bottom!" At this point, Sharon, who had been snoring gently on the sofa, a thin dribble of saliva making its way down her chin, perks up and begins to pay close attention.

"I know", I say, "I have never been faulted for my knowledge of anatomy."

She gives me a hard look and draws away a little. I settle for stroking her back as we dance, gently bringing her closer once more. I am on fire with desire. I catch a glimpse of Sharon, still sitting silently on the sofa, eyes glittering. Somewhere at the back of my mind, I realise that there will be hell to pay one day. I am soused with lust and drunk. I shrug it off.

We dance to a few more tracks. Then Sharon manages to prise herself off the sofa and into a standing position. She wobbles, steadies herself, and declares that it's time to go home. I walk them both upstairs. Sharon is several paces ahead. I take a chance and whisper a subtle invitation.

"Stay. Don't go. If you stay, I'll fuck your brains out."

She literally rolls her eyes in disbelief and disdain.

"Oh shit", I think, grinning inwardly at my astonishing crassness, "I really blew that one".

I close the door behind them and head up to my room to sleep it off. Miriam is fast asleep in her room. I will have a hideous hangover in the morning. I lie in bed, the room swaying slightly, and relive the closeness, the sensuality, of dancing with Amelie. There will definitely be hell to pay. I don't care. It was worth it. I fall asleep, lost in the warmth of her body, her womanly scent and the softness of her skin.

REFUGEES

It is less than a week before we are due to leave for Sydney. Our stuff has been crated up and shipped. We are camping out in our own home. I walk outside the front for a cigarette. I see Amelie, a little way off, outside her place, throwing out the rubbish. I walk over and offer her a cigarette. We talk a little, subdued, neither knowing what to say. I wonder if we will meet again after we leave for Australia. I yearn for some confirmation of our feelings. It all comes together in one inept question.

"Will I sleep with you before we leave?"

She shrugs. On impulse, I lean over and kiss her once, gently, on the lips. Up to that moment, our relationship has consisted, overtly, of a few brief dances, an perfunctory squeeze of her bottom, a profoundly crass invitation, a cheerless enquiry and a single, curiously chaste kiss. Covertly, it has been a whirling, subtle dance. We are, I realise, falling in love.

Finally, a little reality seeps in. I dare not pursue this relationship. I hope and pray and tell myself that moving to Sydney is the only hope I have of saving my marriage.

The last few days are hell. We spend sixteen hours a day sorting belongings and throwing out rubbish. On our last day in Dublin, the front garden is piled high with black bin-liners.

The day rushes into night. A friend turns up in his massive station wagon, and we pile in our luggage. We are late. We have to leave. There is no time for lingering goodbyes. A few farewells called out to the blur of faces standing on the curb, and we are off, refugees, making our escape in haste, at night, unprepared.

We have been in Sydney for three months before I initiate contact with Amelie. She has started work. I find out her email address and risk a message. After a few failed attempts, I get it right.

[BINGO!
Hi Amelie – I miss you very much indeed. Think of you often.
Lots of love. Pat X]

Things have changed a great deal in the intervening few months.
Her reply is swift and stark.

[Hi Pat, I miss you all too and think of you often. I hope you are
settled in well, and things are working for you. It's 'all change'
over here, I'm afraid. You know things were not going well
between Fausto and me. Well, Fausto and I have finally
separated. I asked him to move out. I know you tried to help,
offering the male perspective and all that, but it's definitely over.
It feels so strange being without him after over twenty years.
Love to Miriam and the boys. A x]

RIDGEBACK

I am four years old. We have recently arrived in Africa. We are living in Ndola, Northern Rhodesia, where my dad has taken a job making documentaries for a large copper mining group.

Dad gets us a Rhodesian Ridgeback, one of the toughest, most indomitable, loyal and downright powerful dogs on earth. We call him Maxi because of his size, massive even for a Ridgeback. I could almost ride him if he'd let me.

Dad says Maxi will look after us when he is away in the bush. Already, he is away a lot. He has visitors to the house when he is not away. They talk late into the night. People come and go at odd hours. This is a very different life from England. Everything seems so new and exciting. The sounds and smells of London seem long ago and very far away.

Today we are going to the hilltop lookout behind the old film studios to stare down into the Congo. This has become something of a family ritual. It is early, around seven o'clock, but already the air is hot and moist and full of the scent of growing things. Sometimes, as I lie on my back and watch huge clouds build and flow across the sky, I feel I can actually hear the lush vegetation growing and feel the spin of the earth beneath me.

Before we left England, Dad took us to Kew Gardens, to the big greenhouses, so that we could smell what Africa would smell like and see the tropical plants. Now that I am here, feeling the hot sun on my skin, touching the smooth bark of the mango trees and filling my nostrils with the raw smells of jungle and savannah, I grasp what a dismal, pale imitation the greenhouses at Kew really are.

Now we live in Africa. Me, my Mum and Dad, my brother Sam and my sister, Minnie. I wait by the car for the rest of the family to tumble out of the low, flat bungalow we are renting from the copper mine. It's a friendly, lived-in kind of house, but nothing really works the way it's supposed to. Mum says it's run down.

Unusually, we manage to get organised and out reasonably quickly. There are the inevitable scurryings back into the house to get hats and books (Minnie) and cigars (Dad), and Mum has to shut the front door properly because Dad says the catch is broken and it's a damn good thing, we don't own anything worth stealing! Mum says you have to have the knack and tries to show him how to fiddle with it. Dad is wandering out to the car, not all that interested in being shown. Mum says we'll all be murdered in our beds for want of a door that locks when you close it! She slams the door hard and turns towards the car. Again, the catch fails to click, and the door drifts open. Mum is really angry now.

"You must get the agent to fix the lock today. Anyone could just waltz in any time they wanted." Dad mumbles reassuring noises and unlocks the car. There is a massive bang as mum slams the door shut with all her might, accompanied by a satisfying click.

We have an old left-hand-drive Borgward station wagon with cracked leather seats. It wheezes piteously when we stop at traffic lights. Fortunately, traffic lights are few and far between. My older brother Sam, sister Minnie and I fit easily into the back seat, and Maxi goes in the back section behind a metal grill. The car smells strongly of dog. Maxi likes to lick my neck and ears through the grill as we drive along, which tickles and leaves me covered in sticky slobber. Minnie is reading 'The 13 Clocks' and is not to be disturbed. My brother Sam is slouching back with his enormous smelly brown feet up against the window. Mum is up front in a cotton dress with her hair all piled up on top because of the heat. She looks like a princess.

Northern Rhodesia lies on a high plateau four thousand feet above sea level. The air is a little thin, and we all still have occasional giddy moments if we get up suddenly or exert ourselves too much. The sun is fierce and hot now, and the roads smell of diesel and dust. A metallic taste settles on the tongue. We have no air conditioning, and the back windows are stuck closed. The drive to the lookout takes about half an hour. Despite the discomfort, we all enjoy it, and as Dad says, it costs nothing.

Ours is the only car in the gravel car park. It is still very early. We all jump out and race to the edge of the bluff. Mum calls after us to be careful and not go too near the edge. Maxi comes charging up to us like a battering ram, tail stump wagging, rubbing up against us, knocking us over like ninepins. Dad locks the car and lights up one of his little cheroots. His routine is always the same. He checks his reflection in the car window. Adjusts his pale pink silk cravat and rolls up the long sleeves of his white cotton shirt a couple of turns. He brushes a speck of dust from his khaki trousers and saunters afters us.

As always, we fall silent at the sight of the Congo disappearing into the infinite distance in front of us. A tide of indistinguishable greens washed up against the dry browns of northern Rhodesia. Sam climbs under the white wooden bar at the edge of the bluff, trying to get a view straight down. Mum starts to have hysterics, and Dad calls him back.

I am four years old. To me, it seems like a cliff going down and down and down forever until suddenly it flattens out into a massive, steamy and impenetrable jungle spreading north, east and west as far as the eye can see.

"Anything could still be alive down there." My dad likes to say that.

"I wouldn't be surprised if they found some kind of dinosaur still living down there, quite happily, munching on leaves."

We have heard it all before, but still, we pause for thought. He is right, we think. There could be anything down there, anything at all. Maxi spots a small movement in some nearby bush and charges off to investigate. There is much thrashing about and a bit of barking. He is happy. The rhythmic sound of cicadas washes over the bush, hypnotic and soothing.

"The part of the Congo we can see from here is called Katanga." my dad indicates Katanga with a sweep of an arm.

"It's completely uncharted." I am not sure what that means. The endless sea of green is beautiful and scary. A boy at my school told me the local Bemba people are terrified of the Congolese because they are cannibals. My Mum says that's just rubbish and he should have more sense.

Maxi starts up barking again, more seriously this time, with growls and savage snarls. The sound is coming from somewhere down near the edge of the bluff. The ruckus continues, getting louder and louder. There is wild thrashing around going on in a little stand of elephant grass and dwarfed acacia trees. Suddenly the terrible noise stops – even the insects falter. Silence falls like a silk cloth. We are all looking around nervously, glancing at each other. Even Sam shows no sign of wishing to investigate. Slowly the insects re-start their endless song.

Maxi re-appears. He is covered in blood. His ear is torn, and he has a gash under one eye. "

Must have been something pretty big or pretty savage to leave Maxi in that condition." Sam kneels to examine Maxi's wounds. Maxi gives us his "You should've seen the other guy look." But he is evidently hurt. He sits patiently by the rear door to the car, waiting to be let in.

With a few nervous looks around the now tranquil bush, we wander back to the car and climb in in silence.

When we get home, Mum gives Maxi a good wash and binds up his ear. He lies in the shade on the veranda for the rest of the morning, clearly feeling sorry for himself. Every now and then, I give him a gentle stroke and say, "Poor Maxi", and he makes a small effort to lick my face.

The afternoon is very, very hot. We play in the front yard showering each other with the hose to keep cool. Maxi hobbles down the few steps off the veranda and wags his stub tail a couple of times, deigning to be sprayed.

The next day, Sunday, there are thunderstorms. The rain pounds the tin roof of our rented bungalow and runs in rivulets across the yard and onto the unpaved road. We play on the veranda, running out into the rain from time to time to cool off. Maxi does not join in our games. Mum says he's sickening for something. Probably got some poison in one of his bites.

He won't eat his dinner and refuses any water. Mum says she will have to take him to the vet if he's not better by Monday night.

We start school at half past seven in the morning and finish at one in the afternoon. I don't really like getting up at six for school, but I love the long afternoons for playing. Monday morning is organised chaos as Sam, Minnie, and I systematically lose our school shoes or books or hat. This happens every school day, and Mum gets into a grump, shoving her one enormous black plait between her teeth and stomping around in irritation.

Maxi is hiding in the deepest darkest corner of the veranda when we leave. He does not look at all well. He is half standing, growling slightly to himself while his head sways slowly from side to side. He hasn't touched his food or water.

Mum is a few minutes late picking us up after school. She says she tried to get Maxi into the car to take him to the vet, but he growled at her, so the vet's coming around later, after surgery hours.

Sam and Minnie charge into the house to change out of their school uniform and get a cold drink and a Marmite sandwich. Mum is carrying a bit of shopping into the house. I walk out onto the veranda to see how Maxi is going. It is very bright in the sunlight and very dark under the creeper-covered veranda. It takes a while for my eyes to adjust to the gloom. I can't quite see Maxi yet, but I can hear him growling low and shifting about. I call his name. I see the shape of his head peering out from behind an old rattan sofa.

"Hi, Maxi!" I say, beginning to walk towards him. Suddenly he is erect, hair bristling down his neck and back. He is growling in all seriousness now, menacing and feral. His lips pulled back to reveal teeth. My mum hears the noise as she is walking back into the house and turns. Maxi begins to move, there is something not quite right about his back legs, but he is coming towards me fast.

"Pat, run!" Mum screams. I hear something whizz past my ear. I see a large tin of peeled tomatoes smack Maxi hard on the forehead. I had no idea my mum had such good aim. She grabs me by the scruff of my neck and all but lifts me into the hallway. Maxi is moving like a streak now, directly towards us, madness in his eyes. Mum slams the door shut. The catch fails to engage. She throws herself against the door with her full weight just as Maxi crashes into it from the other side. The catch clicks and engages. There is an almighty crash as Maxi throws himself against the door again and again. We both look at the catch.

"Into the kitchen!" She screams. The kitchen is at the very back of the house. The hallway is long and narrow. Sam and Minnie open the kitchen door, alerted by the screaming and banging. They begin to run to towards us to see what all the fuss is about.

"Get back!" Mum screams again. Her voice achieves some ancient instinctive tone that cannot be refused. We charge down the hallway, praying we will make it before Maxi smashes his way in. Mum pushes us all into the kitchen and slams the door. It has a large bolt which she slides across with a snap. She leans, panting against the kitchen table. There is a single small glass panel high up above the door. We hear another crash against the front door and then another. And then another. The door flies open, and Maxi charges in. Mum is standing on a chair, watching through the panel. Sam and Minnie climb up on chairs too and stare over her shoulder. I can't see a thing. I can only hear the sounds of Maxi charging around and snarling.

Mum tells Sam to watch Maxi through the panel while she calls Dad. It takes a while to complete the connection as mum's voice has a distinctly hysterical edge to it, and the local operator is having difficulty understanding her. She gets through. I hear her say.

"It's Maxi. He's gone mad! He has me and the children cornered in the kitchen, and he has smashed his way through the front door." I can hear my dad's voice but not what he is saying.

"No, we bloody well cannot wait! There's a mad dog in the house!" I hear my dad's voice again.

"Just come home now!" Mum hangs up. I have never seen her so angry. She opens a drawer and pulls out a large carving knife. Sam, Minnie and I stare at her in barely comprehending terror. If it came to a straight fight at that precise moment, I'd have to put my money on Mum.

"He's gone into the dining room." Sam is still standing on the chair, keeping watch. "Shall I quickly pull the door closed on him?"

"No!" Mum's face is white as a sheet.

"Okay, Okay, it was only a suggestion."

Minnie jumps down off the chair and goes into the little pantry, closing the door behind her. I take her place on the chair next to Sam, hopping up and down to catch a glimpse through the glass panel.

We wait for what seems like hours until we hear the sound of the old Borgward wheezing up the drive. We hear the car door close. The silhouette of my dad appears in the front doorway. He has something in his hand, a piece of wood or something. There is a noise in the dining room. "He's in the dining room!" We all begin to scream at once. With a savage snarl, Maxi appears in a blur of muscle and speed, charging down the long hallway towards Dad.

Unbelievably, Dad stands his ground. He takes the piece of wood in both hands like a baseball bat. He waits. At the last moment, Maxi leaps off the ground straight at Dad, seeking his throat. Dad brings the lump of wood down with full force on Maxi's skull. There is a sickening crunch. The power of the blow deflects the dog. He crashes against the wall and slides, stunned into Dad's shins. Maxi is up in a moment, snarling and snapping at Dad. There is a moment of hand-to-hand combat, and then the makeshift wooden club comes down again and again and again. Dad is driving Maxi up the hallway towards us. Dad backs Maxi into the dining room and pulls the door closed.

Dad stands for a moment, panting, leaning against the wall. Blood runs down his arm. His white cotton shirt is dripping with blood, and his pink silk cravat is spattered. We jump down from the chairs, and Mum opens the door. She grabs Dad and helps him to a chair by the kitchen sink. She rips the arm off his shirt and begins to wash the wound. He has a deep bite down his left forearm. Mum pours heavy-duty bleach and scouring powder over the wound and begins frantically to scrub.

It must hurt like hell. Dad is not objecting, not even flinching.

"Did you see his mouth?" Mum whispers.

"Yes, probably just a coincidence. Mad dogs froth for lots of different reasons."

Mum washes off the bleach and scouring powder and bandages up his arm. Dad goes out onto the back veranda and takes out a cheroot. "Can you call the police?" he asks, "See if they've got a dog catcher."

There's a noise in the dining room. Sam pushes home the bolt in the kitchen door.

Mum is on the phone to the police. Yes, there is a dog catcher. Yes, they'll send him around. No, there's no charge. It's paid for by the municipality.

Minnie emerges from the pantry with her book. Mum makes Marmite sandwiches for the kids and a cup of hot black instant coffee for Dad. She makes him take some antibiotics she has left over from something else.

We sit quietly in the kitchen, eating and waiting. There are occasional smashing noises from the dining room. Eventually, the dog catcher turns up. My Dad goes out to meet him and explain things. Mum keeps us holed up in the kitchen. I watch Dad and the dog catcher talking at the end of the hallway. Dad shows him his bandaged arm. The dog catcher takes a look. He asks Dad a series of questions and then disappears into the brilliant sunlight.

Dad comes back into the kitchen.

"He is going to build a cage around the dining room door to take Maxi away in." He rubs his wounded arm absentmindedly.

"He will have to chisel through the hinges and push the door back into the room. He says Maxi will rush into the cage, and he will close a sliding door to lock him in."

The dog catcher appears in the hallway carrying some sections of heavy metal mesh and various tools. We watch as he builds a steel cage and prepares to fix it with three-inch screws to the door frame.

"Is that really necessary?" Mum is concerned about repairs. "This is a rented house, and the damage will have to be paid for."

"Ridgeback, your husband said."

"Yes"

"Then yes, this is all really necessary." The dog catcher begins to screw the metal cage to the door frame. The noise level in the dining room begins to increase. Occasional crashes and bangs give way to a whirlwind of noise. Maxi is going berserk in there.

Finally, the cage is fixed, and the dog catcher, with a long steel chisel and a club hammer, begins to cut through the screws holding the door hinges in place. He takes a long piece of wood like a broom handle and pushes the door back and into the dining room. It falls with a crash followed with blinding speed by a blur of teeth and fur smashing against the back of the cage with such force that the door frame itself begins to shift. With practised ease, the dog catcher uses his broom handle to flick the catch on the sliding door. The door slides down with a loud metallic bang. Inside the cage, Maxi is turning himself inside out in blind, mad rage.

The dog catcher unscrews the cage from the door frame and drags it along the hallway with a long hook. Two long wavy scars appear in the parquet floor as the sharp edges of the cage gouge their way along the corridor. We follow as he pulls Maxi out into the sunshine of the veranda, down the steps and into the front yard. Before anyone can so much as think, the dog catcher reaches in through the window of his truck and pulls out a rifle. He levels the gun at the blur of rage in the cage and fires four or five times. The sound of the gunshots is deafening. Suddenly there is silence. Maxi lies still and bloody and dead.

"You folks newly arrived?" The dog catcher asks with a grin.

"Yes." Dad is nursing his bitten arm.

"Well then, welcome to Africa!"

This is when I burst into tears and run back inside the house.

Another car pulls up in the drive. It's the vet.

Maxi is taken off to be tested for rabies. It will be five days until the results are known. The treatment for rabies, multiple painful injections directly through the stomach muscles and into the lining of the stomach must begin within twenty-four hours. Dad has completed the treatment before the test results are known. The results arrive before the weekend. Maxi did not have rabies after all.

FOR HIM, BUT NOT FOR ME

Miriam is dressing for her end-of-year dance at the design school she attends. She will be leaving the school at the end of this term. She is taking very great care. I will not be going. She has asked me not to go. There is this guy she fancies, she has been attracted to him all year, and this will be her last chance to get his attention. I watch her dress, and undress, and dress again. Shoes are matched to skirts, tops to jeans, and accessories to handbags. A ritual.

I am at a loss, bewildered by her audacity as much as anything. Is she just being modern in the face of my oafish chauvinism? Would I be unreasonable to voice an objection? Why does she think it's ok? I don't know how to respond.

She stands naked by the mirror, examining her body, scrutinising the perfect nineteen-year-old curves. Frowning, she strokes the smoothness of her belly and caresses her pert little bottom. Satisfied, she slips into her foundation, the underwear, building from the inside out, layers to be enjoyed and removed, all in good time.

We have been living together for over a year. She selects the core of her outfit, the underwear, her best, very sexy. She begins to dress again, the final run this time. I watch, helpless.

I watch as the silky lace fabric slides softly across her skin, for him, but not for me. I am transfixed as she positions her bra, her full teenage breasts heaving against restraint. She has chosen a little white cotton dress that emphasises her slim waist and shapely calf. A deep-cut neckline and push-up bra do the rest.

I am slowly hollowed out as she applies her make-up. The ritual is the same, watched and admired so many times. Not for me this time.

"What time do you expect to get home?"

"Oh, late, don't wait up."

"That's ok. I won't be able to sleep until I know you are back home safe."

"There's really no need! I might be very late. I may not be coming home tonight."

"Do you have enough money? I can let you have some cash for a taxi."

"I'll be fine. I have to go now."

With a final flourish, she sprays herself with Rive Gauche (duty-free from a holiday in France). I watch as she scampers down the stairs, hesitating a moment at the front door. She takes a deep breath.

"Have a good time. Be careful".

"Bye," she is gone with a flounce. The door left open for me to close. I am furious, raging, and betrayed. I am unfamiliar with these feelings. I do not know their names. I close the door gently. The house is empty.

Quickly I open the door again and rush into the street, hoping for something, perhaps a backward glance. I cannot see her. She must have sprinted to the corner. I return to the silence of the house. It is dark and warm. The scent of her perfume has stolen down the stairs and now permeates every nook and cranny. I open a tin of baked beans and empty it into a cleanish saucepan. Pop two slices of Mother's Pride into the toaster and turn on the TV in the sitting room.

Banal sound sweeps through the place. Smells of toast and tomato sauce begin to overpower the lingering scent.

I sling a teabag into a mug and turn on the kettle. I take refuge in familiar actions, trivia and routine.

I watch an obscure movie on the TV for a while, seeking distraction. The film, 'Thunder in the Sun', turns out to be rather wonderful in an incomprehensibly silly Hollywood way. The story concerns a group of Basques (the kind from Spain) attempting to cross the United States by wagon train with vines that they wish to plant in California. As they travel through the mountains, they are beset by natives, BUT, being Basques, they are all too familiar with mountainous terrain and reveal their hitherto unsuspected and, frankly, bizarre fighting skills, which involve leaping from rocky crag to rocky crag whilst ululating maniacally. Their secret weapon is a sort of curved wicker basket, which they strap to their arms and use to hurl stones with terrifying speed and Iberian accuracy. Fortunately, they win through the mountains to the plain. At which point, I lose interest and set to torturing myself by imagining exactly what Miriam is doing right now.

I imagine her seeking him out at the dance, assuring herself that he is there. I see her wandering over nonchalantly. Saying 'Hi'. He sees her as if, for the first time, she looks gorgeous. He asks her for a dance. 'Sexual Healing' is playing slow and sensuous. He leads her onto the dance floor. Slips his arm around her, pulling her close. He feels the warmth of her body, her willingness. He catches her scent. She rests her head on his shoulder. He caresses her back. They move together to the rhythm. He kisses her shoulder. She snuggles closer. He kisses her neck, working his way sweetly past her ear to her cheek. She pulls away slightly. He slips his strong hand behind her shoulder, drawing her in firmly. She gives in to the slight pressure and allows her face to come closer and closer to his. He lifts her chin gently and kisses her slowly, attention focussed absolutely on the kiss, on her. He feels her heart beating fast against his chest.

"Bollocks!" I jump up and stride angrily around the house. I check the cupboards. There is nothing to drink. It is too late to go to the bottle shop. I stomp out into the back yard and look up at the late June London sky. The orange light of a million sodium streetlamps casts a cancerous glow across the city. There is a slight breeze - warm. I stand for a while, listening to the sounds of London wafting across the back yard. The ceaseless rumble of traffic, which you never normally notice, is punctuated by car horns and a distant siren fading into the night. The wind picks up. I allow myself to get cold. I consider jumping into a cab and simply turning up at the dance. I have just enough common sense to rule that out. He's probably gay, I tell myself.

I make a hot mug of coffee, determined to wait up, imagining the confrontation when she returns, experiencing the sick dread that she may not. I watch the late news, taking disproportionate pleasure in the misfortunes of corrupt and incompetent politicians. There is a sex scandal, of course – a tiny, apparently sexless MP is not denying having taken a tall, voluptuous courtesan to an official engagement, he is, however, denying all knowledge that she is tall, voluptuous or a courtesan, and he is fervently denying having been intimate with her. Tragically, whilst no one accepts that he was in any doubt as to her calling, it is all too easy to believe that he has never slept with her, or anyone else for that matter. A cruel news editor juxtaposes pictures of the pair – he will not be required to resign, poor little bastard.

It is past one in the morning. If she were coming home, she would be home by now. I wonder where she is. Did he take her back to his place? Is she with him now? I hear her giggling as he shushes her up the stairs at his apartment, trying not to wake his flatmates. I see him lay her across his bed. He kisses her ankles as he removes her tiny stilettos and tosses them casually to the floor. He brushes her calves with his lips. He slides his hand across the warmth of her thighs, resting on the silk lace of her panties. She throws a languorous arm around his neck and pulls him on top of her. They kiss with fiery passion. Suddenly each is fumbling desperately at the zips and buttons of the other's clothing. They rip each other naked. She cups his balls firmly in one hand, kissing his chest. He grabs her by the scruff of the neck, urging her down. She teases, kissing his stomach slowly. With his free hand, he explores her, pressing his strong fingers into her, stimulating her. She goes down on him.

The door slams. I leap up from semi-sleep. It is her. She has come home. She looks tired and fed up, and crestfallen.

"He wasn't there?" I venture.

"He wasn't interested."

I am awash with turbulent emotion. I am elated that he rejected her and that she was hurt by his rejection. I am moved by her sadness and dejection. I am angry with her, and I want her.

I put my arms around her and say soft things. I lead her upstairs to bed. She is a little wobbly, a little drunk. I undress her. I enjoy unwrapping her. It's like an unexpected birthday present. I unhook her bra, noting the rise and fall of her breasts. I place two fingers on either side of her panties and slip them off. She is aroused, and I am suddenly angry again. Enraged by her intended betrayal. I am determined she will cry out with pleasure tonight, but not for him, for me!

I take her savagely, without tenderness. She responds in kind. We fuck hard, sustained by rejection and loss. Satiated, we sleep.

MULBERRIES

Felix, the hugely muscled Swahili labourer who works on our newly acquired 'farm' seven miles from Luanshya in Zambia, is singing to himself as he dismantles some kind of machinery in the shade of the mulberry trees. Minnie is sitting cross-legged in the car tyre swing opposite the garage reading a book while Ingrid plays in the dirt nearby. Sam is nowhere to be seen. I am sitting at the top of a mango tree, chatting with my friend Sawa, Felix's youngest son.

Felix and his entire family (wife and five children) more or less came with the farm when my father bought it. Felix, although all but illiterate, has one of those incredible minds. He has this amazing ability to just figure things out, all sorts of things that you would have thought someone would need a college education for. Today, it's the electricity generator that has broken down again. My dad is away as usual, and we have been without power for several days. Felix is patiently dismantling the thing piece by piece to find the fault.

He lays out each part on the purple-coloured clay path along the avenue of mulberry trees, which leads from our back yard to the maize field at the back of our house. The avenue is probably one hundred metres long, dyed a deep rich purple by the juice of the mulberries falling to the ground and being squished by passing feet.

Each component is laid out in the order that it has been removed from the generator because, as Felix explains, "How else will I know how to put them back?" The process takes hours as I sit with Sawa, watching him. Eventually, Felix has produced a long line of components stretching almost all the way to the cornfield. My mother approaches, seeing the dissected machine lying in pieces along the path.

"It's ok, madam," Felix is a little uneasily, "I'm just fixing the electricity generator."

My mother looks down at the snaking row of metal laid out neatly on the mulberry path and back to Felix. She looks up and smiles.

"Thank you, Felix."

Half an hour of further dismantling and a metre or two more of generator parts and Felix suddenly holds up a small square piece of blackened metal.

"I found him." He smiles at Sawa and me, both now covered from head to toe in mulberry juice and grime.

"Don't touch anything!" he admonishes Sawa before turning to me and asking, "Bwana Pat, will you ask madam to get another one of these?"

I scamper off down the edge of the path, with Felix striding behind me toward the low white bungalow, its red corrugated iron roof visible occasionally through the trees. My mother is sitting on the back veranda, shelling peas. It is intensely hot in the still summer air and silent but for the intermittent high-pitched drone of the cicadas. My dad insists on calling them crickets.

"We've found it!" I cry as she hoves into view. Brandishing aloft the offending part, "We've found the broken bit".

Felix strolls up a moment or two later. My mother puts down the bowl of shelled peas and emerges from the shaded veranda to see what I am holding.

"This one is broken, madam. Can madam get a new one?"

It is soon agreed that my mother and I will venture the seven-mile drive into Luanshya in her extremely old and psychopathically unreliable green Morris Minor to see if a 'new one' can be obtained. I am particularly keen to accompany her as a trip to town will mean a visit to the magical cornucopia 'Theo's Multi-Racial General Store, Cocktail Bar and Tea Rooms', a tiny general store run by a Greek man that sells everything from the local delicacy, tins of condensed milk, through to mantles for gas lamps and a small, dried fish from lake Victoria, called 'Capenta' in the local Bemba language.

THE HILL

The seven miles into Luanshya will take about half an hour. The day is very hot. Huge clouds promise torrential rain this afternoon. The ancient green leather seats of my mother's Morris Minor car smell strongly of old leather polish and dust. Minnie is staying home to read her book and look after Ingrid. The drive is very bumpy. The shock absorbers having long since given up the ghost. I am looking forward to just one thing. The lovely bit where the road suddenly pitches down a precipitously steep hill before crossing a small river via a decrepit wooden bridge wide enough for one car at a time (this is where my mother always vents her new-found Catholicism by muttering "Holy Mary Mother of God, Blessed are thou among women and blessed is the fruit of thy womb Christ Jesus, bring us safely to the other side", and then there's the inevitable visit to Theo's.

Mum's Catholicism seems to have rubbed off on Minnie a bit too. She has a white dress like a wedding dress and a white veil that she says she will wear when she gets 'confirmed'. I have only the vaguest idea what's she's going on about, but the other day she crucified one of her dolls, which I thought was a bit odd.

I stare out the window, enjoying the feel of the wind in my face. I catch the acrid smell of the smoke from charcoal burners visible amongst the trees off to either side of the road. I recognise the huge tree we all call 'the bunch of grapes' due to its shape, leaning over the road ahead. The steep hill and the bridge are just around the next bend. My mother recognises it too and begins to clear her throat. We both watch the white lines in the middle of the road flicking past, each one bringing us closer to the hill, closer to God.

We approach the lip of the hill where it starts, innocently, to dip. My mother grabs one thick plait of black hair in one hand, thrusting it between her teeth in some very personal, piratical gesture of defiance, aimed if not at God Himself, then at the very least, at His creation.

We begin the descent, oh joy of joys! The car picks up speed. There is nothing on the road ahead. We can see, for at least a mile, down this side of the hill and all the way up the other. In the very far distance, at the extreme end of sight, I think I can see a snake making its way across the road. I cannot tell which way it is going. Its thin, rope-like body disappears into the bush on either side of the road. It will be long gone by the time we get there.

The car is now juddering and rattling alarmingly as we speed down the hill. My mother begins to apply the brakes. There is little noticeable effect. We speed on. A truck appears at the brow of the hill opposite – a very long way off. We are a fair way down our side of the hill, but the truck is beginning to pick up speed too. It is loaded with long straight Congo Oak trunks for the sawmills on the Kitwe road. Truck drivers like to pick up speed on the descent as it helps them to make it up the other side and saves on diesel.

The truck is coming on fast. It is not clear to me if we will cross the bridge before the truck gets to the bottom of the hill or if it will beat us to it.

My mother is attempting the same calculation. Suddenly she slams her foot against the brake pedal, pushing it all the way to the floor. This time there is a noticeable change. We do start to slow a little. We both review our speed against that of the oncoming truck and the remaining distance to the bridge. Too close to call.

The truck driver seems suddenly to have made the same calculation. Perhaps he estimates correctly that the brakes on our car are almost shot. He begins to accelerate hard. Plumes of dust and exhaust fumes swirl out behind the cab.

He is not going to make it! Suddenly the mental calculus comes clear. He is not going fast enough. My mother makes her decision. Large trees line the road. There is nowhere to pull off. We cannot stop. She takes her foot off the brake and floors the accelerator. We pick up even more speed. I can see that it is going to be very, very close. I have no fear. I am six years old. I am immortal.

The truck driver realises what my mother has done, reviews his own chances and changes gear. We are close enough now to hear the sound of his engine approaching. Unbelievably he has *increased* his speed. He is accelerating towards us.

"Holy Mary Mother of God, Blessed are thou among women and blessed is the fruit of thy womb Christ Jesus, bring us safely to the other side".

I heartily agree. We are on the narrow bridge. We can hear the sound of the truck's horn blaring out and the raging hiss of compression braking. We are almost across. I notice the writhing segments of a dead snake whipping the road halfway up the hill ahead, cut to pieces by the truck.

We are across. The road widens slightly, and my mother wrenches the steering wheel to the left, willing the car out of the path of the oncoming juggernaut. It rages past with only inches to spare.

"Yeeehaaww!" I am elated. That was fantastic, the best ever!

My mother's face is white as a sheet. Her knuckles are white against the steering wheel. Our momentum is carrying us nicely up the other side. I fall silent. She is beginning to shake.

We crest the hill on the other side of the bridge. She pulls the old Morris Minor over onto the red earth at the side of the road. There is sudden, absolute silence. Red dust thrown up by the racing truck swirls around, smelling of hot quartz and directionless rage. My mother throws open the door and leans out, retching and gasping simultaneously. I look on awkwardly, knowing I should help but not knowing how to. I open the passenger door and run round to her side of the car. I offer her the last quarter of my bottle of orange Fanta, warm and almost flat. It is all I have. She waves the bottle away and throws up in earnest. Specks splash my bare feet. I hardly ever wear shoes.

She gets her breath back and controls the shaking. She gets out of the car, walking to and fro, throwing her arms around her body and then out, repetitively, hugging herself. She is wearing a white cotton dress with enormous red roses, very tight across the body, very flared and pleated from the waist. Her hair is black, her lips are red, and her face is white.

"You look very beautiful", I tell her, and she does, actually.

She swoops down and lifts me up, hugging me tight, saying, "Brave boy! Brave boy!" over and over again.

We get back in the car and continue the journey. The clapped-out old engine wheezes into life and we set off on the few remaining kilometres to town. The dead snake has finally stopped wriggling.

ONE ZAMBIA, ONE NATION!

The banging and singing have been going on for hours, hypnotically, on and on. Men working, men banging, men singing. Steel and bamboo, the scaffolding stage grows, shaded by the tall Congo Oaks sprinkled across our front lawn. I watch, with Sam and Minnie, out of the way at the top of the mango trees that line the drive from the road to the house. We are excited. Nothing like this has ever happened before. The song is rhythmic. It marshals the men, coordinates their effort, synchronises their bulging muscles, swells their chests, expresses their unity, and gives them voice. We breathe in time to the rhythm of the men. Our bodies vibrate, and our hearts beat to the rhythm of independent Africa, to the rhythm of *Zambia*.

Pickup trucks slow on Jacopy Road as they pass the boundary of our land. Afrikaners mainly, and European white settlers. They are not happy, not happy at all. We, children, are oblivious. There is going to be a huge political rally in our garden. Ten thousand people will come, twenty thousand! My father has agreed to allow Kenneth Kaunda's Party, UNIP, to hold a rally on our farm. He says Northern Rhodesia should be independent. He says the Africans should run things themselves. My friends at school, and their parents, are worried. They remember the Mau Mau in Kenya and the Lenshina Riots in our own country. I am torn. I know my dad is right that the whites cannot own Africa, that Africa is not theirs, but this is my home. I live here. My friends live here. Unspoken fear underlies excitement. Dispossession waits silently in the wings.

Some say Kaunda himself will come. He will visit our home and have tea with my mum and dad. It is bewildering. I go along with it.

Time for lunch. I shim down the mango tree and run around to the kitchen at the back of the house to make myself a sandwich. I find my mum up to her elbows in giant trays of peanut butter sandwiches. The men are hungry. I am to help her carry out the trays of food.

There is a momentary awkwardness as the realisation spreads that a white woman is bringing them food. Then all smiles and "Thank you, madam". The men rest and eat. The stage is almost complete. Trucks arrive carrying public address equipment and a huge generator. I catch a glimpse of one of the huge green lizards that live in the trees, glaring balefully down, unimpressed.

A small crowd has gathered on the road. Several pickup trucks have stopped. Men are standing on the flat boards at the back, carrying shotguns and rifles. One of the men shouts something. My dad reacts, worried, trying to avoid any 'nastiness'. The stage builders melt away, only to rise moments later, like flood waters, around the trucks. The 'waters' continue to rise around the settlers, silent, smiling, unafraid. Engines start, and trucks move away slowly. Crisis past.

The next morning, we are all awake early. Minnie sets aside the book she is reading to go outside and enjoy the excitement. By the time I wander outside, about six fifteen in the morning, the day is already hot. There are people everywhere. Silent, relaxed, expectant. The generator coughs and comes to life. People rush about the stage setting up chairs and microphone stands. The inevitable 'one-two, one-two' booms out across the garden. My friends and I run around under the stage, between the bamboo and steel poles, beneath the spot where Kenneth Kaunda himself will later stand. Music suddenly blares, loud and tinny, from the PA speakers. People in the crowd get up and begin to dance. It is still early morning. It is party time.

People keep coming all morning. Additional PA speakers are rigged up in the field behind the house, out of sight of the stage. Still, the people come. Every inch of space is occupied long before the dignitaries arrive. People are sitting on the shed roof, in the mango trees, everywhere, in their thousands. It is impossible for me to guess numbers. My dad says there are about twenty thousand people crammed into our eight-acre farm.

There is a long line of large black ladies, many with children strapped to their backs with shawls, forming around our house. My mother has decided to offer the women the use of our single toilet. There is much joking and amusement among the women and much dignity as they wait their turn in the blazing sun. The line goes around the house and down the mulberry path all the way to the maize field.

Dignitaries begin to arrive and take their place on the stage. An air of expectancy gathers, and people begin to sing political songs. The rally begins. Someone explains that Kaunda cannot be with us in person. He is held up on important business in Lusaka, but he is certainly with us in spirit. The crowd is disappointed. The speaker calls out to the crowd. If Kaunda cannot be with us in person, let us at least make sure he can hear us all the way to Lusaka.

Call and response. The cry is taken up, first by one, by many, by all. The sound and rhythm pound the air like a fist. Our chests reverberate with the depth and power of the sound.

ONE ZAMBIA,
ONE NATION

ONE NATION,
ONE LEADER

ONE LEADER,
ONE KAUNDA

CHICKATAY
CHISOKONAY
N'DOOM!

And with each N'DOOM! The upheld fists of the revolutionaries are brought down against their chests in a gesture of defiance, implacability and strength. Africa is not ours. I realise. We cannot stay here.

Miriam is going on holiday with her family to Provence. They always go to Provence. They have a small villa set in orchards near a pretty little hill town by the sea. Apparently, the perfectly preserved medieval hill fort was built by the Cathars of neighbouring Languedoc, who were prone to persecution at the time by the Catholic Church. She will be gone for two weeks. I have just started a new job and cannot go with her.

I am not looking forward to two weeks working in the airless polluted heart of London in July while Miriam is away sunning herself in the South of France. Miriam keeps rubbing it in, quoting from Ode to Provence, "Oh for a beaker full of the warm South!" and such like. Extremely irritating. Our relationship is still quite young. We are girlfriend and boyfriend rather than the more grown-up 'partners'. Frankly, I wish she'd just piss off and leave me to it, but this is the evening before she flies out, and I have to be nice. I decide to be gallant about it and buy a bottle of Vin de Pays d'Oc. Miriam does not like red wine all that much, so I will get the lion's share. It only takes a glass to get her tipsy and a second to get her horny. There is method to my madness.

We have French bread and pâté and drink red wine at room temperature served in small, perfectly round glasses. Joni Mitchell is on the record player wailing about California and goat herds. We begin to dance and then to smooch. Miriam has a great arse, small and pert and perfectly round. We become somewhat entangled as we dance, ultimately tottering into an unceremonious heap on the sofa. Miriam is lying across my knee, giggling, face down, out of breath. This is one of our good evenings. We go to bed happy.

Miriam is bright and breezy in the morning, very matter-of-fact. I have to face an hour and two changes on British Rail to get to work. I give her a little kiss and say, "Have a lovely time, send me a postcard." And then I am out of the house. The early morning is clean and clear as I walk to the station. My friend Andy calls to see if I am up for a party on the weekend. Miriam will be away. What the hell? I write the details in my diary and dive into the working week.

It is surprisingly boring at home without Miriam. I can do anything I want. I don't want to do anything. I stamp around in the evenings making fried egg sandwiches with tomato sauce. Leaving the plates to collect in the sink. I miss her. I keep thinking of that last night, of her pert round arse across my knee. I lie in bed at night, reliving the glorious sensuality of it, relieving my own frustrations over and over again. I can't wait for her to get back.

Saturday duly arrives, and I head off with a gallon drum of Watneys Red Barrel Bitter for the boys and a six-pack of Baby Cham for the girls. The party is at Andy's mum's place, but she is not there. Instead, Andy's mature and responsible cousin Leanne has been drafted in to supervise. This is something of a vain exercise as she is one of the biggest pissheads I know. Great girl, though, drives a sports car and shares in all the usual debaucheries.

I arrive early to help set up and share a couple of joints with Leanne. Setting up means clearing enough room on the kitchen table to set up the booze. I can do that.

By the time actual guests begin to arrive, we are all wasted. Leanne and I are deep in an apparently philosophical debate as to, perhaps, the meaning of life, the nature of existence and life after death. Andy is digging holes for the fairies at the bottom of his mum's garden – no one knows exactly why the fairies need this done, but Andy is determined. The evening is getting off to a wonderful start.

At some point, Leanne and I become very close friends. We find our way to Andy's mum's bedroom, and we get into some seriously heavy petting. I am sparing no thought for the Cathars, Provence or Miriam. I am getting down and dirty with Andy's mature and responsible cousin Leanne. We fuck like tigers until we pass out.

In the morning, we part company as friends, with no regrets. Leanne drops me at the tube station. I watch her drive off. Nice girl. I have a final cigarette before venturing into the abyss of London's underground rail network.

During the week, it finally dawns on me that what I have done is called 'being unfaithful' and is generally considered wrong. I know well enough how I would feel if Miriam did it. I agonise momentarily over whether or not to tell Miriam. I am a bloke. Of course, I'm not going to tell her. Instead, I call Andy to see how he is going. He is in somewhat bad odour with his mum regarding fairies and the fact that someone had slept in her bed.

"Possibly several people judging by the state of the room!" according to her.

I ask if Leanne had a good time. He says he thinks so, hasn't actually heard from her and was still asleep when she left. All is well. No point in mentioning it. Miriam is due home in a few days, and I realise I am really looking forward to seeing her impish little face.

The days drag. London has an unexpected heatwave revealing hideously white and sunburned young women in all their pallid glory. I don't suppose I look much better myself. I spend Friday night washing the dishes and vacuuming the floor.

Saturday morning, I drive to Miriam's parents' place to pick her up. I arrive a little early and sit on the doorstep, having a cigarette and a bit of a daydream. The next thing I am aware of is the sound of their voices getting out of the taxi. Shit! I spin around, looking for a place to get rid of the cigarette butt. There is nothing nearby except an empty milk bottle. I drop it in and stand up. A happy, welcoming smile across my face.

"Hi, did you have a good time?"

"Yes, we all got a bit sunburned, and Daddy had a tummy upset."

"Here, let me help you with your bags".

"Come on in and have a cuppa." Miriam's mum is always hospitable, "Oh, be a dear and run around to the corner shop for some milk, would you? I am sure I left a note out for the milkman."

All eyes are turned to the lone milk bottle on the doorstep, smoking lazily in the morning sun.

"Back in a mo", I beat a hasty retreat.

By the time I return, the house is in its usual pandemonium, and I slip in unnoticed. We have a cup of tea and a bit of a chat about Provence and foreign climbs generally. I am beginning to feel a little overwhelmed by the family atmosphere. The power of the clan is very strong and can stifle. I manage to drag Miriam out of the house and into the car.

Now that I am with Miriam again, I begin to feel jittery about the thing with Leanne. She is starving. We stop on the way home for salt beef bagels at the 24-hour bakery in Brick Lane. I am particularly solicitous to Miriam's needs. I throw in a piece of cheesecake.

"Gosh, you really did miss me, didn't you?" she laughs uncertainly, "I hope you didn't get up to any mischief."

"Chance'd be a fine thing. We had a heatwave while you were away, would you believe?"

We munch on salt beef bagels for a while before I remember.

"I hope you were a good girl in Provence. Didn't get up to anything I might consider naughty?"

"Of course not! What are you suggesting?" The tone has turned cold and suspicious.

"Nothing. Only joking". Silence descends once more.

Saturday morning traffic through the East End is surprisingly light. Tower Bridge approach road is clear. We are soon safely back in South London.

"I didn't get up to anything on holiday", Miriam volunteers from out of nowhere, "you are always so suspicious."

Life soon returns to normal. I go to work, and Miriam goes to college. We both go to the pub in the evenings and play pool. We come home drunk and have fumbling sex. Thus is the even tenor of our days.

About ten days after the Leanne thing, I notice an uncomfortable itch in my groin. Upon investigation, I discover an infestation of small lice-like critters. Although I have never had this particular problem before, I am pretty sure these are known affectionately as 'crabs'. Thank you, Leanne!

As always, when presented with a problem of this magnitude, I refer to my much-thumbed copy of the 'Alternative London', a cornucopia of unusual and illicit information for the accident-prone. It recommends 'painting yourself all over with "Ascabiol" from chemists, without prescription'. I jot the name down on a slip of paper torn from the Readers Digest.

Miriam is still asleep. I rush down to the chemist in the high street, arriving as it opens. I sprint to the dispensing counter, praying I will be served before the endless elderly patrons waiting outside manage to Zimmer-frame it through the store.

"Please, may I have a large bottle of Ascabiol?"

"What are you using it to treat?"

I realise that a little more preparation might have been good. No one expects the Spanish Inquisition.

"My dog"

"Your dog?"

"Yes, the vet recommended it."

"What for?"

"For the dog" clearly, I am engaged in a verbal fencing match with a master.

"What is wrong with the dog?" Shit, I really have no answer to that. What if I say the wrong thing? This bastard clearly doesn't believe a word I am saying. I stare at the scrubby bit of paper in my hand, 'Ascabiol'.

"Scabies!" best guess I can come up with.

Reluctantly the pharmacist shuffles off to get the stuff. I am relieved and elated. I have won. I have beaten the nosy bastard pharmacist. He is gone quite a while before returning with a four-litre flagon of white liquid.

"Take a hot bath and rub this on all the inflamed and itchy areas." He smirks. I am surrounded by elderly Zimmer-frame athletes, snickering to themselves.

When I get home, I have a second problem. Miriam is now awake, has made her own tea and is not in a great mood. I hide the family-sized bottle behind a large plant pot in the front garden and try to enter the house surreptitiously. Pointless. No sooner is the key in the lock than she comes hurtling down the stairs.

"You're up early." Eyes narrowed, nasty suspicious tone.

"Yes, went for a walk, woke up early and couldn't get back to sleep."

"Hmmm." No immediate forfeit, then. I slope off to make myself a cup of tea and some toast.

Miriam is going shopping later with a friend. After she leaves, I wait a full fifteen minutes before peeking out of the front door. The coast is clear. I sprint across to the flowerpot, retrieve the enormous bottle of white lotion and rush back into the house, all in under a second. I run a bath as quickly and as hot as possible and jump in. The goo comes out in enormous goops, which I spread liberally around my genitals. The effect is repulsive. I shan't describe it further. I am not sure how long I have to leave it on. I stand in the bath, dripping goops of white goo from my genitals and shivering. I notice a growing warmth in the affected region. The warmth swiftly increases to a fiery glow and thence to blowtorch intensity. I throw myself down in the bath and scrub hysterically for twenty minutes. I let the water out and hose myself down. The skin of my nether regions is scalded a fiery scarlet. I am without dignity, whimpering slightly. I find the loosest underwear I have and slip gingerly into it. How on earth am I going to keep this from Miriam?

By mid-afternoon, the scarlet has faded to an excusable pink. I hide the bottle under an oily rag in the boot of the car.

Miriam returns with bargains and is very happy. I say nothing. Time passes, and still, I say nothing. The blowtorch appears to have done its job, at least. Three or four weeks later, I realise that Miriam has mentioned nothing either, and neither has Leanne.

METHANE AND WEAVER BIRDS

It is one of those cold clear spring days in the mountains, up above the tree line. The Swazi winter is over, the six-foot snow drifts have cleared, the fireplace is cold and silent, golden weaver birds are busy in the willows overhanging the pond, and my brother, surprisingly, is willing to endure my presence. School has not yet started, and he is bored. I will do.

Mum has gone for a long walk taking my sisters Minnie and Ingrid with her. Sam and I wander down to the pond and watch the weaver birds building their nests. Hundreds, perhaps thousands, feverishly building their little city of golden grass purses. Each one hanging from the outermost, apparently least permanent, twig they could find.

The colony appears to grow before our eyes, extending like a time-lapse film to fill every inch of available real estate. We are standing on the concrete dam itself now, peering down into the icy, crystal-clear water. The spirit of the mountains sniffs this way, and a chill wind blows over the mountainside, whipping the grassy slopes this way and that like a giant pallet knife. The dassies are up and about. New life is everywhere.

In the deepest depths of the pond, it is possible to see platannas gliding purposelessly, marginally above the deep organic silt. Minute swirls of mud are flicked up by an unexpectedly powerful push of their long, mottled legs, clearly visible, prehistoric, some twelve feet below.

Occasional bubbles of gas push free of the mud and begin their slow, wobbly ascent. We watch as they pick up speed, only to pop when they reach the surface.

"Methane." My brother raises an eyebrow to indicate that this is a concept way beyond my meagre mental capacity.

"What?"

"Methane."

"You-thane what?"

"No, those bubbles. They are methane."

"What's methane?"

"Kind of gas"

"What kind?"

"Methane!"

"Well, what's so special about it?"

"It's inflammable." My brother is four years older than I am and is familiar with words like that.

"What's that mean?"

"Inflammable means that it catches fire."

"The air in the bubbles catches fire?"

"Yes."

"When?"

"When what?"

"When does it catch fire?"

"When you set fire to it." This is all getting a bit circular for my tastes.

"Show me."

"What?"

"Set fire to a bubble."

We don't have any matches, so I wait in the limpid sunshine while he runs off to pinch some from the kitchen. I catch a bubble as it rises, cupping it in my palms. The gas has a funny smell, not horrible exactly, but kind of earthy. My hands are frozen. The banks of the stream that feeds the pond are still dotted with patches of snow, shaded from the sun, left over from a recent fall.

My brother reappears with a box of matches and proceeds to hold lighted matches above the surface, waiting for a bubble to appear within range. Several matches blow out, and a couple burn down to his fingertips before he drops them hissing into the pond. We watch with rapt attention as a large fat bubble wobbles its weary way from the murk to the surface, popping obligingly next to the concrete dam wall. There is a brief, satisfying flare as the gas catches fire.

We lay next to each other on the dam wall, considering this new phenomenon. Watching the clouds swirl past, reflected in the dark, clear water. Listening to the bustling weaver birds. I have a brilliant idea.

"If we could collect a bit more of it, we'd get a better flame."

My brother agrees. We think about collecting methane. I remember an old terracotta flowerpot left over from my failed attempt the previous summer to create a vegetable garden on the nutrient-free, stony soil of the heath. I scamper off to get it.

When I get back, my brother has found a long bamboo pole with which he is stirring up the mud and silt at the bottom of the pond. A steady stream of bubbles is rising to the surface. I lean over the water, holding the flowerpot almost completely submerged in my right hand. I am in constant danger of toppling into the freezing water, and I am starting to giggle uncontrollably. I place the palm of my left hand over the hole in the centre of the upturned flowerpot, covering it well enough to allow the gas to build up.

It is agonisingly slow work. My arms begin to lose all feeling as the bubbles work their laborious way to the surface. I move the flowerpot slightly this way and that, trying to catch every bubble. After a few minutes of this, and at the point where I am losing all feeling in my arms, I believe I have collected what must be a reputable amount of methane. I bring the flowerpot around towards Sam. He sees what I am doing and pulls up the bamboo pole, discarding it on the bank. Keeping the flat bottom of the upturned flowerpot just above the water's surface, my hand still tightly pressed over the hole, not allowing any gas to escape, I wait while Sam fumbles with a box of matches.

The bottom of the upturned flowerpot is poking an inch or so above the water. My brother leans over and lights a match. I am clinging to the submerged rim of the flowerpot with one hand, trying not to fall in, still covering the hole with the other. My face is only inches from the hole.

"Quick, move your hand." My brother holds the match to the hole. There is an almighty gout of flame, perhaps a yard high and a loud 'whoosh'. The pressure of the water forces the gas out in a powerful stream. My face is hot. The stench of burnt skin and hair is in the air.

I see my reflection in the water. I have completely burnt away my fringe and peeled some skin from one finger, fan-bloody-tastic! Total success! We rush off to tell our father all about it.

He is sitting at the kitchen table, drinking tea, reading the newspaper. He looks up as we run in. Looking to my brother first, his son and heir, then seeing me wet and burnt and laughing with excitement.

He was a captain in the Royal Engineers. That methane is inflammable is not, it seems, news to him. He is impressed at my brother's use of water pressure to prevent blowback.

"What's blow-back?" we both ask simultaneously. He explains (his remarks intended more for my brother than me) that if we had lifted the flowerpot almost all the way out of the water, there would not have been so much pressure pushing the methane out, so we would not have got such a good high flame, and it might have been possible for the flame to blow-back inside the flowerpot.

"What would that do?" I ask.

"Well," he explains, talking directly to me this time, "If the flame blew back into the flower pot, you might have had an explosion rather than a big flame."

"An explosion?"

"Yes, very dangerous."

Brilliant! We rush off to investigate.

CUTTY SARK

I am living alone with my father in beautiful downtown Balham, London (Gateway to the South). He is intensely lonely. I don't know what to do. Always tending to deep depression, he seems cursed in some subtle way. He was born in the wrong era. He is alienated from this modern world. Wrong for it, as it is wrong for him. I sometimes wonder if, like father, like son, I will follow in his footsteps. I am aware of a kind of narcissistic conceit in that, but I can't shake the feeling.

Sam is away in Cambodia, living with rebel Cambodian or Vietnamese irregulars along the border of the two countries. Last year he was in Thailand pretending to be a Buddhist monk. Next year – who knows? Minnie lives at Aunty Alice's just around the corner, but she never visits. She never comes near the place. Sometimes I see her crouching down behind cars to avoid being seen by Dad or me. You can always pick her out in her purple and green clothes – a horrible colour combination. Not sure why she does it. Not really sure what's going on with her at all. Mum and Ingrid are living in a tiny flat in North London. Mum has a new boyfriend, a young Aussie bloke who lives downstairs to them and plays the piano. He seems ok, and she's happy. At least I don't have to worry about her.

Dad and I watch TV together most evenings and share a bottle of Cutty Sark whiskey (he likes it with water, I take it straight). On more affluent occasions, we drink Jameson's. He is silent except when he tells stories. He is a wonderful raconteur. He is also, intellectually, one of the most brilliant people I have ever known. I am not brilliant. I do not do well at school. I don't give a shit about anything. I am a teenager.

I am short, reasonably athletic, with long dark hair to my waist, and not bad looking with a devilish, cheeky grin. I smoke too much and dabble in the less devastating drugs. I have good friends. I hardly ever think about Africa. I am inured to city life. I am ok.

My friends come around as much to hear my dad's stories as to see me. I am proud to have such an interesting dad. I am afraid for him too.

On the weekends, I prowl around London with my mates, drinking in The Windmill pub on Clapham Common, gate-crashing parties, and randomising. There are plenty of girls. We have no responsibilities. My three-year relationship with the exceedingly pretty Alice Pretty has ended due to my philandering and general idiocy, and I have taken up with a series of Tracy's. These are.

- Tracy, the junior British figure skating champion (fantastic body)
- Tracy, the actor I met at a drama club in Stepney (amazing grasp of the colloquial)
- Skinny Tracy, sister of one of my classmates (threw a cup of coffee over me)
- And Tracy Cumberbatch (not all that good-looking but incredibly sexy)

My Tracy period, though not the high point of my career, nevertheless displays a pleasing regularity – like a row of complementary ornaments. Feckless swine, my brother is right.

COMPANIONSHIP

We are walking together somewhere, Miriam and me. We walk together through the remains of our childhood, through adolescence, early adulthood and into middle age. We are spinning the threads of our lives together. We have our hands full with life. We are on an upward trajectory, climbing, exploring, and living life. We are overloaded with *things* as we reach the top of the arc. The view is splendid and terrible. We set things down, one by one, meaning to come back for them later, friendships, locations, sweet summer afternoons in Shropshire, memories, and love. I do not realise, neither one of us realises, that our lives end and are renewed with each passing instant. There is no going back.

We accumulate new things along the way. Like characters in a virtual reality game, collecting equipment, attributes, ambitions, achievements, successes and failures - pruning and replacing all the while. Things get easier. We do not notice the slope downward now. We are thankful each step requires less effort.

A slight hollow appears in the path, muddy and wet. We walk on together on either side, unconcerned. Over time the hollow becomes a mountain stream, tumbling and laughing between rocks. The stream widens and deepens as we walk on. It is still easily narrow enough to step across. The downward slope increases. The fast-flowing stream has eroded the soft limestone, cutting deep. We are walking in the Dolomite mountains in Italy. It is full summer. Our paths occasionally diverge, and we lose sight of one another for a moment, or two as one path or other diverts around rocks and trees. The stream ends suddenly in a pretty waterfall, cascading out of sight into a steep ravine. The paths on either side continue, more or less level, the gap still bridgeable.

We develop interests of our own. Our paths diverge further. The gulf becomes unbridgeable. We see, a little way ahead, a place where our paths converge once more, jutting rocks on either side of the gorge and, far below, a deep, broad river. As we come to the spot, we realise that the rocks do not meet. There is still a gulf, but it can be crossed. One or other of us must leap the gap. We go to counselling together to discuss the problem. We have a rope. I could attach it to my side of the gorge as a lifeline for Miriam. I look around for a fixing point. The rock is smooth and featureless. There is nowhere to attach the rope. I say I will wrap it around my waist, and the rope will hold. I look down at my body, fat, out of condition, middle-aged. Miriam doubts that I am strong enough to hold her weight. Secretly I doubt it, too, though I make encouraging noises. Miriam dares not make the jump, with or without a lifeline. We consider alternatives. There is a stump of an old tree on Miriam's side. I toss the rope over to her. She works for a while, attempting to secure the rope on her side. Each time she ties the rope, it slips off. Miriam cries out in frustration that it's not fair my expecting her to tie the rope. I have always done that sort of thing for her. She tosses the rope back in frustration. I grab one end and fumble. The rope slips off the smooth rock and falls into the ravine.

Way off, years ahead, we can see a spot where our paths appear to converge once more. We have no choice. We cannot go back. We walk on along our separate tracks, talking, making plans, and keeping our spirits up. We move to Sydney. Over time we talk less. Conversation stops. I go on a business trip to a conference in New Orleans. Suddenly, around a curve in the mountainside, the gorge opens out into a canyon, and wild spume and mist obscure our way. Our two paths snake off on either side, disappearing into the blue haze.

We can still speak across the gap without shouting. We make plans and take stock. We set down our various burdens and make an inventory, listing our assets. I realise that the things we have set down along the way, meaning to return for, are irretrievably lost. These are friends, family, relationships, and, of course, love. I am terrified to admit it. I gaze into the void. It lacks the meaning that I had always assumed. I search again, checking and re-checking. Lost, dejected, I mention it to Miriam. She is incandescent, furiously denying what I am saying, furious with me for saying it. She checks on her side, rummaging for ages through the debris of our lives. Finally, triumphantly, she brandishes aloft an iron cash box, rusted and without a key.

"It's in here." She may be right, but neither of us can open it.

Halfway between waking and sleeping. Musing on the past, on all that has happened. Dawn over Western Australia, slowly breaking. Remembering wild lightening across the Indian Ocean coming nearer, silently, through the darkness, approaching. Trying to recall *why did we ever come to Australia?*

Summer in Australia. We are on holiday from Ireland. Staying in Perth, Western Australia, visiting my mother and sisters. Having left school at sixteen with no visible qualifications, I have, finally, completed a degree (2:1 Politics and Philosophy, useless, but better than, say, Ancient History and Archaeology), and we have moved to North Dublin to live in a curiously tall and narrow decaying terraced townhouse that my grandmother left me. I am working in Social Services for the city council on what is known by my co-workers as 'The Dirty Squad'.

"Ah, you'll love it, Pat", the supervisor told me on my first day. I am a 'Domestic Environmental Health Officer' (don't ask).

Miriam and I do not yet have children. We are spending three months in Western Australia, re-acquainting ourselves with my family. It has been twelve years since we last saw them. My sister Ingrid was twelve when last I saw her. Now she is a woman of twenty-four. She works as a beautician, hairdresser and manicurist. Minnie says she lives in a bubble of certainty that the world loves her and will take care of her. Men, according to Ingrid's cosmology, will obligingly fall at her feet when required. The gulf seems unbridgeable. I do not know who she is. I am uncertain how to join her in her current reality. She seems nice.

It is a few years since Minnie visited them, and we are the first rellies from overseas they have seen since then. We are standing in the sitting room of my mother's house in Balga, a blue-collar suburb of North Perth, Western Australia. The area is still respectable, but it will decay into thuggery and drive-by shootings in the years to come. I have just discovered that I have another sister, a foster sister, Laura. I accept this automatically. If Mum says I have another sister, then I have another sister.

Mum and John, the Aussie bloke she picked up in London, are headed off on another one of their Great Outback Tours. We are considering joining them on part of it. Ingrid and Laura have moved out of the house in Balga and are now hanging out in Updike Street, a notoriously dodgy street in a notoriously dodgy area known as Northbridge. It is very close to the city centre, but at night it serves as Perth's red-light district.

Mum and John are planning a trip up north to Marble Bar (on average the hottest place in Australia! Mum beams) across to the Northern Territory diamond mining town of Lake Woods (Most isolated town in Australia!) and thence to Cooktown and Lizzard Island in Queensland (The first real European settlement on Australian soil *and* worst roads anywhere in Australia!). Minnie was right. Mum really only likes places that make even the truest, bluest dinki di-est Aussies shudder in horror.

The conversation turns to our upcoming trip out east to Kalgoorlie and the Gold Fields, down south to Esperance, back west to Albany, then north back to Perth. A trip of around two thousand kilometres.

Foster sister, Laura and her bloke are planning to make a similar trip but in the other direction, counter-clockwise. We are studying the map, mouthing the names of some of the places we will be passing through, Jerramungup, Munglinup, the unlikely 'Speddingup', and Salmon Gums.

An uncomfortable sensation steals over me. I feel the familiar 'separation' in my mind grow stronger, and the curious, all but inaudible, high-pitched whine that accompanies dissociation grows louder. And suddenly, here we are again, me experiencing the corporeal world and me observing. I am staring at the map, at the place marked 'Salmon Gums'. Just for a moment, I glimpse Miriam and me meeting my sister and her husband. I know it will happen. The sensation begins to grow weaker. For once, I have the presence of mind to say something.

"We will meet you here." I say, plonking my finger down on the map. I lift my finger a little to show where I have pointed.

"Here", I point again, "just south of Salmon Gums." I am certain. No need for thought, I know.

There is a moment of baffled silence before Greg - Laura's bloke – shakes his head.

"No way, mate. We're heading out ten days before you. We'll be up around Paynes Find or Mount Magnet before you get as far as Coolgardie."

We all study the map, calculating time and distance. Greg seems to be correct. We will not meet up.

We decide to go watch a ruinously loud Aussie rock band playing a nearby biker venue. It has been over forty degrees Celsius all day (around one hundred degrees Fahrenheit). Now, in the cool of the evening, it has dropped to around thirty-two. Stifling.

The biker club is like a scene from some American movie. Rows of bikes line the dirt track road. The venue turns out to be a disused corrugated iron shearing shed on the edge of the 'city' of Marangaroo, a market gardening district increasingly corroded by encroaching suburbs. Unlike its archetypal American equivalent, the mood is upbeat. People are happy. No one wants a fight.

Ingrid, Miriam and Laura disappear off to do whatever it is groups of young women do on these occasions, and I am left to chat with Greg. We have absolutely nothing in common, except, insofar as we have her in common at all, Laura.

"Beer?" he asks, breaking the uncomfortable silence. I stop scuffing my toe against the red, pebbly earth.

"Yeah, great." The band plays anthemic rock'n'roll. Acid House music, just emerging in Europe, has gained no purchase here. We take the only avenue available to us and get very, very drunk.

It's all going off in the shearing shed. People are gyrating vigorously, blithely unaware of the rhythm. Hard-bodied young men stand around the walls in clusters, exuding cool, ranking the women. Occasionally one of them, egged on by his mates, will make a foray onto the dance floor, sidling up to one or other group of handbags and young women, at first dancing adjacent to them, attempting some threadbare chat-up line against the din, having to repeat himself three or four times. The separation of the sexes is extreme. Contact is clumsy and fleeting. The shed smells of hot metal, sweat and spilled beer.

I make my way outside for a cigarette and a breath of fresh air. Huddles of mates are discussing the imminent AFL (Australian Rules Football) final. Consensus is reached that last year's winners, Hawthorn, will prevail, although Carlton, winners in three of the previous ten years, is also a team to be watched. I couldn't care less. The game is incomprehensible. The very use of the word 'rules' appears oxymoronic.

There is a brief scuffle near the entrance to the shed. A standoff between two groups of young men. This looks more interesting. I wander over to snoop. A young fella in some distress is led off to the side by one of his mates.

"She's not worth it, Stevo."

"You're better off without her."

"Shane's a wanker anyway," Stevo shrugs, "she's welcome to him."

There is a brief silence as the group considers the wanker Shane and his new girl. One of the group pipes up.

"You remember Cindy?" Nods.

"She was straight up, but she spent all my money, so I had to get rid of her" and after another moment's silence, "I love her, but".

The wind picks up strongly from the east. I trust vaguely that the night will cool down a bit, but I am wrong. The wind is hot, blowing from the desert heart. It's like being in a tumble dryer. Greg turns up with a couple more pints of EB (Emu Bitter). We have, somewhere during the previous five or six pints, come to some kind of an accommodation. The silence sits easily between us. We are here purely at the convenience of our women, and we know it. Greg offers to explain AFL to me. I decline. My sister Ingrid appears, giggling. She is smoking a joint. I do not know her at all. I have memories of her, fragments, of a little girl in Zambia and in Swaziland, but not in England. I barely recall her from London at all.

I remember her first sentence. She would have been about two years old. I am standing on the back veranda with my mother when she appears, soaked to the skin, with long, dark, frenzied curly hair, lank, like rats' tails. She fixes my mother with a defiant glare and to everyone's immense surprise, says:

"Change dress, cause wet, cause couldn't turn off tap".

Is this the same girl, now a woman?

My mother used to talk to us a great deal about philosophy when we were little. She was particularly fond of Spinoza. I remember Ingrid patiently explaining, in response to some telling off.

"If this is the best of all possible worlds, and I am the best of all possible Ingrids, then even if I did it, I was still being as good as I possibly could be". (Jostein Gaarder, take note – it is a risky business introducing children to philosophy).

MIDLIFE CRISIS

I snap back to some present. This present. Not New Orleans this time. North Rocks, Sydney. I have been living on my own for almost a year. Miriam has finally served the court papers on me. We are finally getting divorced.

We are arguing about money, well, not arguing, really, Miriam is asking for pretty much everything I have, and I am saying "No". Suddenly everything is coming to a head. We are due back in the family court in a few weeks. I have an interview for Australian citizenship in a few days, and the sale of our house in Dublin appears finally to be going through. Miriam and the boys have been on holiday in Ireland for the last month. They will be home in less than a week. Parallel lines, the threads of my life that once appeared to meet at some distant future, are converging now.

The reality of divorce sits heavy on my mind. I love my two boys with an increasing rawness. Emotional eczema. An inflammation of the sentiment, sensitive to everything. A grating soreness.

Of course, I look back on my life, my quarter-century marriage. Of course, there were good times. I am desolate, infinitely lonely, but resolved. It was my decision to walk out, to rush out, to run screaming from that little house in Pleasantville. It came upon me unexpectedly, not so much a thief in the night as a blinding, disillusioning revelation. One instant, I was inextricably immersed in a marriage that had stood the test of time with a companion who, of all people in the world, knew me best. The next instant, it was over.

We have used up and spat out three counsellors of varying capabilities and degrees of simpatico. We have made no progress at all. Miriam characterises everything I say as 'Crap'. I have had enough. I am, were I to give it a moment's thought, monumentally fucked off and definitely feeling sorry for myself.

Miriam's explanation is that I am mentally ill, there being no other feasible rationalisation. She has given me the book 'The midlife Crisis' to read, and I have read it. It is quite obvious that I am having a midlife crisis. So what? Am I not entitled?

It is hard to remember why we, why I, wanted to come to Australia in the first place. Something about the infinite emptiness of Western Australia, the implacably barren red deserts, the huge, unending sky. And the stars. More a mood than a career choice. I struggle to remember how we felt. I want to return to my own personal dreamtime.

I decide to buy an old but mechanically sound car, just for while we are in Western Australia. The car lot in Marrangaroo has a red, four-door Holden Kingswood sedan with a five-litre engine and automatic three-speed transmission for $4,995 dollars.

The guy laughs.

"Sure, they have problems, but anyone can fix 'em".

"It has some poorly repaired crash damage on the passenger side front and wing."

"I can let you have it for $3,995 and I guarantee a fair trade-in on return if it's still in excellent condition when you return it."

I want to point out that it is not in excellent condition to start with, but that seems churlish. The deed is done. I return 'home' to my mum's place driving a massive, petrol-guzzling Kingswood sedan, guaranteed good for 5,000 miles, with 176,589 miles on the clock. Laura and Ingrid are sitting on the step drinking homemade milkshakes when I arrive. Mum and Miriam come out as I pull into the front yard. Miriam runs her hand along the bonnet. Mum stares.

"It looks just like my old Kingswood, the one Laura stacked!"

Laura and Ingrid bestir themselves to come over and take a closer look.

"Bugger me!" Laura nods, "It doesn't just look like your old Kingswood. It *is* your old Kingswood! Look, see where the arsehole at the servo stuffed up the repairs. The number plate has been changed, is all."

I remember Minnie said something once when I was back in London about how she had picked Laura up from hospital after Laura had stacked Mum's car. There is much 'My my-ing' and many 'who would have believed it's'. Laura runs her hand over the damage.

"Where were you going when you stacked it last time?" I am mildly curious. She does not answer straight away. After a few moments, she responds.

"Oh, just for a run, to put it through its paces. Mum had only just bought it, you know."

"Think it will get us to Kalgoorlie?"

"Probably." Laura smirks, "It did last time". She turns and walks back towards the house. Things not said and never to be said swarm this way and that.

It is still early. I suggest a sightseeing trip to historic Guildford.

Mum shivers, "Déjà Vu." She jumps in the back. Ingrid and Laura slip in next to Mum, and Miriam takes the front passenger seat.

After a while, Laura points out a low hill a little way ahead.

"That's where I stacked the car last time!"

Fortunately, the trip to historic Guildford goes off without incident. Mum, Miriam and Ingrid raid the local charity shops while I am left to peruse the real estate agent's window and imagine never going home.

SOUTHERN CROSS

We are heading inland across the desert and scrub, following the Great Eastern Highway. The water pipeline from Mundaring Weir all the way to the eastern goldfields, snakes along beside the road, mile after mile, decade after decade. The Kingswood is going like a dream. It seems made for the long straight Australian highways. We have been driving for two days heading for Kalgoorlie. Tonight, we are sleeping under the stars in a speck of a town called Southern Cross. The Milky Way is a brilliant carpet of stars across the night. Breathtakingly lovely. The streets of the town are implausibly wide, sufficient, we are told, to turn a camel train. Camels are not able to walk backwards, apparently, and, as they were the essential mode of transportation when the gold fields were opened up, the town was designed with them in mind. The streets are all named after the stars that make up the Southern Cross constellation. They are lined with tiny, two-storey timber shops fronted by raised covered boardwalks with balconies above. At any moment, a cowboy could leap to his horse below and high-tail it out of town.

Southern Cross, for city slickers like us, is a deeply romantic place, redolent of Australia's Wild East. We are enchanted. It is too hot to sleep. We stare up at the stars. Even Miriam seems content. It feels good to be alive.

Over a month has passed, and I have heard nothing from Amelie, no email, no text messages, nothing. I know that something is wrong. I can feel that she is angry and hurt. I turn myself inside out, imagining what it is, what has happened, fearing that she has suddenly come to her senses and realised that we have no chance of happiness together, that I was just a distraction. Then I receive her email. I am floored. I am miserable. I want to smash something.

[I have been re-reading through some of your emails, and it has made me wonder why you continue to talk to me. Why we text each other why you phoned me?! A]

Fearing it is the end, I send a sort of farewell message. At least she will know that I am sincere, that my feelings are real and that I am finding my way too. It is nearly thirty years since I have been in this hideous no man's land of desire, self-doubt and hope. I am a teenager again, awkward and out of my depth. I do not expect to hear from her again.

[Dear A, I have felt at times, like Farmer Boldwood in Far From the Madding Crowd, that the symmetry of my existence is "slowly getting distorted in the direction of an ideal passion." I have felt emotions recently that I have never felt before or have not felt for so long as to amount to the same thing. I have revisited dimly recalled passions, and I have awakened to an uncertain future. At times I feel like a wandering traveller, and at others, like a meandering road. I have learned, and I am learning a great deal, and I just wanted to thank you. Pat, x]

I hear nothing for a couple of days. I write again.

[Amelie, I am afraid you will let me become just a pleasant reverie, the sound of my voice gently attenuating in your ear until finally all that is left is the memory of a sound once heard a long time ago on some vague summer's weekend, someplace, sometime...]

I have heard nothing for a further two weeks. I am going stark staring mad. Life with Miriam is taking on a surreal edge as I live increasingly in this bizarre fantasy life. It is beginning to dawn on me that my marriage has failed already. I am at a loss to explain how I didn't notice it. I have no idea what to do for the best. I am wearing out. I have little enough strength to keep going myself. There is precious little left to support Miriam. Her endless gloom and despondency sap my strength. I have no idea what would make her happy, and, I realise, I never have had.

Monday morning. There's an email from Amelia, polite and formal.

[Hello, I was not expecting to hear from you again. By the way, has our liaison rekindled your relationship with Miriam at all? Thanks to you, too, I have always known we are simpatico. Love, A, xxxx]

I can't help but laugh. Why is she asking? What does this suggest about her relationship with Fausto? What 'rekindling' has she been enjoying while I have been raging through all the canyons of madness and self-pity? The question is so transparent, in a way, so innocent. I assume I have whipped her into a frenzy of sexual desire and sent her home to Fausto. There is a second email.

[Now I am curious. What have you learned? How are you, like Farmer Boldwood? Trust I'm not like Bathsheba!]

Fan-bloody-tastic! I set aside my jealousy. She is continuing the correspondence. It is her birthday. Casting caution to the winds once more, I decide to go for it.

[Happy birthday, beautiful one. Sorry that this email was not waiting for you. I started to write it about five this morning but didn't want to send it until it was ready - it's still not ready!!

I relate myself to Farmer Boldwood only insofar as I, too, feel that the whole centre of my life is being realigned. Like it is being done *for* me by some invisible hand. I do not relate you to Bathsheba at all (except in that you are beautiful and headstrong - in a nice way).

I have been forced to face up to and re-learn my emotions. I am not typically very emotional at all, so all this came as a surprise. I must see you! I am flying to Dublin in July. I can't wait for you to become my lover - I imagine that I might kiss you, caress you, undress you, feel your skin against mine, stroke your face, lose myself in the deep pools of your wonderful eyes and make love with you for the first time. I feel like a giddy teenage boy, bashful and shy and full of wonder. Pat, x]

In response, I receive two blank text messages in quick succession. I am thrown once more into paroxysms of self-doubt and fear. I have gone too far! I have made some unacceptable presumption! I have committed some unknown offence for which I cannot even apologise. I struggle to interpret her meaning. Two blank messages – what can it mean? What is she trying to tell me? Over a week goes by before I hear from her again.

[Ran out of credits on my mobile. Will buy more after lunch. So excited you are flying to Dublin. Talk soooon! A, xx]

Relief floods through me – the blank messages were just a glitch. There was no subtle reproach, no disapproval. In a torrent of relief, I write back.

[I am yearning for you. I want to see you so badly I could explode. I can't wait to be with you. Pat, x]

Her reply is businesslike and arousing in equal measure.

[Hi Pat. I don't want a seedy hotel. It's important we spend time together somewhere nice. We haven't really spent any time alone together! I will feel like a virgin again. A, x]

[Hi A, Irresistible to think that I knew you before you were a virgin.]

[Pat I am very nervous about everything. Not about meeting you but about being so secretive and cautious. Not something I've ever had to do before. All my Love, A. XX]

[Hi Sweet Pea, I am feeling nervous too – both about meeting you and about the secrecy. I feel I should warn you that I snore and I am somewhat rounder – I hope the reality doesn't disappoint too much. I am longing to see you, though – like a little boy with butterflies in my tummy. Lots of love, Pat x]

[Darling A, Only six weeks to go – I'm all at sixes and sevens. I just can't wait to see you. X]

I run into a frantic period at work. I dash off a quick note.

[Hello, you gorgeous, wonderful woman. I am fine - long weekend due to King's birthday - much domestic stuff. I am desperate to see you. I will sort out accommodation and let you know. Lots of love, Pat, x]

I call her mobile too, despite the risk that Fausto will answer, despite the risk that she may be unable to talk. I just have to hear her voice. I am so excited! I get her voice mail instead and leave a brief message. I am totally crestfallen. I leave for a day of meetings in central Sydney. While I am out, she replies.

[Pat, so sorry to have missed your call. I have run out of credit again. Call me on my work extension up to 1 pm. No privacy, but I would love to hear your voice. A, x]

I do not receive her message until the following morning. I call her immediately on her mobile phone, fumbling, misdialling, eventually getting the right number and getting through. I hear her voice, still soft with sleep, low, sultry.

"Hi, it's me."

"Oooo, Hello, how lovely to hear your voice."

"How are you feeling?"

"Excited, terrified. I shan't be able to meet you at the airport. I need to sort out the children first."

"No worries. We can meet up at the station."

"How are you?"

"About the same, mixture of terror and anticipation. I just can't wait to hold you in my arms."

"I can't either."

"I wonder how we will be together. Will we feel the same face-to-face, do you think?"

"I don't know. I've been wondering that too."

"Well, I have to find out for sure, one way or the other."

"Me too. Fausto's in the kitchen. I can't talk long."

"I just had to hear your voice. I'm sorry about the mix-up today. I didn't get your messages until just now, so I called you straight away."

"Oh, bugger! I have to go now. Can't wait to see you."

"Me too. I will be jet lagged, you know."

"Don't worry. I'll be gentle with you."

"Not too gentle, I hope!"

She giggles. I am intoxicated.

"Bye for now."

"Bye."

I hear Fausto's voice in the background. The line goes dead. I sit for ages holding the phone, recalling the lovely, gravely sound of her voice, wondering if we will be awkward together or if it will seem natural. Savouring the anticipation. I have to head home. Miriam will be wanting me to make dinner.

I send another email the moment I get to work the next morning.

[My Darling, It was wonderful to hear your voice last night. I want to have time to gaze into your eyes and kiss you. I want to make love with gentle languor and with rough passion. I want, very much, to kiss you from the nape of your neck to the small of your back. I want to drift off to sleep with you in my arms and wake next to you. The sooner you are curled up in my lap and purring, the better, Pat, X]

[I share your thoughts. A, x]

I get on the Internet and make a firm booking. I email her the details and log off. In the morning, I get her reply.

[It's not really what I had in mind, but beggars can't be choosers. It will have to do. We really need a big room with a king-size bed and an open fireplace. Love, A, x]

I can't stand that she is disappointed. That I have made a poor choice, something sub-standard. I will change it. She can have anything she wants. I call her number. Fausto answers. I have called her home, not her mobile phone. He recognises my voice immediately. I make up some idiotic excuse about having accidentally dialled the wrong number. I say I was intending to call my mum. He is not convinced. We have a brief conversation. He knows things are not going well with me and Miriam. I talk a little about that, then make my excuses and hang up, cursing myself for an absolute bloody fool. Of course, it will all come out one day. He will remember the call and put two and two together. He's not stupid! Bollocks, she will be furious. I have been careless. Can't be helped.

I send her a text message to tell her that I have accidentally spoken with Fausto and an email confirming the booking.

[A, The place is booked. It was all I could find, but I don't want you to be disappointed. Let me know if you want me to change it. It was very odd talking to Fausto last night – I felt awful. I am counting the days now until I see you. Lots of love, Pat, X]

[Hi Pat, Things with Fausto are bad again. He is drinking and taking other things to plug the gaps. He really is a decent man, and he adores us completely, but I can't bear much more. We have been together for over twenty years, and I think I have tried everything! It got better after I asked him to go. For a little while, he realised how much he had to lose. I can't bear the trauma of telling him to leave again. Still looking forward to seeing you, but had a terrible sinking feeling after chatting with Miriam. I am ignoring my conscience. It is my choice. I am going to meet you anyway. Love A, x]

[A, I know I can't really have you for more than a few stolen moments, but to me, that is worth it. You know you can change your mind if it gets too much – I will understand absolutely. I am ignoring my conscience, too, because the chance of being with you is irresistible. You are irresistible. I will be at Wicklow station around lunchtime on Friday – does that suit you? I will still be a bit jet-lagged and bedraggled. I long to hold you in my arms. I think about you all the time. *I can't wait to see you!* Lots of love, Pat x

That's all I have, all I can piece together, the shards of my broken life. How do I begin to understand this tempestuous, ill-advised, sudden love? How can I ever explain it. To my boys, to Miriam, to anyone? The world has been reborn strange and new, and I am lost in the vastness of possibility.

MONKEY JERKY

The sand is white-hot. The sea is blue and cool. I am drying quickly in the warm breeze. Particles of salt, visibly growing on my skinny little legs, sparkling like tiny jewels. The monkey man comes past again, selling small bags of money jerky.

"Bush meat", he calls out, swinging what is unmistakably a roasted monkey arm this way and that.

"Very good!" He smiles. Enormous white teeth gleam delightedly in his red-brown mouth.

"Try some", he smiles broadly, "No charge".

"What does it taste like?" I ask, not sure if people eat monkeys or not.

"Very, very good!" he proclaims to the small crowd of Afrikaner families beginning to pay some attention.

"Very, very good indeed!" His teeth are bigger and whiter than anything I have ever seen. His smile fills my field of vision. Slowly and with great ceremony, playing the gathering crowd, he removes a small white cotton sack from his large leather shoulder bag. He holds the tiny bag aloft, the cotton seeming impossibly clean and white and pure against the acetylene blue sky. Deftly, reverentially, he unties the drawstring on the little bag and removes one tiny brown morsel of smoked and dried monkey flesh. The roasted arm abandoned pokes tragically from the big leather bag. He holds the morsel of flesh towards me in his big hand, relaxed, waiting, not forcing it on me. I reach out and take the piece of monkey. It is warm and dry in my hand, rough textured. Not unpleasant. It smells very slightly of wood smoke. Without thinking about it, I pop it in my mouth and chew. It is actually rather nice, in a way.

"What do you think, young man?" he asks, turning to the crowd, making sure they are still engaged.

"It's nice", I say, "I like it, sort of smoky."

"Smoky it is!" he looks around at the seated Afrikaner boys, "Just like biltong".

The crowd stirs, and young men reach for their wallets, bringing out small piles of change.

"Tiki a bag!" the man calls out across the beach, "Only a tiki a bag!" Young Afrikaner men, laughing nervously, approach and form a little queue. Each holds out a few coins. None hold back, afraid to be outdone. If a little kid will eat it, and an English 'Roy Neck' kid at that!

All the bags are sold except one, the one my piece had come from. The monkey man sits on the sand next to me, occasionally picking a piece of smoked monkey from the bag and popping it in his mouth. The waves are breaking over the coral reef a few metres out. Boys with pocketknives and half lemons are sitting in the surf breaking over the reef. Eating oysters raw.

"Here", he holds out his hand, offering me what's left, "On the house". I take the bag and sit down next to him, listening to the waves and the gulls.

"You are not South African". It is not a question.

"No, I am English".

"English"

"Yes"

"I am from Angola."

"Where the war is." He doesn't speak for a while. I think he hasn't heard me.

"Yes, it is better here, on the beach."

"Will you go back when it's over?"

"No, I can never go back."

"Would you get into trouble if you did?" He looks up at me, serious for a moment, then smiles.

"No." He shakes his head. "I would not get in trouble."

"Why not then?" I ask, "Why can you never go back?"

"There is nowhere to go back to." He stands, brushing the sand from his legs and arms.

"Will you go back to England one day?" He asks.

"No." I answer, bristling and angry, "I can't go back either."

"Well then," he gets to his feet, "I will see you tomorrow".

My Dad decides to eat at the hotel that night. My family gives every appearance of respectability and conventionality – to some extent, by actually being both respectable and conventional. But we are not Afrikaners. Unlike them, we are not part of Africa or part of the solution to Africa's problems. We are, in fact, part of the exit of Europeans from Africa, part of Britain's exit strategy.

A man joins us for dinner. Very smartly dressed in a way subtly unlike us Europeans, and nothing at all like the exotic dress of the Africans. My father introduces him as 'Gideon'. He is very tall, not very black, and he is an American, not an African. He is from a place called Washington, DC.

I am surprised and a little confused. The simple rule I have always gone by, that black people are Africans, has been shot to pieces. I thought American = Cowboy. Other than the occasional DC comic, I have never encountered an American. My friend Renee is Canadian, which, she has impressed upon me in no uncertain terms, is different, and I think perhaps 'better', as far as she is concerned.

Gideon speaks excellent English and tells very funny stories. After a while, he and my father stroll off into the courtyard so my father can smoke a cigar. They talk for a long time. Sometimes their voices are heard above the murmuring of the diners.

The Afrikaners at nearby tables give us funny looks. They haven't seen an American before, either.

The next day we go to the market in town to buy stuff while my father and Gideon look for a typewriter and a working telephone.

The market is brilliant! Thousands and thousands of stalls selling everything you could possibly imagine in a million years. The noise is deafening, with all kinds of African and Western music blaring from every stall. It is a very hot day. Huge white clouds grow more and more massive as I watch. The smell of raw and rotting meat makes us all gag, and after seeing lamb carcasses so covered in flies that they appear to shift and move as if still alive, I do not feel like eating anything ever again.

One stall sells Chinese fireworks for a couple of centavos each, another has hundreds of pocketknives shaped like fish or animals in every possible colour, but best of all is the stall selling bows and arrows and all kinds of hunting knives. My brother gets a fantastic full-sized bow with a dozen arrows for two escudos, and I get a wooden-handled hunting knife with a snakeskin sheath for fifty centavos. Minnie and Ingrid each choose a little China box for putting special little things in. One is green, and the other is blue, and they have pictures of beautiful Chinese ladies on them wearing long dresses and carrying big feather fans.

Suddenly my father reappears wearing his wide-brimmed floppy straw hat, his white long-sleeved cotton shirt soaked with sweat. Gideon has managed to find a working telephone but has had to rush back to Washington, DC, as his mother is ill.

My father guides us to a long row of stalls where Honey Buns, a local delicacy, are made. Each stall has a small clay oven at one end. Trays and trays of Honey Buns in various stages of development cover the narrow trestles. At the end, furthest from the oven, are the cooked buns, now cooled and packed in transparent polythene bags. Next to them are trays of cooling buns, and nearest to the ovens are the sticky doughy honey cakes engulfed in swarms of bees attracted by the honey.

"Currant buns" enthuses my father, "fresh from the oven! What could be better?" He is very pleased with himself about something, "Or more wholesome". My mother buys two large bags of buns, one escudo each, and we head back towards the beach for a swim.

The clouds now fill the sky, massive fluffy castles piled billowing layer upon billowing layer until, at the highest levels, they flatten out against a transparent ceiling, spreading to form an even, inverted bowl across the sky.

We are still about half a mile from the hotel when the skies open. Large raindrops fall like liquid eggs around us, plopping into the dust with a soft *thwumping* sound, throwing up small clouds of golden dust.

Mum opens up one bag of currant buns and passes them out. They are still slightly warm and sticky. We munch in silence as we walk through the steadily increasing rain. The currants are not particularly sweet but very crunchy. It is very hot. Maybe the rain will cool things down a bit.

The hotel is in sight. We are all soaked. Minnie suddenly lets out a pitiful wail. "There's a bee in my bun", she cries, "It's full of bees".

Each of us examines the insides of their bun.

"These some in mine!"

"Mine too!"

"And mine"

"They've all got bees in them!"

"They're not currants at all", I say, "they look like currants, but they're really burnt bees!"

"What could be better?" my mother enquires, "or more wholesome?"

DYLAN THOMAS

We are in Spain when my father dies. I know before we leave that he will die while we are away. I do not want to be there when he dies. I do not want to see him dead. I cannot bear to see his light go out of this world, his wonderful stories, his beautiful intelligence.

As he gets sicker, he becomes increasingly desperate to get out of the shabby little workman's cottage he shared so briefly with my mother. The reek of sickness and cold sweat lies across the place like a dirty blanket, gritty and unwholesome to touch.

One night he and I listen to a recording of Richard Burton reading Dylan Thomas 'Rage Against the Dying of the Light!' Miriam is out. Just me and him and a bottle of whiskey. He smiles. I feel nauseous.

After that, he begins increasingly to make mad plans to move. A houseboat on the Thames at Kew or a cottage in Kent. He has no savings and only a small Civil Service pension. It is hopeless. I am afraid he will do something rash. He is becoming more and more desperate. He wants to die somewhere nice. The situation is impossible for him in London. We decide to move him in with us in Dublin.

I am looking after him as slowly, he dies from the inside, eaten away by cancer and despair. Miriam is good. She makes him endless cups of tea and snacks. Stifling her occasional resentment. Minnie has been over a couple of times to visit. She never stays long. It is as though she is monitoring his condition.

I am mentally and physically exhausted by his slow descent into misery, watching him decay over seven years from the time my mother leaves him. Seeing him smoke and drink himself to death. His last two years are harrowing. He has had numerous heart attacks and strokes. Now he has cancer of the jaw. They take him into hospital from time to time to remove more of his face. His features collapse inwards by slow degrees. His light flickers.

Shortly before we leave for our three-week holiday in Spain, my brother comes over from Manchester to visit. He is visibly shaken. There has always been a deeper bond between my father and him, than with the rest of us. Samuel, the eldest, after Eden died of leukaemia (endless x-rays in the womb), has always been my father's favourite. It is a simple fact, understood, not for me a matter for debate or resentment. Ingrid, Minnie, and I come second. That is our allotted place. Minnie has never been able to accept this. She is full of rage and resentment.

They talk together for hours in the sitting room. I wander in every now and then with cups of tea and plates of biscuits. I know I am not to be privy to this conversation. My father is saying goodbye to his eldest son. I hear occasional snippets of conversation as I open the door. It dies as I enter the room. I hear my father say, "I don't want to die like this, Sam, not like this." What can my brother say? What can anyone say? He wanted to die, just not like this.

My brother emerges from the room, a little white, a little shaky.

"Why didn't you tell me he was so bad?"

"He seems better this week."

"Last time I saw him, he looked fine!"

"Sam, I have been with him every day for years. Perhaps I don't notice the tiny changes day by day."

"You should have told me."

"What could you have done?"

"I could have been here for him!"

"Sorry."

"It must have been hard for you, too, I guess."

I feel a lump growing painfully in my throat, the beginning of tears.

"Yeah," is all I can manage. I retreat to the kitchen to do the washing up. My brother carries a step ladder upstairs, banging it hard against the banisters with every step, chipping the paint. After a while, I hear him rummaging about in the attic where all his stuff from my dad's house is stored. Occasional loud thumps as he chucks down a box or suitcase of stuff from one or other of his many trips to the Far East, South Pacific or South America. Dust begins to settle on the stairs, banisters and balustrade. He drags everything down into the kitchen and begins to sort through the accumulated crap of half a lifetime spent on the hippy trail. I am not sure if I resent him his travels or not. I have stayed put, hardly venturing out, except for two weeks of annual summer holiday in Spain. I am fully domesticated. He has tasted adventure. I have not. I am working at the local Social Services as a Visiting Officer, checking up on people. He is working in Manchester, for now, doing something or other.

Most of the junk from the attic has been eaten away by some kind of weevil. Tatters of lovely silk shawls and batiks litter the floor. A leather jacket desiccated and torn, an Afghan coat, his pride and joy, falls to pieces as he handles it. A few things survive. Brass gods from India carved animals from Peru, bits and pieces.

He clears up his junk as best he can, leaving grey smears on the white paintwork and a faint whiff of patchouli oil.

Sam is gone again in a day or so. Our melancholy routine continues. Our death march. My father watches as we pack for our holiday. He and I both know why I am leaving. We both know we will never see each other again. Nothing is said. I am leaving him to die alone. I am just not strong enough.

The taxi pulls up outside. I give him a gentle hug, almost lifting him off his feet. He is light and frail, like a bird.

"See you in three weeks."

"Yes, have a good time!"

He watches as we clamber into the taxi. He waves as we pull away.

We live it up in Spain. Drinking, eating tapas, swimming and partying. It's a febrile charade. We have been away two weeks when the inevitable telegram is delivered. It's from Minnie. She went to visit him in hospital. He had been admitted the day after we left. She was the last member of the family to see him alive. How ironic.

[So sorry to tell you, dad died last night in hospital, Minnie]

I call the airline, and we get flights home late the next day. I drink everything we have in the fridge, wine, beer, cheap Spanish brandy, indiscriminately. Miriam joins me in the ritual. We spend the two-hour coach journey to the airport and the flight home vomiting into plastic carrier bags.

The house is cold, empty. Just the lingering tang of sweat, decay and urine coming from his room. I walk into his bedroom. Piles of newspapers everywhere. Each one has a note or comment scribbled in the margin, or an article circled in red biro, a writer's habit. I grab a roll of black plastic bin liners from the kitchen drawer. Miriam has collapsed upstairs.

In a frenzy of guilt and loss, I strip the room, stuffing newspapers, and junk into bags. I strip his bed. Chuck the bedding into the washing machine. I go through his threadbare wardrobe, discarding almost everything. Under his bed, I find a small wastepaper basket squashed full of tissues encrusted with dry brown mucous. I empty it into a bin-liner. The tissues fall out in one piece, like a jelly mould.

I rush to the lavatory and throw up, over and over again, until there is nothing but green bile. I collapse on the cold tiled floor and cry, heaving sobs.

"Sorry, Dad. So sorry!"

I have him cremated. The funeral is a dismal affair. A handful of family and friends. His body lies in a hospital freezer for nearly a fortnight and then a chapel of rest for a weekend. I do not visit him. I do not want to see his body. I do not want to have that memory.

A mere month later, Miriam and I are married. Her family has provided me with a haven. Her family are truly my family now.

THEO'S MULTI-RACIAL GENERAL STORE, COCKTAIL BAR & TEA ROOMS

The aged Morris Minor makes it up the long hill. The bridge over the river is visible behind us in the distance. The rest of the journey is made in silence. Soon enough, we arrive in Luanshya. The roundabout by the Municipal Swimming Pool is covered in brown and gold marigolds. There is a slight scent of chlorine in the air. We park outside Theo's. The open doorway is protected by an ancient and broken bead curtain, ostensibly keeping out the flies. My mother pushes through it into the gloomy interior. The shop falls silent. It takes a moment for our eyes to adjust. The place smells of stale beer and smoke. I notice three men playing cards on an old Formica table on the mezzanine floor at the back of the shop. They are all gazing at my mother. A black woman in a white cotton apron sweeps the floor. Theo scurries over, his warm smile momentarily lifting the sadness from his eyes.

"Good morning, madam." He glances at me and then back to my mother, "How may I help you?"

My mother rummages through her shiny black patent leather handbag, eventually retrieving the broken piece from the electricity generator.

"I need a new one of these, please." She holds the small square of black metal in front of her for Theo to see.

"What is it?"

"It's from our electricity generator." Pause, "It's broken".

Theo calls over to one of the card players. A fat man in a black suit, ambles down the few steps and into the main part of the shop. He is smoking a fat cigar. He wafts Eau de Cologne and old sweat. My mother holds the broken piece up in front of her.

"Westinghouse Diesel," he mumbles, "It's a brush. These come in packs of four."

"I'd like a pack, please". The man makes his way slowly through to the back of the store. The back wall is covered by a huge array of small wooden drawers, each bearing an illegible label, dimly lit. The meaningful etiquette of some past lost civilisation. Its bare bones commandeered for a new purpose.

A few moments later, the man returns with a grubby plastic pouch containing four small metal squares.

"You'll need a mechanic to fit 'em", the man holds out the little packet for my mother to sees, "or an engineer."

My mother thanks the man and places the brushes in a cardboard box on the counter. She gets out her shopping list. Flour, margarine, marmite, long spaghetti in purple-blue paper packaging, the usual things, all piled in the cardboard box as she calls them out. Mum picks out a girl's magazine for Minnie and a little doll for Ingrid. Sam gets a Superman comic. I pass her a small tin of condensed milk and a pack of Wrigley's spearmint chewing gum. She pops them into the cardboard box without a word. When we are done, the black lady in the white apron carries the cardboard box out to the car.

After the shopping, my mother wants to head over to the Luanshya Club. She says she needs a drink. I will have to wear shoes. My mother scrabbles around in the back of the car to see what she can find. She thinks there's an old pair of Minnie's flip-flops somewhere. With a bit of scrabbling around, she finds them. They are a little too big, and they have pink glittery bits. Great! When we get to the club, Mother orders a large gin and tonic, and I have an Orange Fanta.

The club is divided into the bar area, which is noisy, full of smoke and men drinking beer, and the salon, which is silent, and all but empty except for two or three small groups of women wearing flowery cotton dresses like Mum's and chatting quietly. The room smells strongly of insect spray.

The wife of one of the mine engineers whom my dad knows slightly, spots us from across the room. My mother swears quietly under her breath before asking, "Won't you join us?" The mining engineer's wife's name is Shirley. She gives me a very nice smile before turning to my mother.

"We don't very often get to see you in town, do we?" There is what even I can detect as an awkward pause.

"How lovely to see you today. We, wives, must stick together while our men are away." My mother nods agreement. Shirley calls the waiter over and orders two more 'G&Ts'. My mother starts to protest but subsides.

I am bored. I look around without interest at the other people in the club. Mainly white men in neatly ironed khaki shorts, white short-sleeved shirts, brown suede shoes and fawn-coloured socks pulled up to the knee. It is cool in the club. Cold air blows from round vents in the ceiling. I ask the waiter where they get the cold air from.

"Air conditioning". Means nothing to me. I imagine they have a huge fridge or a room upstairs full of ice that they blow the air through to cool it down.

I notice some kids on the first-floor terrace throwing things at passing vehicles. Sounds a bit more like it. I take my Fanta and head outside. The heat on the terrace is unbelievable after the cool of the club room. A couple of the boys are from my school. We exchange brief greetings and begin, meditatively, to throw mango stones at the large shiny hub caps of passing trucks. The sky is heavy with massive clouds. No one notices the glittery bits. It is quite a while before a very red-faced man stamps angrily onto the terrace shouting at us to stop and go back inside.

When I get back to the table, my mother is on her fourth 'G&T' and is telling Shirley about our near miss with the truck. She seems to be having fun.

We have to leave. Mother is in a very good mood. She likes Shirley. They agree to meet up again sometime.

We manage to get home without incident. My mother drives very slowly down the hill and up the other side. We are only two miles from home when the sky opens, and the afternoon's torrential rain begins to fall.

STOPOUT

Friday night after a long week. I stop by the bottle shop to buy a case of beer on my way home. Miriam is going out for drinks with her workmates. They are currently surveying the public transport travel habits of the population of a small North Dublin suburb. They have been at it for nearly a year, and the project is now only a week away from completion.

The routine is the same every day. They meet for coffee in a local café before wandering off to their allocated locations, typically a range of bus stops across the suburb, where they question public transport users as to the frequency with which they use public transport, the form of transport they use and the distance they have travelled this journey.

Around mid-morning, their supervisor makes his rounds checking that all his charges are at their posts. Once he has gone, they meet up in another café in the next-door suburb, where they fill out a day's worth of typical answers and chat amongst themselves.

Around five p.m., they wander back to the collection point, where the supervisor picks up the completed survey forms and takes them back to headquarters to be keyed into the database.

This is a very important survey. A great deal of public funding, based largely upon this laboriously collected information, will go into refining the public transport network and improving the service to Dubliners. Tonight, they are going out to celebrate the end of their labours. I was perfectly willing to tag along, but Miriam preferred, as it was a works outing, to go alone. I shall sit at home and drink beer. Fine by me.

I hope, vaguely, that she will not be too pissed to climb the stairs when she gets home. Whatever. I flick through endless channels of crap before settling for a documentary about Peregrine Falcons. Not that I have any particular interest in Peregrine Falcons.

The evening's TV drags on, and I finish the case of beer. Around midnight I stagger up to bed myself. She can sleep on the sofa. I fall into a drunken sleep almost immediately.

When, finally, I do wake, I am more concerned about the pounding in my skull and the heat behind my eyes than I am about Miriam. I manage to make it into a sitting position. The room spins slightly and then stops. Not too bad. I manage to glance blearily around. I notice that Miriam did not make it upstairs. I tip-toe slowly down to the kitchen, making no noise. I shush myself a couple of times, still drunk, not wanting to wake her too soon.

I put on the kettle and sling a couple of tea bags into mugs. There is some milk in the fridge, so things are definitely looking up. I open the back door and step out into the tiny yard to have an illicit cigarette (I gave up smoking years ago). I have taken to smoking Sweet Aftons in the belief that there is something refined and poetic about them. They are quite reasonably priced, and they have no filter. I cough my guts up. The pain in my head is so severe that I feel like crying, just for the relief.

No one stirs in the sitting room next door. I finish making the tea, accidentally dropping a boiling hot teabag on my foot. The pain is instant and excruciating. Things are really not going all that well after all. I carry two mugs of tea through into the sitting room, opening the door with an elbow. There is enough light filtering through the curtains to see that the room is empty. I am not yet alarmed.

I open the curtain and look around. No doubt about it, she didn't make it home last night. I decide to make some eggs and drink some tea and wait for a sheepish phone call. I watch kids' TV and smoke another cigarette. By about half past ten, I am beginning to get a wee bit concerned. I call her boss. It's the only work number I have for her. He picks up on the second ring.

"Hi," I say. "This is Miriam's husband. Looks like the team had a pretty good night last night." I say, "Miriam still hasn't made it home."

"She probably stayed over at Tasha's. I left at about nine, so no idea where they went on to. I'll get you her number, just a mo." I hear background scrabbling noises for a few moments. Then he comes back on.

"Here you go. They were in full spate by the time I left, so I expect they'll all have terrible hangovers". I write down the number.

"I'm not feeling too clever myself," I say, "Thanks a million".

"That's OK, bye".

I hang up. I decide to have one more cigarette before calling Tasha. Don't want to wake her too early or come the heavy husband. The sun is up, and the day is warm for September. I laugh quietly to myself, thinking about the sorry state Miriam must be in. I am beginning to feel a bit better.

I call Tasha. She picks up after about nine rings. A sleepy voice answers. "Hi, who's that."

"Hi Tasha, it's Miriam's husband, Pat, she never made it home last night, and I wondered if she was still with you?"

"Oh shit." I hear her mutter under her breath.

"Sorry to bother you so early."

"Ah no, that's ok", there is a cagey tone to her voice. "How did you get my number?"

"Your boss gave it to me. Hope that was ok?"

"Oh, yeah, sure. I'm afraid Miriam isn't here. She didn't stay with me last night". There is something in her tone, something in her choice of words. I feel a knot begin to form in the pit of my stomach. Some nasty intuitive part of me knows something is up.

"Who *did* she stay with?" I ask, trying to sound more bemused than suspicious.

"We left the club in a taxi", she is distinctly guarded now, "They dropped me on the way."

"Who else was in the taxi?"

"A couple of the others. I don't really remember."

"I am quite worried about her" The horrible feeling in my guts is beginning to separate into strata, jealousy, and suspicion above, concern for Miriam below, oil and water, nauseating.

"She didn't come home, and she hasn't called."

"I don't think she had any money." The guarded voice suggests.

"Why not? She only just got paid. She could just go to an ATM."

"She lost her purse".

"How did she lose her purse?" I smell a rat now, and I am beginning to get really agitated. My stomach is roiling and twisting itself into knots. I remember her college end-of-term party a couple of years ago. I remember the gutless rage. It is all coming back.

"Someone threw it out of the taxi".

"Why? Who?" I am managing to keep my tone reasonably neutral – fury still contained.

"Iain."

"Who's Iain?" Anger starts appearing in my voice now, "Why would he do that?"

"He works with us. He didn't want her to pay for the taxi."

"Who else was in the taxi?"

"Just Miriam and Iain."

"I see. Why didn't you stop the taxi and get her purse back?"

"Dunno".

I cannot think of anything to say. I don't want to make these odd snippets of information add up. I can make it all add up only too easily. I know exactly what has happened. Icy coldness washes through me, seeping into my bones.

"Where does he live?"

"I don't have his address."

"Do you know roughly where he lives?"

"Rathmines somewhere."

"Where about in Rathmines, roughly?"

"The street opposite the cinema. I don't know what it's called, and I don't know the number, sorry."

"Do you have his phone number?"

"No"

"OK, thanks, Tasha, thanks for your help." Trying not to sound sarcastic. My heart is pounding, fight/flight in full spate, balanced for now.

"Look, Miriam was very drunk. She was just dancing with him, that's all. I'm sure nothing happened."

I hang up. I am stunned. I don't know what to do. I will kill him. I will smash his face in with a tire lever. I will kill them both. I seethe with impotent jealous rage. I know the road she means, opposite the cinema.

I get dressed and get in the car. I do not own a tire lever. I do own a small crowbar. It will do. My head is clear. My hangover is gone. I open the window and light a cigarette. I am alert, frozen between purposes. I start the engine. The motor turns, coughs and stops. I drive an ancient, bright orange, emphysemic Mini.

"Not now." I scream at it, "Not bloody now!" Dammed rage gushes forth. I slam the dashboard and the steering wheel with my fists. I turn the key a second time. The terminally under-serviced engine catches. Rathmines is not too far, maybe ten minutes at this time of day. Long enough to work myself further into a frenzy of self-doubt, fear, uncertainty, and a killing rage.

I find a parking spot at the bottom of the street, where it joins the main drag. I have run out of cigarettes. There is a petrol station across the road. I buy a bottle of water and another pack of Sweet Afton.

"I really must give up again", I think, "Miriam is bound to find out."

I wander up and down the road, chain-smoking. I rehearse the previous night's events in my mind. I imagine every scenario in horrible detail, torturing myself, feeding my sense of injustice and hurt, and picking at imaginary sores.

They drop Tasha off. They are alone. She turns to him and giggles. She is quite drunk. He reaches across and caresses her thigh.

She smiles, snuggling against his shoulder and slips forward slightly in the seat, allowing him further access. His hand slides up, lifting her skirt, feeling the warm softness of her. He kisses her gently, tenderly, relishing his moment. Their lips part, soft wet tongues caress. She sighs.

No. Earlier. It must have started earlier in the pub. They dance at a respectable distance at first and then closer. Slowly they slide into a close, sensual embrace. He grinds his pelvis against hers to some sultry Reggae number – Lover's Rock. She responds. His hands drift downwards, inevitably, sweetly. The small of her back, then lower. His hands are on her small, pert bottom. Pulling her closer to him. Squeezing hard. She is aroused. She is drunk and happy and enjoying the attention. He kisses her neck. She feels his firmness as he presses against her. She caresses him. They murmur words of hot desire. They want each other. It is somehow decided.

They stumble out of the taxi. He pays with indecent haste, practically throwing banknotes at the driver. He fumbles with his door key. Eventually, it bursts open, and they fall into the hallway. There is much mutual hushing as they struggle up the stairs to his flat. Another key. More fumbling. They are in! They undress themselves and each other in comic haste. He kisses her breasts, caressing her nipples with his tongue. She reaches down and grasps him, stroking him gently with the tips of her fingers.

I am delirious with jealous fantasy. Perhaps she was less complicit, I suggest to myself. Perhaps he overcame her maidenly resistance. He invites her up to his flat for a coffee promising to call a cab for her. He puts on some music. They sit together on the sofa, waiting for the kettle to boil, listening and chatting easily. He pours her a drink, a nightcap. The coffee will be ready soon. One thing leads to another. He suggests she stay over – she shall have the bed, and he the sofa.

Whatever – I am going to kill him. And her.

Perhaps forty-five minutes pass, perhaps an hour. I return to the car and drink some water. I am about to light another cigarette when I see, in the distance, too far to make out any detail, a couple at the brow of the hill walking down the street towards me. They are walking close together, talking animatedly. I know it is them. Long before I can really be sure, I am certain. I watch, fascinated, as they approach. I feel hollow at the sight of him. What was merely fantasy is now suddenly real. I feel broken and pathetic. I can see them clearly enough. It is Miriam, and some skinny younger bloke, a few years younger than we are, I'd guess. Very early twenties. I feel nauseous. I can't believe she would do this to me! The evidence is right there, in front of me, in all its spotty splendour. Miriam sees the car. Recognises it. Sees me. She steps away from the bloke, Iain. She says something to him. He looks up, straight into my eyes. I understand. He tries to grab her arm. She pulls away. He is talking very fast, loudly, almost shouting. I catch snippets.

"You don't have to!" he is urging, almost beseeching.

"Yes, I do".

"Please!"

"No. I can't. You must leave me alone now."

He looks directly at me. They are no more than twenty yards away now. He wants to fight me. I can see it on his face. He wants to smash me to pieces and take Miriam away. I get out of the car to face them. I am ready for this little shit. I leave the crowbar on the driver's seat, in easy reach. I look him up and down disinterestedly, allowing a slightly amused smirk to appear on my face. Actually, I realise I have no idea how I must look. Probably demented. The realisation that my amused sneer may look like constipation deflates me completely.

Miriam tries to get ahead of him. He strides faster to keep up.

"Hello," she manages, "Sorry. Were you worried?"

"Who's your friend?"

"This is Iain. He's a colleague from work."

Iain stares defiant rage at me. He has lost. Whatever game he has been playing, he has lost. I do not understand what has happened. He has backed down. I am massively relieved. I cannot trust my voice not to shake. I give him a nod. There is a pause of some indeterminate duration. Things realign.

"Hop in." I get back in the car and starting the engine. Thank God it catches first time. Miriam gets in. Smiles at Iain and tries to open the window to say something. Bollocks to that! The main road is busy at this time of day, notwithstanding which I hit the accelerator and race out into the traffic. Someone beeps. So what?

The journey home proceeds in frosty silence. I am *not* going to be the first to speak. Explanations will be all one way! Now I am furious and ethically superior and the absolute owner of the moral high ground. I am also hollow and lost and betrayed.

We are near home when Miriam clears her throat.

"You must have been worried. Sorry."

"Why didn't you come home?"

"I lost my purse. I had no money."

"Why didn't you call?"

"I told you. I had no money."

"You could have reversed the charges."

"Sorry. I was drunk."

"You could have simply dropped Iain off and come home in the taxi. I would have paid the fare." Silence.

"You stayed with Iain?"

"Yes. No. Not *with* him. I stayed at his flat."

"He must have a phone."

"He said it was broken."

"Could you get a dial tone?"

"What do you mean?"

"On his phone. Could you get a dial tone?"

"I don't know."

"Why not?"

"He wouldn't let me touch the phone."

"Wouldn't let you?"

"No. He said it was broken."

"Did you sleep with him?"

"No! How can you think that?"

"Did you sleep in a spare bed then?"

"No, Iain doesn't have a spare bed. It's only a studio apartment."

"Where did you sleep then?"

"On the sofa, I guess."

"You guess?"

"I think I'm going to be sick!"

I pull over into a side street while Miriam retches into the curb. We head off again.

"Why did you stay at his place at all? Why didn't you get out of the taxi with Tasha?"

"How do you know I shared a taxi with Tasha?"

"She told me. She also told me that Iain threw your purse out of the taxi."

"What else did she tell you?" I have never heard that tone from Miriam before. I feel physically sick. There *was* more to it. Obviously, it must have been going on for some time.

"What else could she have told me?"

"Iain is just a colleague from work."

"He was begging you to leave me for him!"

"I know. I don't know why he was doing that. I didn't know he felt that way."

"He took you back to his place, and you willingly stayed the night with him."

"Not willingly. I told you I lost my purse."

"You didn't lose it. He threw it out of the taxi, so you would have to go back to his place." I am desperate to believe her, desperate for what she is telling me to make some kind of coherent sense. I know it will not. It cannot. Miriam's inner world makes very little sense. How could her description of it do better?

"I had no choice."

"You could have walked away when you got out of the taxi."

"I was drunk. I just wanted to sleep."

"So, nothing happened then, that's what you're telling me?"

"No, nothing happened. You do believe me, don't you?" I don't know what I believe. I know I don't want to pursue this to the bitter end. I don't want to know the truth. I am deeply disappointed that Miriam cannot at least construct a plausible story. She owes me that much, at least some plausible explanation. Somehow this hurts worst of all. It is like a kind of laziness, a total lack of care for me. She can't be bothered even to make up a convincing lie.

"What bloody choice do I have?" We proceed in icy silence. I don't know what to think. Miriam is plainly seriously hung over. I doubt she would have been up for much by the time she got back to his place. I don't even know if this is the first time she's been to his place.

"I don't know how you expect our relationship to work if you don't believe a word I say," she ventures, "Nothing happened. I was drunk. I fell asleep on the sofa. Now I feel like shit, and I can do without your suspicious questioning. End of story."

I don't know how she does that. I don't know how she always manages to turn things around so that I'm the one in the wrong.

"What I can't understand, is why he would think it would be OK to take you back to his place like that? Why would he think you would accept unless you already had some kind of relationship beyond mere colleagues?" Miriam is giving me the silent treatment now. Soon I shall have to apologise for doubting her.

THE DEAN OF ECONOMICS

I have just turned twenty-six years old, and we have been living in Dublin for a bit over a year when I realise, I had better get my life in order and obtain some kind of qualification. I have to my name: A certificate for swimming a width of the local baths and another certificate for swimming a length. Also, two uninspiring School Certificates, one for English Language and the other for Physics. I am well aware that this is a bizarre combination, but I can offer no explanation for it other than that I quite liked English and Physics when at school. Both Sam and Minnie have hundreds of qualifications. They are academic. I am not. After extensive research, I set my heart on a degree in economics. I have only the sketchiest idea of what economics actually is, but my research has told me that people with economics degrees make lots of money, and I am earning practically nothing and working worryingly hard. Surveying the range of Universities and Colleges accessible by public transport, I decide upon the most excellent and August, University College Dublin. It's a nightmare of a journey, north to south, right the way across Dublin, but it is at least accessible by bus.

I have a reasonable degree of common sense, i.e. I am somewhat street-smart, and I know they will not accept me if I simply bowl up and ask nicely. I set about constructing a cunning plan. I phone up and ask who actually runs the economics bit. The economics bit is, I learn, called the School of Economics, and is run by a dean. It is a relatively simple matter to obtain his name, phone number, plus directions to his office.

I am set back momentarily when I discover that the minimum course requirements (what you have to have to get on the course) are five school certificates, at least one of which must be in Mathematics. This strikes me as something of a problem, but I read on and discover a reference to 'Mature Student Entry Requirements' and the exquisite concept of 'prior experiential learning'! I am not slow to realise that this is what I need. I find it most agreeable that this fine institute of learning has fallen upon such an abstract and malleable yardstick. There is a leaflet that tells you what sort of thing counts as experiential learning. I am sure I have loads of it and start writing down all the experiences I have had that would count. It does not take as long as I had hoped. I need a more scientific approach. I review the course requirements and begin to develop a patter. I do at least know what makes for a good patter.

During my research into the reading list, I discover that the dean has written a book on economics. Gut feel tells me I have found my lever. All I need now is a decent fulcrum. The fulcrum is not too long in revealing itself. The College, it seems, attempts to embody egalitarian principles, and has a mission to educate street urchins. This is very good, very good indeed. I am certainly the quintessential street urchin. I stand in front of the bathroom mirror and practice Artful Dodger facial expressions and mannerisms.

I am ready. My plan is deceptively simple. I shall go and ask the dean for a place on his economics degree. My execution is exemplary. I arrive at the College at around 11 a.m. I go straight to the library and ask about the dean's book. I am pointed to a long low shelf with about one hundred and fifty copies of a small green textbook.

"That's it", the librarian sighs.

"You certainly have a lot of copies," I venture, "is it in great demand?"

"Never read so far as I'm aware", he grumbles, "we only keep it in stock because the dean wrote it."

"I have an interview with the dean after lunch", I lie. "Do you think I might borrow a copy if I promise to return it straight away?"

The librarian hesitates.

"I'm being offered a teaching role", I lie again.

"Well, alright, I suppose." He shakes his head. "It's not like we'd miss a copy."

I thank him profusely and exit before he has time to change his mind with a small green textbook under my arm.

I sit on the College steps in the late spring sunshine, smoking a pack of Majors (the Sweet Aftons made me cough too much – no filter) and attempt to decipher the chapter headings. I am baffled. Some things look ok, 'The Theory of the Firm' doesn't sound too bad, but 'Giffin Goods in Post War Europe?' defies comprehension. Well, one can over-prepare.

I arrive outside his office at precisely 12 noon and sit across from his door on an oak slab set into a deep window recess. At exactly 12:15 p.m., his secretary leaves her office (adjacent to the dean's) and goes to lunch. I wait a while to make sure that she has really gone, which is just as well as she returns a few moments later to get her umbrella. I wait another five minutes and then saunter across the hallway to her office. I begin to bang hard on the door. A be-spectacled old gentleman emerges from the dean's office and asks if he can help me.

"Oh, no thanks. I just wanted to speak to the dean's secretary."

"Well, she's probably gone to lunch."

"It's ok. I'll wait."

"Well, you may be waiting quite a while."

"Not a problem. Sorry to have disturbed you." I make to return to the window recess to wait.

"Well, err, I am the dean. Actually, perhaps I can help."

"That's very kind of you, but I don't mean to trouble you. I'll wait for your secretary to come back."

"No trouble at all. Come on in."

I follow him into a dimly lit cave constructed of old books and dust. I had expected a few piles of books and manuscripts, grime and watery sunlight through cracked glass etc., but this was an order of magnitude more impressive. Only a college dean could possibly manage this level of chaos, and even then, probably only in Ireland.

Contrapuntally, he has a sleek-looking Habitat desk lamp – a gift from a worried student, I imagine.

"Now, what can I do for you?"

I glance shyly at the floor.

"Well, thank you so much for taking the time to see me. It is very good of you. I don't mean to impose."

"No imposition. What can I help you with?"

I sense I may be overdoing it a little.

"I wanted to find out how I can get a place on the economics degree." I give him an earnest look. "I love economics, but studying at home no longer satisfies me intellectually. I need the demands of formal study and the competition of other opinions and points of view."

We discuss my deep love of economics as I surreptitiously place his book front cover up on his desk. The Dean's glance hovers over it for a moment before moving on. I am not sure if my approach is a little too crass. I imagine my father saying, "Ah, no, Pat, that was just crass enough!"

I confess my lack of detectable qualifications. The dean perks up enormously. We investigate all the many and various ways in which I have valid, even compelling, prior experiential learning.

The dean removes a small pad of fleshy pink notepaper from his desk drawer.

"I'll write you a little note." He scrabbles around for a moment, looking for a pen. "Should suffice."

I wait patiently while he scribbles on the tiny square of Basildon Bond. I know enough to stop talking once I have closed the sale.

"I'll send this to the course director. You should get an interview within the next few weeks."

I thank the dean profusely and leave. I wander out of the rolling green College grounds. Dublin traffic roars this way and that. I am in something of a daze.

The interview letter arrives only three days later. It is terse and to the point.

"Interview 9. a.m. Monday, Course Director's Office". There are some brief instructions as to how to find it and a phone number "should I prefer to withdraw my application". Not a happy course director, not happy at all.

I turn up to the interview in what I believe to be a very smart new suit. I knock lightly on the door.

"Come!" A loud, no-nonsense voice booms out.

"Oh shit." I think, "This is going to be hard".

The course director sits in an enormous leather chair behind a deliberately intimidating mahogany desk, wearing a very expensive dark blue pin-stripe suit with extravagantly red braces. He takes in my new suit in an instant. Inscrutable, I can't tell what he's thinking.

Oh shit, again, this is not some dusty academic. This is the real deal. On the terrifying mahogany desk sits a small pink note, absurd, embarrassing against the vast expanse of tooled Moroccan leather.

I change my game plan on the spot. I meet his eye, coolly or as coolly as I can manage.

"OK," I say, forcing myself to look him straight in the eye, "What's the deal?"

He gives me a long appraising look. Some of the ire leaves his face. He flicks the tiny note with an expensive-looking fountain pen.

"You can have a place, but the moment you realise you are too far out of your depth, you come and see me, got it?" His home-counties English accent is slightly jarring in the hallowed halls of University College. I nod acceptance.

"What then?" I try to hold my ground. "What will you do then?"

"Find you a better course."

"OK." I nod my head once with what I hope looks like confidence.

"OK," he smiles. "I've done it!" I realise, but I have no one I want to tell, no one to call, no one I want to share it with.

COUSIN ELIZABETH

Miriam's cousin Elizabeth from Toronto is coming to stay. I have only met her once before, when she was over in London before we moved to Dublin, singing with her band. She is a kind of mirror image of Miriam, a photographic negative, opposite in every way. Whereas Miriam is quite tall, Elizabeth is of average height or slightly less. Miriam has short spiky dark hair. Elizabeth's is long and wavy and blonde. Miriam's skin is pale, whereas Elizabeth is tanned. Miriam has piercing blue eyes. Elizabeth's are a beguiling deep dark brown. Miriam is serious and somewhat academic – Elizabeth is into singing and songwriting and acting and art therapy. Elizabeth is also very, very sexy. Err, not that Miriam can't be if she sets her mind to it.

Elizabeth has been given the job of converting the traditional English pantomime Puss in Boots for the Toronto audience. She will be staying for six weeks. Miriam and I are both looking forward to it.

Miriam insists that we go to the January sales to get all new bedding for the spare room. I am not so sure this is necessary. Sounds very pricey. However, I am left in little doubt. It is my job to pay for these things, not to choose them. The weather is absolutely foul outside. The Weather Office has issued a severe weather warning - wind gusting up to 75 miles per hour and driving rain.

We make a deal. Miriam will go alone to the January sales, her gold credit card poised to strike at any and every bargain that comes within range. In this way, she assures me she will save me enormous sums of money. I am so pleased. Also, I get valuable Brownie Points without having to venture out to the hideous sales. I do have to put up a shelf in the spare room, however.

Miriam, though airily unaware of the true economy that pervades our lives, has an iron grasp on what I can only describe as her own private economy. Learnéd books could be written on it. A whole area of economic theory is just waiting to be uncovered.

Miriam's economy, which I have coined the 'Brownie Point Economy', consists of two counterbalancing forces or currencies, one positive and the other negative. First are the Brownie Points. They have a small positive value and are reasonably easy to obtain but are subject to a ruinous inflation rate leaving them virtually worthless after about eight hours. Then there are the negative demerits. The demerit is the more mercurial of the two currencies having a highly variable exchange rate against the Brownie Point. On some occasions, the Brownie Point has been known to approach parity with the demerit, but not on many. The typical exchange rate is about twenty Brownie Points to one demerit. I can't help feeling there should be some equivalent of a bond, but perhaps I've been reading too many economics primers.

The even more mercurial aspect of the demerit is its capability, unique amongst world currencies, spontaneously to rekindle. Having been redeemed in July, say, for the sum of approximately twenty Brownie Points, the exact same demerit may spontaneously rekindle months later, according to some arcane and ancient matrilineal law predating the Babylonians, as though it had never been redeemed at all. Further, demerits attract hideous rates of compound interest, requiring immediate and strenuous efforts at repayment if a life of indentured servitude is to be avoided.

Putting up the shelf in the pantry will be a source of mega Brownie Points if I get it done. However, as far as I am aware, I have no outstanding unredeemed demerits. Secondly, I need some bits from the hardware store, and there's the awful weather outside.

I get out my laptop and open the specially crafted Spreadsheet model of the Brownie Point economy. This is not a back-of-the-envelope calculation. This is a detailed economic model incorporating concepts such as 'value at risk', 'net present value', and Modigliani and Miller's notion of the 'passive residual'.

The core of the problem can be expressed algebraically thus:

$$mh = bp^n/dm$$

Key.

Mh	My Happiness
Bp	Brownie Points
Dm	Demerits
n	n represents the function sb/ex where
Sb	Satisfaction with sales booty, and
Ex	Expectations of progress on the shelf front

It is plain from the above that n (success on the sales booty front divided by expectations of progress), being a highly leveraged multiplier, is the crucial term in the equation.

I set the potential for earning new Brownie Points against the fact that I have earned a few Brownie Points already today.

- I have taken the brand-new toaster, which I bought before Christmas, back to the store because it burnt everything in its general vicinity, and obtained a replacement lacking this feature, *and*
- I have put a hat-and-coat hook up on the door next to where we keep the ironing board (job outstanding for about eighteen months), *and*
- I am not complaining too much about her going to the sales.

It is probably also worth chalking up a couple of intangibles. Miriam's lie-in (ten o'clock) plus two cups of tea and two rounds of marmite toast (made on the pyromaniac toaster). These are each fairly small things, but they do add up to a certain number of highly valued, if ephemeral, Brownie Points.

Add to this my reasonable expectation that returning with large amounts of booty from the sales may reduce expectations of progress *and* moderate the propensity (otherwise fairly powerful) to issue demerits. The issue really becomes, will my failure to put up the shelf result in the egregious allocation of a demerit or not? As I have no current outstanding demerits, I do not really need to earn any more Brownie Points today. My strategy is clear. I will sing the prowess of the hunter-gatherer on her return. Obviously, this means that every item of loot must be eulogised as an ideal combination, merging and interpenetration of utility and beauty in a perfect harmony of form and content. In other words, a fantastic bargain. My tears will be tears of joy at the huge sums Miriam has saved me.

At the same time, I must plan the necessary expectation management on the shelf front. When my opinion is sought (via her mobile phone) regarding the acquisition of an identified target within range, I must use the opportunity to highlight unforeseen challenges that have arisen on the shelf front. (N.B. Make a list and keep it by the phone.)

Matters are taken out of my hands. The doorbell rings. It is Elizabeth, one week early.

"Elizabeth! Hi. It's lovely to see you, of course, but you are one week early, aren't you?"

"Oh, didn't I tell you I changed my flights?"

"Don't think so. Anyway, you're here now. That's the main thing." I grab her small suitcase and usher her in.

"Is this all you've got." Miriam would have had twice or three times as much.

"Yep. Always travel light. Laptop's in here." Elizabeth taps the small expensive-looking rucksack she is carrying.

"I'm afraid Miriam is out at the January sales. She'll be back in a couple of hours, I should think."

"Not to worry on my account."

"I'll show you to your room. You can sort yourself out, and I'll make a nice cup of tea. Oh, or coffee." I lead Elizabeth up a couple of flights of stairs to her room. She flings her suitcase onto the bed.

"There. All done". I like her.

We go back down to the kitchen, and I fuss about making tea and toast while Elizabeth tells me all her news, all her hopes and fears, all her doubts and opinions of any sort and on every topic. She is an awful lot of fun, but she doesn't half talk a lot.

I see a taxi pull up on the street outside.

"That'll be Miriam."

"Oh, can I go? Can I, please? Let me. It'll be such a surprise." I follow Elizabeth upstairs and wait a few yards down the hallway while Elizabeth crouches down with her hand on the doorknob. After what seems like ages, the doorbell rings. Elizabeth leaps up and throws open the door.

"Surprise!" she yells, arms outstretched, left knee bent slightly, hips swivelled to best advantage. Where do girls learn that?

"Oh, my God! Elizabeth! Fantastic. But you're a week early!" Miriam shoots me a withering look over Elizabeth's shoulder.

"Yes." I chip in, "She only arrived a few moments ago. I tried to call your mobile phone, but it was switched off or unobtainable." Shit! I can really do without a demerit just because Elizabeth has arrived early. I help Miriam in with all her shopping. I am desperate.

"Wow. Just look at all these bargains." My happy face is firmly in place, "You must show us what you've got!" The ploy works. Miriam looks smug. This means she has saved me thousands and thousands of pounds. I can't wait.

I make more tea and toast while Miriam unpacks in the sitting room. She has many bargains, many, many bargains. I am so happy. Elizabeth is wonderful, however. She 'oohs' and 'aahs' over every item, correctly estimating some massively inflated price which Miriam is able disdainfully to cut by at least half. The savings just pile up. Both ladies decide to carry the stuff up to Elizabeth's room and give it a makeover. Far as I can see, it will end up looking like a Belgian brothel. None of my business, I'm sure.

The next several weeks pass in a haze of fun, frivolity and outings. Elizabeth really is the perfect house guest. We get to go see

Puss in Boots over and over again. Elizabeth and Miriam discuss the ins and outs of the storyline and characterisation in detail. Elizabeth develops a Canadianised version incorporating various sporting and political personalities we have never heard of.

All too soon, her last night in Dublin arrives. We go to a posh jazz club for dinner and to listen to the band. The food is pretty good. They have a French chef, and the jazz is wonderful. The band takes a break, and Elizabeth goes up to have a chat. They establish some mutual acquaintances from the Montreal Jazz Festival. Elizabeth is in her element.

After a while, the band starts up again. The sax player begins to introduce the next song.

"We're very fortunate tonight to have in the audience a dear friend and a regular on the Montreal Jazz scene. It's her last night in Dublin. She's jetting back to the ice and snow in the morning, but I guess if we ask real nice, we may be able to persuade her to come up on stage and sing us a song." The crowd cheers.

"Hey Elizabeth, why don't you come up on stage and jam with us a while?"

The spotlight sweeps the crowd. Alights on our table. Illuminates Elizabeth. She shakes her head at the sax player, feigning reluctance, and then shrugs acceptance of her fate. The crowd roars.

"Ladies and gentlemen, please welcome to the stage Elizabeth Babel." The applause continues and then subsides. The band starts up a well-known song. The sax player introduces it anyway.

"Ladies and gentlemen, a foggy day in London town." The crowd is silent. Elizabeth is still, focused, and centred. She is magnificent, transported and transformed. I remember the words from a review she showed us once 'a cool blue diamond, tracking a red-hot groove.' True enough. Miriam and I are both smitten.

The journey home in the taxi is silent. Each person alone with their thoughts. It has been a wonderful six weeks. Miriam and I have not had so much fun in years.

The next day Elizabeth is gone. It is as though a light has gone out of our home. We both find ourselves wandering from room to room, almost in search of her. She is so full of life, so giving of joy. We agree that we must go to Canada in the summer.

ST MICHAN'S CHURCH

We are over from Zambia, visiting my grandparents in Dublin. It is just before Christmas, and it is very, very cold. I am seven years old and Zambian. This freezing damp air is just plain wrong.

I know my grandparents have bought me a very large, very expensive battery-powered fire engine for Christmas. I have seen it in its big square box under their bed. What can they be thinking? The present is far too young for a person of my years. My grandparents seem very nice in a way, but they are very distant, not like anyone I've met before, an earlier order of humanity. They are not really sure what children *are* exactly, what amuses them, what they are supposed to say to them, or supposed not to say. Their own daughters, my aunt and my mother, were safely taken care of by governesses until they were old enough to be introduced to society. My father is at home reading the newspaper. "Catching up on European current affairs" as he puts it, and my brother has gone rambling in the Carrick Hills. My grandmother and mother decide to go off shopping. They are taking Minnie and Ingrid with them. My grandfather and I are doubtful about that course of action. He very kindly offers to take me off and look after me for a couple of hours. We are standing by the Liffey, looking back towards O'Connell Street and Temple Bar.

"I know." my grandfather checks that the womenfolk are safely out of sight, "Let's go exploring the dark and dangerous North of the town. You'll have to keep your wits about you now, Pat. There's footpads and thieves a' plenty once you cross the Ha'Penny Bridge."

We cross the bridge in a few moments and enter deepest, darkest North Dublin. My grandfather seems to know exactly where he's going.

"Have you heard of the Crusaders?" My grandfather offers me a conspiratorial look. We are in a narrow, cobbled backstreet with high brick walls around us. It is an echoing place. Shreds of mist hang in the corners and stairwells of ancient warehouses.

"You mean like Richard the Conqueror?"

"Yes, that sort of thing. The soldiers who went off to war in the Holy Land."

"Yes." I'm not sure where this is leading.

"Well." My grandfather, fixes me with a steely eye, "Would you like to meet some of them?"

"Meet them?"

"Yes!"

"Wasn't it a long time ago?"

"It was that Pat, that it was."

"So how can we meet them now, then?"

"Just you wait and see!" He is gleeful and mysterious in equal measure. We pass through a couple more narrow streets and round a few more corners before coming out in front of a very unremarkable-looking church.

"Here we are. Now, are you feeling brave, Pat? Are you up to it?"

"Up to what?" I ask, not liking the way this is going at all.

"Visiting the dead!"

I am sure I am not up to visiting the dead, not at all, not today.

"Not really." I venture.

"Right you are, Pat, right you are." He leads me swiftly down some steps. I wonder briefly if words have different meanings in Zambia and Ireland.

"I'm not really sure…"

"Ah, you'll love it! You can tell all your friends about it."

A bored man reading a newspaper by the light of a single bare bulb takes the entrance money from my grandfather.

"It'll be the full tour, will it?"

"It will. It will." My grandfather pats me on the head. "This young man is my grandson. He insists on seeing everything you can throw at him."

I don't. Really, I don't.

"So be it!" The man is no longer bored.

We set off down some more stairs into a gloomy hallway under the church.

"We're in the crypt." The man grimaces in comic terror, "Where the dead live."

The next forty-five minutes become a blur of images and tales, speculation and downright lies. We see beautiful old coffins covered in gold filigree, coffins broken open to reveal the preserved bodies of the dead, lips drawn back, leering, wisps of hair. We venture down narrow, echoing corridors where lights are shone into tiny chambers and the names and dates of the dead recited. The cold begins to seep into my bones. We are introduced to executed rebels and the handless and footless corpse of a long-dead soldier.

"It's the dry air and the limestone," the man reaches out and touches the wall.

"What is?" I wonder, lost in Irish myth and an unaccustomed familiarity with the dead.

"Now here's a fella that's been waiting a long time to meet you!" We are in an open room with white crystal-encrusted walls. Several bodies lie on the floor, illuminated by uncovered neon tubes.

"Will you shake his hand?" the man asks, pointing at the nearest of the dead people, "It's ok, he won't bite." My grandfather and the man have a little chuckle about this. I have lost all sense of reality. I step forward and take the brown, dead, leathery hand in mine.

"Pleased to meet you." I shake the hand once and place it gently down.

"You'll be ready for a nice cup of tea and slice of cake, I imagine." The man turns to my grandfather, "There's a grand little place around the corner. Tell 'em I sent you." He gives my grandfather a conspiratorial wink and leads us back into the light of day. It is freezing outside. It has begun to drizzle, and an icy wind blows off the nearby river.

I am more than ready for a nice cup of tea and a slice of cake.

"What did you think of that then, Pat?"

I look up into my grandfather's face, not knowing what to say, for once utterly lost for words.

TYING THE KNOT

After my father's funeral, Miriam and I decide to get married. I do not really know how this decision is made, what thought we are putting into it, or why we feel the need to get married. I am confused. So deeply confused that my normal mental functioning seems to be switched off or asleep. It is as though everything is suppressed into my subconscious, even conscious thought, or perhaps it is more that conscious thought has been temporarily stunned into insensibility by the death of my father. I am running on intuition and body knowledge alone, without the interference of the conniving ego. I do not know if getting married is a bid for security, comfort, and support or simply the path of least resistance. It could very well be either or both. All of the above. It would make sense either way. It seems like a perfectly straightforward thing to do. It seems quite insane. It seems like a cry for help and stability in a cruel and uncertain world.

Surely, we should give ourselves more time. Give it a year and see how we feel about it rather than being spooked into marriage by the spectre of death. We have been together for five years. We can wait. Why should we wait? If we are not ready by now, we never will be. If it ain't broke, don't fix it. We are fine the way we are. And on and on and on.

The date is set a month hence. A whirlwind of arrangements, compromises, promises and refusals ensues, sweeping away doubt, leaving little space for introspection. There are still times, though, in the wee small hours of the night, when I can't sleep, and my defences are low, that I hear, or think I hear, attenuated and thin, and far, far off, a little voice inside screaming primal doubt, a little boy crying in the loneliness of a dark and shuttered room, hidden and afraid.

We pay for the event ourselves. Miriam's mum chips in for the reception. Miriam and her mother choose the dress, choose the place for the reception, choose the guests, and choose the reception menu. I watch all this from a distance. I am separated. Alienated from it all. Increasingly there is some conscious part of me that doubts. Some part, that I chose to ignore, that warns. It is a lonely voice without friends. No one else questions the decision. No one else seems to think it odd that we are now suddenly getting married just a few weeks after my father's death.

The allotted day is suddenly upon us, and I am in a Dublin taxi on the way to the church with my brother Sam and my best friend, Kurt. The back of the taxi smells of stale fish and chips. The three of us are feeling somewhat delicate after the previous evening's bachelor night celebrations. Streets and buildings, faces and advertising hoardings sweep past in a blur. Several times, when the taxi stops at traffic lights or pedestrian crossings, I think of jumping out and just running away. I feel the pressure mounting like gorge in my throat. I force myself to think. I do have strong feelings for Miriam and her family. I do love her. At least, I think I do. How do you know if you love someone? When the chips are down, and you are in the taxi on the way to the church where your bride-to-be, your friends and relations, indeed your entire family await, how do you know what love really is? And what does it matter, really? What difference does it make?

My old friend, the feeling of dissociation, of separateness that envelopes me from time to time, chooses that moment to seek me out. I find myself staring out of the taxi window at a Dublin that no longer makes sense to me. I have decided marriage it is. It makes no difference. I feel a little nauseous, but nothing a cigarette won't fix.

Our wedding day, though in late autumn, is blessed with gorgeous, unseasonal sunshine. It is downright hot for Dublin. My inner 'observer' is with me once again. I am simultaneously doing and observing. The day's events unfold. I watch, no longer a participant. The taxi pulls up with half an hour to spare. Friends and relatives are milling around, and children are running in and out of people's feet. Older folk are sitting or standing quietly. I wander off down the narrow path at the side of the church, proudly Anglican in a Catholic city. I couldn't care less either way. The narrow way opens up to reveal an old stone bench and a haggard-looking apple tree. It is a perfect, sheltered spot. I sit on the bench and begin to smoke a cigarette. The sounds of guests talking and laughing, and the low hum of the traffic are audible but do not impinge. It is very peaceful. My whirling thoughts race hither and thither. I observe them indulgently, like an aging grandparent secure in the knowledge that the little dears can soon be handed back to their adoring parents.

Kurt appears around the side of the church. He comes and sits next to me. I offer him a cigarette. He lights up. Nothing is said for several minutes, and then Kurt pipes up.

"Better get you inside and find the flower for your buttonhole." I suppose he is right. We both stand and walk back around to the front of the church. The place is heaving with people now. There is lots of waving and greeting and handshaking and kisses. I watch my feet move by themselves, one in front of the next, automatically. I make my way up the aisle to the front. The air in the church is cool and very dry. There is a faint smell of wood polish in the air. I am reminded of the church in I visited once many years earlier with my grandfather.

Minnie, despite all odds, has decided to attend. She is currently a radical lesbian separatist living in London. She has forgone the purple and green of the suffragettes for the pink and black of the modern dike-about-town. Kurt reckons even lesbian chicks just can't resist pink. Minnie is resplendent, all in black except for the pink boots and pink triangle earrings. My grandmother, my dad's mum, is sitting right up front near the altar. Minnie is standing in the aisle as far back as possible. She has brought along her girlfriend Kate for moral, or perhaps political, support. Kurt wanders over to say 'Hi'. They talk for a few moments, and I see Kurt pointing out where my grandmother is sitting. Kurt turns to me and calls out.

"Do you know the one about the bridegroom whose sister's a pinko, commie queer?" The question rings out across the church, finding its way into a momentary silence. I am horribly embarrassed. I decide to make a joke of it. The organist is in the middle of "Jesu joy of man's desiring". I shout back.

"If you hum it, I'll get him to play it." The organist pretends not to hear. All very undignified.

Sam is already in position. He is my best man. He has the rings in his hand. He keeps putting them back into his waistcoat pocket and then retrieving them. He seems more nervous than me. I realise he *is* more nervous than me. I am not nervous, not at all. I am not really here.

The guests are all finally seated on the correct sides of the aisle. Sam has stopped fiddling with the rings. The organ music starts. Miriam and her father appear at the door of the church, silhouetted against the brilliant sunshine outside. Everyone turns to watch the bride approach. She looks gorgeous in ivory silk and satin, a wimple-style hat perched precariously on her head and a very long veil. She smiles at everyone as she walks up the aisle. I wonder briefly if her Jewish heritage is of any concern to her.

Her father, very tall and dignified in his yarmulke, nods gravely at all and sundry. He can't really understand why his darling daughter has married out, but he's making the best of it. Miriam looks devastatingly lovely, young, alive and full of joy.

Miriam is standing next to me at the altar. I look deeply into her eyes. She smells strongly of Channel Number 5. It suits her. I see her as though for the first time. I really see her. She is very beautiful. I know her and her family as well as anyone can know anyone. They are my family too. All dutifully arrived from London on time and in good order.

We are a good match. Everybody says so. The service begins.

We say the words and sing the songs. I am not really Christian, and Miriam is not really Jewish, well culturally but not religiously, but a church wedding just seems so much more 'meant'. We sign the register. Posing this way and that for the photographer.

Mercifully the set-piece photographs are relatively few as none of us can really be bothered, and the requisite relatives are not to be found. We soon head off to the reception.

There is a pub with a large beer garden just across from the place where the reception is being held, and our guests are well on the way by the time we arrive. There are a great many guests. I am not certain we have enough food to feed them. This is where being a genuine Christian might really come in handy.

Everyone leaves the beer garden and piles into the wedding reception. Inside, there is a bar presided over by a rather pretty, rather tubby American girl. The drinks begin to flow. There are far too many people for the reception area. People spill out into the street, across to the pub and into a side alley. The food is laid out buffet style, but, as suspected, it is insufficient and is soon gone. Miriam, quite rightly, is the centre of attention. This is her day, and she looks wonderful. I find a stool at the far end of the bar and begin to drink slowly and steadily. No one approaches me. I do not have to converse at all. The American bar person gives me a nice smile. She has very even white teeth. I light another cigarette and watch the day unfold. The deed is done. No going back.

I notice the two gifts from Minnie, one each for Miriam and me, wrapped in black paper and secured with black ribbon. Very symbolic. I know she will have made some kind of point. I have to open them. She has given Miriam quite a nice twenty-six-blade Swiss Army knife, and for me, there is a little electric heating element sufficient to boil water for one cup of tea. "For when she leaves you," the note says.

By bedtime, I am too tired and too hung over for sex. Miriam is disappointed, more, I think, from the point of view of fulfilling the proprieties than from any actual carnal desire. I am sorry. We fall asleep quickly. Both zonked.

SALMON GUMS

We are bouncing along in the red Holden Kingswood, heading south from Norseman. It is late afternoon, and we have already had our third front wheel blow-out in a week. The tarmac on the roads, where there is tarmac, is tacky from the heat. We have no air-conditioning. The windows are wide open, and a hot breeze is blowing through the car. We make our way through occasional sparse townships and settlements. Dundas, Bromus, and Beete. We are approaching Salmon Gums.

At one point, a herd of wild Brumby horses charges out of the woods to our left and runs alongside us for a few hundred metres before veering off back into the scrubby bushland.

The road is arrow straight for hundreds of kilometres at a time. This is outback country. The bush is peppered with occasional eucalyptus forests and scrub. In the distance, we make out a curious dark cloud swirling low over the road. We watch it for nearly an hour as we approach. We can see that it consists of hundreds and hundreds of birds wheeling and looping, spiralling round and round.

We slow to a crawl as we approach the flock. They are beautiful black cockatoos with red markings, thousands of them forming a stable twister bird cloud over the highway. We stop the car and get out to watch. It is eerie beneath the birds. We can see straight up through the clear space at the eye of the storm. The sun is almost blotted out, and a deep shade hangs over the road. We have no idea what they are doing, why they are doing this. We watch for perhaps fifteen minutes before driving on. In the rear-view mirror, we see the birds merge back into a flock and the flock into a dark cloud. Ahead real clouds are driving in from the south. Huge cumulonimbus towers hundreds of feet tall. They are growing and spreading almost visibly as we drive towards them. The clouds combine into a thick dark blanket very low against the horizon. There is going to be a wild storm, and we are driving straight towards it way off in the distance.

We pass a wonky sign bearing the legend 'Salmon Gums'. The township is tiny, hardly more than a dot, maybe six hundred souls. We whistle through it in a second and are out the other side before we know it. As we pass the sign proclaiming that we are now leaving the township of Salmon Gums, Miriam and I exchange glances. Despite my prediction, we did not meet up with Laura and Greg.

We head on into the storm. The cloud cover has at least cooled the tarmac, and we are making good time. Suddenly the sky opens, the cloud sinks to within a few metres of the road and rain lashes down. We slow to a few kilometres per hour with the windscreen wipers on full. We can hardly see the road ahead.

A few cars and utes pass us heading North, and then suddenly, out of the rain, appears a white van with its headlights on full. I am temporarily dazzled by the headlights as it sweeps past in the rain. But as it passes, I catch a glimpse of the driver. I shout out to Miriam, "It's them!"

"It's who?"

"It's Laura and Greg."

"Can't be." My comment is summarily dismissed, and we drive on for a while. Then suddenly I stop the car and turn around.

"This is where a five-litre engine should come in really handy. It *was* them, I'm sure of it." I drive back northwards as fast as I can.

After a few minutes, we see their taillights in the distance. We are slowly making ground. I am driving like a maniac against the wind and rain. There is a mineral taste in the air, like wet stone. I manage to get up close behind them and begin to flash my lights and sound the horn. We are both barrelling along at around eighty kilometres per hour. They take no notice. Who would stop in these conditions in the middle of nowhere?

I get alongside and wave to them to stop. They stop, and I get out and run to the driver's window. Greg rolls the window down an inch or two as I approach, and then they both recognise me.

"Hi guys," I can help grinning. There's a sign saying 'Welcome to Salmon Gums' just visible ahead, lit up by their headlights.

"What happened?"

"Broke an axle near Esperance and had to wait there a week for a spare to come from Perth."

We stood there, staring at each other for a few moments and then, realising there was nothing more to be said, turned around and headed off again in opposite directions. All the time, I could hear a smug voice at the back of my mind saying, "Told you so".

Miriam and I stumble off to bed. We are quite drunk. Amelie and Fausto have left. There is an empty brandy bottle on the coffee table, and all the ashtrays are full. The stench of alcohol and tobacco smoke permeates everything. Bloody good evening all around.

We manage the four flights of stairs with a modicum of decorum, the necessary level of stumbling, and zero dignity. We attempt to be extra quiet as we pass by the children's bedrooms. Of course, this results only in extra shushing and outbursts of giggling. We are both relieved and somewhat surprised that the ascent is achieved without significant misadventure.

As Miriam undresses, I stand on the balcony, set high up in the roof of our four-storey townhouse, gazing out over the Dublin skyline. The rain has stopped, and the black slate roofs glisten. Forests of chimney-stacks rise in serried ranks, street upon street, inviting Mary Poppins and Bill Sykes to dance over them, singing "Chim.. chimaney... chim chimaney.. chim chim cha roo....!". A cool wind blows from the west, ruffling the feathery tops of the trees. I can just make out O'Connell Street Bridge far away in the murky streetlight. The endless susurration from the High Street has reduced to a purr. The unique oily smell of Dublin after rain penetrates my awareness, gaining my attention. I have grown to love this stinky, dirty, huge, unplanned, and utterly magnificent city.

I light a cigarette, pondering the meaning of life for a bit. We had fun tonight. Odd that it should seem notable. I almost want to tell someone about it. Behind, in the bedroom, I hear the small noise of something being dropped on a wooden floor, followed swiftly by a resounding "Fuck" from Miriam. I suppose I'd better show willing.

"What's up?"

"Dropped a bottle of cleanser. Nothing broken."

Miriam is standing naked, scrutinising her face in the mirror above the basin. Occasionally dabbing here and there with a soggy ball of cotton wool. She seems to know what she's doing. A distant siren coming from the High Street almost demands attention.

From outside on the balcony, I watch Miriam at her pagan ablutions. The scent of watermelon, or something redolent of sunshine and blue skies, reaches my nostrils. She is almost done. A quick obeisance to Artemis or perhaps Oprah, and she will leap into bed.

Miriam leaps into bed, literally. She takes a short run up and then hurls herself into the air from about three feet away. I am not always quick to identify these eccentricities as foibles demanding any kind of explanation, so it takes me about ten years before I think to enquire as to why she does that. I still remember the "Isn't it obvious?" look she gave me. "Someone might grab my ankle," she explains. Ours is a Victorian steel framed bed, the mattress positioned high above the floor, leaving ample space for a footpad or other n'er-do-well. Obvious!

I shuck off my t-shirt and jeans, observing the entrancing violin curve of Miriam's waist and bottom. She bends down to get something else from her vanity case, presenting as if by accident, a very round, very pert bottom. Although I am tired and would really prefer just to go to sleep, chivalry requires a response. I feel myself harden a little. I lean over and give her a resounding smack on that fine, entreating arse.

Wrong move.

This, apparently, is not what was required. Miriam spins around in swift, sudden anger.

"Don't you dare hit me! How dare you? What gives you the right?" I have miscalculated. She is not happy.

"It just seemed the polite thing to do." Sometimes humour works. Not often, but what else have I got?

"Well, don't you ever hit me again, or I'll have you up for domestic violence!"

The balcony beckons. It's time for another cigarette. I listen to the night sounds of North Dublin. Another distant siren wails, police or ambulance. Can't tell which.

A small movement catches my eye in an adjacent garden. There it is again! Out of the shadows, a fox appears, cautiously sniffing the air. It makes its way out onto a small earth mound and sits in a pool of moonlight, looking back into the deeper shadows. More movement. Very slowly, and at first, very cautiously, two tiny cubs emerge to sit close by their mother. The vixen sniffs at them and gives them a bit of a lick. The cubs gain in confidence as I watch and begin teasing each other, tumbling this way and that. The vixen watches indulgently. Quietly, I call Miriam.

She deigns to appear, but upon seeing the foxes, hauteur is replaced by enchantment. We watch together, entranced. We have seen urban foxes often enough in London, but we have never seen them like this in Dublin. Suddenly the vixen and cubs disappear. A crack of light appears at the back door of the house across the way. We hear the grumpy old git who lives there grumbling to himself. "Piss off, bloody vermin."

The spell is broken. The world is suddenly cold and unwelcoming. We hear the sound of squealing brakes and skidding tyres, very close this time, followed by shouting. Miriam goes back inside. I finish my cigarette. The nearby altercation comes to an end. I shut the balcony door on the outside world. Unbidden, from some demanding seat of desire, I recall the clear pink handprint left on Miriam's very fine arse. I am instantly hard.

Miriam is getting ready for sleep. I shall have to work quickly, Miriam's desire for sex, never much in evidence, falls away quickly. Still, it's worth a go. I kiss her shoulders and manoeuvre gently, snuggling up to her. She wraps her arms around my back, giving me a half-hearted peck on the cheek. She is already cooling. I feel the desperation rising in me.

It may very well be an intriguing irony for some that women need to feel loved to have sex and men need to have sex to feel loved, but now, at this exact moment, I just need sex, raw, shameless, physical fucking. Right Now! I begin to lick her nipples and caress her thigh. There is some positive response. She opens her legs a little granting further intimacy. She is somewhat aroused. With the single-minded intensity of a street shark fleecing a mark, I work her body, covering every angle. Somewhere deep in my gut, I acknowledge the fear that the game demands a level of commitment and skill that I cannot hope to sustain. I see my fingers growing icy and numb as I hang above the ravine of rejection. One by one, my fingers give. I am losing the battle. I am not desired. At best, I am used, as is she. Below consciousness, I am enraged, a beast howling at the moon. I have no rival. The game is not 'his' to win but mine to lose.

"Fuck it"

Quick flickering strokes fan the flames of her arousal. I take a nipple firmly in my teeth, not enough to cause pain but sufficient, if I have calculated correctly, to retrieve the situation. She tastes of body lotion, slightly bitter. Yes! She takes my cock in one hand and caresses my balls with the other. Game on.

I step up the speed and intensity of my caress. She is holding my balls firmly in the palm of her hand, squeezing gently. Her breath comes in shallow gasps. Her orgasm is imminent. Timing is everything.

She goes rigid, stifling a small cry. I have only seconds to act while she is still aroused before she turns her back.

I slide on top of her, gently parting her legs with my weight. As I begin, I feel my own cadence is out of tempo with hers. Raw male desire surges through my loins, obliterating any sense of mutuality on my part. I pump away, lost in a world of sensation and desire. She is always silent when I am inside her, never a moan of pleasure nor a whisper. Nothing passes her lips. I look down at her face. Her eyes are closed, her mouth pinched, fixed in a rictus of disgust. Bile rises in my throat, the incongruous taste of brandy on my lips. It is always the same. I am revolted by it all. I disgust myself, so weak, so driven and controlled by instinct and desire. I can barely stand to see that familiar look on her face. I cannot stand it. What hope is there? She is repulsed and disgusted. At last, I come. She doesn't even push me off, just waits patiently for me to roll over. She is already half asleep. The room smells of watermelon.

I say nothing. We say nothing to each other. The issue lies between us every night, yet we can neither of us find the courage or the words to raise it. Like magic, once the word is spoken, the incantation made, there is no going back.

I venture back out onto the balcony for a final cigarette. The lights are on at Amelie and Fausto's place. I can see smoke wafting from the open kitchen window. A golden glow, intimate and inviting, spills out across the lawn. I can hear snippets of music across the cold night air, 'when a ma-an loves a woman, she can't do no wrong…' I imagine the scene down below in Amelie's kitchen, the warmth and gentle intimacy she must enjoy. I finish the cigarette, musing to myself.

I arrive at Amelie's front door at eleven a.m.

"Burglar, burglar, madam." I call out. She rushes to the door, the kids (a boy and a girl) in tow. There is no shyness this time. We can't wait to hold each other, to feel the warmth of our bodies.

"Oh, thank God", I hear myself saying, "Thank God". The kids are bouncing all around. It is wonderful to see them, so intelligent, so full of life. I find I have opened my heart to these children. They drag me off and show me their stuff, one a fairy grotto, the other a skateboard. One so like Amelie, the other so like Fausto. I feel at home. I feel I am home.

I sit down on the hall floor to explore the fairy grotto. One by one, the fairies are brought out with ceremonial seriousness to be admired and discussed.

"This one has a broken wing, but mummy says she'll help me fix it." I agree that it will be good as new with a dab of glue. The next fairy has a glittery face and white wings.

"She's the queen", I am told. Each precious treasure is brought out for my inspection and approval. I feel I have been allowed into a special, secret world. I feel honoured by this little girl's trust. At the same time, somewhere at the sly edge of perception, I sense the Observer shuddering a little at the mawkishness of it all.

Amelie's kids are going to stay with their grandparents while Amelie and I take the Dun Laoghaire ferry across to Fishguard and drive down to Cornwall for a few days. Although I have been travelling for days now from Sydney via Atlanta, and I am in my usual sorry state, I am nevertheless full of energy and life. I want everything to be perfect. This is our fourth time together. It's been four months since Madrid. I am on my best behaviour. The ferry crossing is slow and foggy. The ship's horn, mournful in the chill air. Glad to be on dry land again, we drive down to Cornwall together in complete contentment and happiness. We cannot stop touching each other. We are constantly stroking each other's arms and legs. Amelie hangs on to my left arm as I drive, absently stroking the dark hairs of my forearm. We stop at a transport café and have a full English breakfast of eggs, sausage, bacon, hash browns, toast, and large cracked mugs of horribly stewed tea. I certainly know how to treat a girl.

The cottage, 'The Owls', is right down at the bottom of Cornwall near St Michael's Mount. We find our way straight to it and settle ourselves in. Amelie is wearing blue shorts and that little black top with red flowers. She looks ravishing.

We sit on the little sofa and drink wine together, taking this opportunity to commune, chatter idly and make simple plans. We will drive to St Ives and see the Barbara Hepworth Gallery. We will walk over the causeway at low tide and visit St Michael's Mount. We will stroll on the beach, holding hands. We will peer into the rock pools and walk along the cliffs. We will be together.

We sleep peacefully that night, like kittens. We snuggle up and canoodle. I brush her hair. It is heaven. At some point in the night, I notice she is no longer in bed. I can see her sitting in the window seat, smoking a cigarette, pensive. I say nothing. We both have our moments of doubt. I lie in her bed, still warm with her warmth, still sweet with her scent.

Next morning, we get up late and have a leisurely breakfast. I watch her sitting cross-legged on the bed, brushing her hair. I know it is a moment I will always want to remember. I snap off a quick photo. She looks about twenty, almost absurdly cute. I am besotted.

Although it is mid-summer and warm, the sky is overcast. We drive down to Mousehole and have lunch in the inn on the quayside. We go for a long walk up and along the cliffs, heading south. Amelie is wearing blue jeans and a red nylon raincoat. She is happy and carefree. We stop often along the track for a hug and a kiss. Being together is so right, so good. Even the simplest little things, like buying a loaf of bread or drinking a cup of tea, seem special, perfect. This is the first time since I was ten years old in Swaziland that I can say I am completely happy.

We drive across to Porthcurno to see if we can get tickets for the Minack open-air theatre perched right on the edge of the cliffs above Porthcurno Bay. By the time we get there, cars are already arriving for the evening's performance. We are stopped by an unhappy and harassed-looking man asking for our tickets. We explain that we want to get tickets for tonight's performance. He is clearly having a bad day and tells us that all the tickets are sold out for weeks ahead. We turn around and hide the car out of his sight at the top of the car park. We sneak back in and make our way to the ticket office, where we are told the same story. Eventually, they agree to take my credit card details and call if two seats become available. We are depressed.

Amelie suggests we go to Sennen Cove for dinner in a pub she remembers. We drive through narrow lanes over the hills and arrive around sunset. The sea is calm, gentle surf rolling with the rhythm of centuries caresses the shore. Amelie hesitates for a moment. She is gazing towards a nearby hill. She is quiet for a little while. I do not intrude. Cornwall is full of memories for her. The pub is bustling, but we find a little table in a corner and sit down. The food is average pub fare. Amelie peruses the menu sceptically, looking for Chicken Caesar Salad or Grilled Blue Eye Cod. We play safe and order fish and chips.

It's so good to be in an ordinary English pub with Amelie. We talk about the harassed man at the Minack Theatre. We wonder if we will get tickets. Amelie tells me about the time she went there with her kids and the magical way the actors seemed to rise up out of the sea, suddenly appearing over the edge of the cliff. She is sharing her life with me, her memories and experiences. I am enraptured. I drink her in, hungry to know all about her, her hopes and dreams, even her arbitrary likes and dislikes. She is happy to show me around her world, to allow me to share its magic and poetry. I adore her absolutely. She is my life, the keeper of my soul. I vow to dedicate my life to her, to be the best person I can be for her. The Observer stirs, disturbed in its slumbers by narcissistic sentimentality.

That night we make love for hours. Her need is imperative, primal. She is in control. I am sitting on the sofa. She straddles me, and we kiss fiercely, wrestling. She pulls my t-shirt up over my head and begins to kiss my neck and my chest. I struggle for a moment with the buttons down the back of her top and then again with her bra. Suddenly those unfathomably lovely breasts caress my skin. We are both on fire. Clothes are jettisoned like shrapnel. I hold the back of her neck and pull her lips to mine. My hand slides down the soft plane of her stomach. I stroke her gently at first, then with growing urgency. My hand slips further. My fingers explore. She is hot, ready. She has my shaft in her hand, her white teeth sharp against my ear. She pushes me back, her mane of hair tossing across her face and shoulders like living flame. She mounts me, grabbing my wrists and forcing my hands up along the back of the sofa. I rise up to meet her, thrusting against her pelvis. She lets go of my wrists and grabs my face between her palms. The kiss is rough, painful. My hands are on her firm buttocks. I pull her hard against me as I thrust deeply into her. We cry out together, louder, and louder. It is so good. Our bodies are in perfect harmony. The pleasure almost overtakes me, and I fight to regain control. I focus on her body, her rhythm. Her arms and legs are around me now, squeezing, crushing me. There is only the intensity of the moment, the rhythm, and then, the shuddering cries.

We are hot and sweaty. Her skin tastes salt. I cling to her as she rocks slowly back and forth and from side to side. We rest in each other. We are one.

We spend the next morning in St Ives, visiting the Hepworth Gallery. We wander through, pointing things out to each other, and enjoying the shared critiquing of art, exchanging points of view. We spend some time peering in at the dustily preserved workshop where

Barbara Hepworth worked. Unfinished pieces are exactly where she left them. The room is pregnant with her absence.

We have a coffee in a little café overlooking the beach immediately below the St Ives Tate gallery. The sea is azure blue, the sand is clean, and there are gulls in the distance wheeling and turning over the cliffs. This has become something of a ritual for us. Drinking cappuccino. I swear that we will one day have a cappuccino together in a little café, in the evening, in St Marco's Square in Venice.

We drive up the coast for a while, more or less randomly, and then take the turnoff for St Agnes. We drive down past the inn and park near the beach. Shoes and socks are off in a second as we scamper down to paddle in the surf. There is a deep cave off to the left, which we explore like children. We walk deeper and deeper into the dark, seaweed-smelling cave and are just about to turn back when we see dim light ahead. We continue on intrepidly and find our way out onto the beach.

We ramble off across the rocks. The tide is low but coming back in. We look for crabs and shells in the rock pools. After a while, we turn off along a path leading up to the cliff top. The view from the top is breathtaking. We wander along the tracks admiring distant chimneys of disused tin mines. We come across a cliff rescue team abseiling down the cliff. They wave us past cheerily. A steep path leads us back to the pub. We discover that we must book a table in the restaurant at this time of the season. It will be an hour until our table is ready.

We stand outside the front, chatting and listening to the conversation of locals. A small group of middle-aged men with leather waistcoats, Cornish accents and Harley Davidson bikes talk animatedly together. Their routine, it transpires, is to drive down to the pub after work, have a couple of pints and talk about motorbikes before heading home to the bosom of their families. Kings of the Road, for a little while.

The restaurant specialises in seafood, and Amelie loves to eat. I enjoy simply watching her. She works with such gusto. Prawns are stripped in seconds. Crabs are made short work of. Her eyes are alight with gastronomic pleasure. I thank God she didn't order the lobster. Wearing a bib, she would have looked like a messy little girl.

We drive back to the cottage after dark. The roads are deserted. Amelie begins to stroke my thigh, her fingers creeping up under the hem of my shorts. I reach across and reciprocate. Our arousal grows slowly. We enjoy each other's sensuality as much as the act of love itself. Amelie reaches over and undoes my shorts and caresses me. We are relaxed, at peace. In one graceful movement, she leans across and kisses me gently. She encircles me with her lips. I feel accepted as a man and as a lover. I feel loved.

We sleep soundly that night, entwined in love.

We have tickets to see Tristan and Yseult at the Minack! Row twenty-five, near the front. The day is spent pottering about. We cross the causeway and explore the lower reaches of St Michael's Mount. We have Cornish dairy ice cream in a waffle cone. We find somewhere for our ritual cappuccino. At about half past four, we set off for Porthcurno. The same angry man is there but in a better mood this time. There is a decidedly average café where we have microwaved Cornish pasties with obdurate capsules of tomato sauce and coffee in polystyrene cups.

The broad circular steps of the arena are filling up, so we make our way down towards the front and find our seats. Someone distributes white balloons for some unspecified purpose which will be revealed. The evening is warm. It looks like the rain will hold off.

A mood of expectancy settles over the natural amphitheatre. Silence falls like snowflakes here and there. We are all suddenly aware of the extraordinary beauty of the place. The sun is setting behind us. The sea stretches away forever. Far below in Porthcurno Bay, we can just make out families packing up and heading home. There is something eternal and timeless about the scene.

The performance is fantastic and brilliantly staged. The play demands considerable audience interaction. We are all part of the event. We are enthralled. The story is a tragedy of star-crossed love and a war between the Irish and the Cornish kings. As the sun sets and darkness falls, the sea becomes a deep blue curtain open to the skies.

It is a deep joy to share this with Amelie, to experience the magic of her world together. She sees with a keener, more discerning eye than some. Her world is full of optimism and possibility. Her's has richer hues, more brilliant sunshine and darker shadows.

That night we are buzzing together like two little bees. Talking about the play, the staging, the performances, the amazing natural amphitheatre, and the vista. We break up in fits of laughter over one actor who played a psychopathic imbecile, berating and threatening the audience with ineffectual rage. We are ablaze. The next day we head home. We will spend the last few days with her kids. I am really looking forward to it. I hadn't realised how much they had come to mean to me.

The long drive back through Cornwall and Wales is one great blur of motorway. We stop at the same transport café for a bit more top-notch cuisine. Amelie acquiesces resignedly. The tea is even worse this time!

We arrive back in Dublin late, exhausted. The kids are due back the following morning.

The next day Amelie and I take a day trip to O'Connell Street so she can buy birthday presents. It is a wonderfully domestic day, shopping for the exact right pair of orange basketball boots. Amelie takes me to her favourite coffee haunt. I have to agree the cappuccino is excellent. We get back late in the afternoon, laden with presents that Amelie tries vainly to hide in her flat.

The next day we take a riverboat ride down the Liffey. I explain to Amelie that we Australians love to see the wonderful old buildings and statues of Dublin. The skyline has changed a good deal in a mere two years since I was a Dubliner. I take heaps of photos, a real tourist in my own 'home' town. We have a lot of fun with the kids.

The time for me to leave steals up on us unawares. The agony of separation silences us both. We are so desperately in love. We dread the loneliness and longing ahead. We kiss goodbye bravely, each being strong for the other. I feel Amelie's heart pounding in her chest. I cannot bear it. I cannot bear to see her pain. Then the moment is upon us. I head for the Dart station. I'll take the train into town and taxi out to the airport and yet another twenty-four-hour flight. I am biting back the tears. I am howling inside, and somewhere at the edge of perception, I fancy I can hear Amelie doing the same.

IDENTICAL TWINS

I have fallen in love with one of two inseparable identical twins. They stay out of each other's way, of course. They are very good about that, incredibly good about it. But it is always going to be challenging. Though they are alike physically, their personalities are very different. Where one is happy, the other is sad. Where one is warm and loving, the other is cold and selfish. Where one is vulnerable and uncertain, the other is arrogant and demanding. Where one gives, the other takes.

I am succumbing to a terrifying illusion, one that has been growing in my mind for many years. One that, even now, I find hard to discuss. They are so alike, you see, same gestures, same manner of speech, same scent, same smile, same eyes. At last, at long last, I have come to see them as one person. The illusion occurs sporadically, with long periods of clarity in between. Over time, however, it comes more frequently. Lasts longer, worms its way deeper into my mind. Today I am leaving, today I have finally realised they are one and the same person. Always have been...

LET THERE BE LIGHT

My mother drives the car straight in under the corrugated iron roof by the hen coop. The sound of the afternoon rain on the roof is colossal, unbelievable. We stop for a moment to watch the rain. Sheets of it, sweeping across the land. Small rivers grow in seconds across the yard. It is an hour and a half before dark, and the generator still lies in pieces along the mulberry path. My mother picks up her cardboard box, and we run as fast as we can across the drenching space between the hen coup and the front veranda.

The sound of the rain on the veranda is muted by the enormous bougainvillea that grows up over the roof and hangs down in festoons of deep purple for most of the year. I can hear shouting and laughter coming from the back of the house. Mother is a little wobbly. She decides to have a short nap.

Out the back, my brother Sam, Minnie and Ingrid are playing chicken with the rain. In Zambia, during the rainy season, the rain falls in narrowly defined areas. It can be raining on one side of the house and not the other. Today the rain is pouring out front of the house and down one side, but not out the back. We run into the downpour to get soaked and then back into the sunshine to dry off. We are only wearing shorts of some very thin cotton. The late afternoon sun is still fierce. It is a good game.

After a while, the rain suddenly stops. The clouds continue to move off, building visibly for the next downpour. Soon the ground begins to dry out. The avenue between the mulberry trees has been spared by the dense overhang of branches.

Felix appears a little way along the mulberry path. I remember the plastic bag of generator parts and run back into the kitchen to get them.

Felix has arrived at the back veranda by the time I have located the box (on the floor in the hallway outside my parent's bedroom) and returned with the bits.

Felix takes the plastic bag and examines the pieces minutely.

"Four. Yes. Is better." Felix smiles. "All new ones." He takes the bag and strolls back in the direction of the mulberry path.

Sam, Minnie, and Ingrid and a few of Felix's older children begin to climb one of the giant prehistoric anthills that speckle the landscape. There is a large concrete water tank on top, and they want to catch the shiny brown 'water boatmen' that swim around in it.

I follow Felix. He has reached the very far end of the row of metal generator parts produced as he dismantled it earlier. He opens the plastic bag and places the four metal 'brushes' on the ground. Felix walks carefully back down the long row of parts, examining each one carefully, seeming to place each part in sequence in his mind. He takes the four brushes and heads off to the pump house where the dismembered generator lies.

It is now just before five in the afternoon. The sun will set around six p.m. Felix only has an hour if he wants to get the generator working again before full darkness. This is going to be interesting.

From a low branch of a mulberry tree, I watch Felix as he makes his way to and fro from the pump house and back. Back and forth he goes, many times. Slowly, almost imperceptibly, but inevitably, the row of parts begins to shrink.

It seems to take ages to select and reconnect each part. The sun is lowering in the west. Felix realises that it will be close but that it can be done. He picks up the pace. We do not particularly need the thing to work tonight. We have been doing without it for weeks. Felix is not doing this for us specifically but as some kind of test of himself.

The last couple of yards are consumed swiftly. Large parts that bolt on easily. I sidle over to the pump house and watch from the doorway. He does not notice me. He is intent. I see Felix place the three original metal brushes in the plastic bag and place the bag on the little shelf above the generator.

He stands and looks down at the rebuilt machine. He checks the fuel level and the oil. And then, with a curiously uncertain shrug of his shoulders, he reaches down and turns the starting crank. It takes a few goes, but then the engine coughs into life and begins to pick up and then begins to stutter. Quickly Felix reaches down and turns a little tap on the fuel line. The engine roars into life.

Felix turns finally and sees me standing there. He is smiling, triumphant! I run across the intervening couple of yards and hug him around his waist.

"You did it! You did it! You did it!" I shout over and over again, but he cannot hear me over the roar of the electricity generator. He picks me up and carries me outside, setting me on his shoulders as he approaches the rear veranda. I hear excited shouting from the water tank on the anthill. Soon there is a small noisy crowd accompanying Felix and me across the yard.

My mother, looking somewhat tousled, appears at the kitchen door. Darkness is falling. Some of the lights must have been left switched on when the generator failed last time. There are a few lights on inside. I can hear the sound of the fridge compressor struggling back to life.

"Well done, Felix", my mother gives him an enormous smile, "Oh, I have something for your wife. Picked it up today at Theo's in town." She runs off and comes back a few moments later with a large bolt of cloth with a red and green African design on it.

"Thank you, madam. My wife will be very pleased!" He is happy. He is acknowledged. It is a quarter after six p.m. The sun has set, and it is already nearly fully dark.

We hear the crunch of tyres on gravel. Headlights bathe the pump house, mulberry trees and the giant ant hill momentarily in brilliance.

My father is home!

NAUGHTY GIRL

The Spanish desert night stretches out across the pitiless, craggy mountains of Andalucía. Wisps of music float up from the bars, still bustling even at this hour in la plaza down below. The scent of jasmine is strong on the slight breeze.

We have been drinking 'La Mumbas' (cheap Spanish brandy with chocolate milk) all evening. The taste coating our mouths is sweet and thick.

As I turn to the basin to brush my teeth, I see Miriam has put on 'something nice'. Um-hum! I know what this means. Miriam is in frisky mood. Rumpy-tumpy is back on the agenda. Ooh Yeah – that's what I'm talking 'bout!

I turn off the bedroom lights, leaving just one small sidelight turned on – enough to see by. Miriam stretches luxuriously in a red satin all-in-one thingummy-what's-it clinging to every curve. I hope things will go ok tonight. Sex with Miriam is a bit of a hit-and-miss affair. There appear to be rules to the game, but I am not privy to them. Like chess, there are specific rules for each move, but as with chess, the interaction is essentially adversarial. The outcome never seems to be 'mutual'. Miriam seems to like the *idea* of sex more than the actual thing. The subtle and not-so-subtle manoeuvres leading up to it she finds exciting and engaging. The 'shenanigans', as she puts it, leading up to the actual 'malarkey'. Thereafter, quite often, things go downhill. Tonight, will be fine. I'm sure. I hope.

I slip into the bed next to her, snuggling up for a cuddle (she doesn't like to be rushed). She is warm and responsive. We kiss gently and begin to caress - generic opening moves at this point, nothing too specific. I start with the small of her back. I think she likes that. Slowly things warm up. Our caresses become more intimate, more directly sexual. Her hand begins to wander down my body – I take this as a sign that we have left the beginning game and entered the middle game. I slip my hand over her bottom and squeeze, gently at first, testing the waters. She arches her back, pressing herself hard against me. Wow, things are going along swimmingly.

Miriam turns to face me for a moment, then looks away.

"Umm"

"Yes"

"Err. You remember the other night."

"Yes," Cautiously, not sure what part of the evening she is referring to.

"When I was cross with you."

"Yes" I have no idea what's coming, but whatever it is, I don't think I'm going to like it.

"I'm sorry I shouted at you like that."

I am bewildered, "That's ok. I shouldn't have done what I did."

"It was just that you caught me off guard, you see. I wasn't expecting it."

"Yes, Sorry."

"No. That's not what I mean."

I am truly lost now, "Umm, well, what did you mean? Err, exactly?"

"Well, perhaps I wouldn't have been so cross if it hadn't been such a surprise."

"Oh, I see." I don't see at all. I have no idea where this is going.

Miriam is silent for a long while. I get back to caressing the warm, soft skin of her inner thigh. Tentatively, dangling between uncertainty and encouragement. I begin to run a forefinger gently across the line where pubic hair gives way to a lily-white tummy. Finally, she takes my cock firmly in her hand and begins to kiss my neck. I commence a deep, slow stroking between her legs. She moans.

"I know I am difficult sometimes. Selfish." I freeze, hoping conversation will end and we can get down to business.

"I can be a bit, well, naughty."

"Yes," I say, "you can be a very naughty girl indeed". Not really sure why I said that. It just seemed to be in line with her mood, whatever that was.

"I may need to be taken in hand from time to time."

"Taken in hand?" What *is* she getting at?

"Yes, when I am naughty when I am being a naughty girl."

"When you're a naughty girl?" Dawning realisation. I really am dumb sometimes.

"Yes, I might need to be punished a little just to bring me back in line."

"And have you been naughty recently?" She is breathing more heavily now. Her eyes half closed. Her lips moist.

"Yes, I have been a naughty girl, and I need to be punished."

"Well," I say, "you leave me very little choice". She writhes beneath the words, scarlet satin sliding across her body.

"You had better come and lie across my knee" I am painfully hard and erect, "You are about to receive a thorough spanking".

She slides across, silky as an eel. I undo the poppers at the crotch of her satin one-piece and lift the material across the small of her back, exposing her lovely round bottom.

"Tell me, young lady, precisely how naughty have you been?"

"Moderately, I need a moderate spanking master."

I bring my hand down with a resounding slap across her right buttock. She is rigid, her hands gripping the sheets. I spank her again. The other side this time. She lets out a tiny stifled "Oh!"

I spank her again and again. She lifts her bottom to meet my oncoming palm. Her bottom is glowing a rosy red. With one hand, she reaches behind and grabs my cock, squeezing painfully hard. I work more quickly, synchronising with her breathing and the rhythm of her hips. I increase the speed, maintaining a strong, steady rhythm. She begins to buck a little – not long now. She makes a curious mewing noise and goes rigid.

Roughly I roll her over onto her back. I kiss her shoulders and manoeuvre gently on top of her. She wraps her arms around my back. I enter her. She is hot and ready as I have never known her. She is full of desire. Her nails dig painfully into my back. I exhaust myself inside her. We kiss and canoodle for a bit. She closes her eyes and her breathing steadies.

I walk out onto the balcony for a last cigarette, unusually, unbelievably, a *post-coital* cigarette. Everything is still in full swing down in the town square. Someone is letting off fireworks down in the valley. Tiny shooting star rockets lift perhaps a hundred feet before returning forlornly to Earth. The breeze is warm and scented with Jasmine.

I stub out the remains of the cigarette and head back inside. Miriam is already asleep.

WHITE DOG

I am given Lady as a replacement for Blackie, who has been killed by a snake. We find blackie stiff as a board under a mango tree one morning. Blackie was a Dachshund crossed with something black and terrier-like. Nosy, loyal and fearless.

Lady is a mature Boxer bitch with big sad eyes and a slobbering gob.

"She's a good family dog," my father pronounces as he produces her from the back of an ancient Land Rover.

"A good guard dog, too, for when I'm away." I glance doubtfully at this big tired old dog. Not exactly a little boy's dream. I offer her my hand to sniff. She produces an enormous pink tongue and licks it, leaving slobber all over my wrist. She'll do, I decide and drag her off to play before it gets dark.

My father is off again the next morning at first light. I do not hear him leave, but I know he is gone. The acrid smell of cigars and sweat clings to his biscuit-coloured corduroy jacket still hanging on the back of the kitchen door.

I decide to take Lady for a walk. Outside I can hear Felix singing to himself as he rakes up leaves in the garden. I put Lady on a lead and taker her out to meet him. She catches sight of him as we round the corner. Her ears fold back, and the hairs on her neck stand on end. She begins to snarl fearsomely, pulling hard against the lead. Trying to get at him.

"New dog", Felix remarks, hardly looking up from his work. As we get closer, Felix looks up. He offers his hand and calls gently to her.

"It's ok. I won't hurt you." With that, Lady goes berserk, straining against the leash, fury in her eyes. I realise I cannot hold much longer. Felix realises too. Just as the lead is about to be pulled from my grasp, he spins the rake around and clouts Lady hard on the forehead. Lady yelps and rears back for a moment before flying at him, raging and snarling like a wild thing. Felix hits her again. I do not know what to do. Lady is my pet, but Felix has every right to protect himself. There is a look in his eye I have never seen before either. A cold rage, icy in the Zambian sun. The dance continues. I have lost hold of the lead now, and I do not dare to intervene for fear of being bitten myself. The one rule everyone learns young in Africa is never to mess with a mad dog. Lady lunges again, barking and snarling. Felix strikes even harder this time. There is a sickening thud of wood on bone, then silence.

My mother comes running out, closely followed by my brother and Minnie. Lady is lying on the ground, apparently unconscious. Felix is breathing hard, gripping the rake in both hands.

"What happened?"

"Lady attacked Felix mummy. She just went for him the moment she saw him."

"Why did you buy this dog?" Felix is furious, "Why did you buy this kind of dog? What do you need it for?" My mother is nonplussed.

"*What* kind of dog? What do you mean? Lady is a replacement for Blackie."

"Not a good dog." Felix growls, "It has been trained."

"Trained? Trained how?"

"It has been trained to protect whites."

"What? How do you know?"

Felix smiles, not a happy smile. He pulls himself to his full imposing height and looks down at my mother. The rake held lightly in his left hand.

"I am black."

My mother knows she is being told something, something important, but she does not understand what.

"How was she trained? I don't understand Felix. I'm sorry."

"Madam," Felix is calm now, "These dogs have a name. They are trained to protect whites, only whites."

"Against what exactly?"

"Against blacks, madam." Dawning understanding crosses my mother's face.

"These are called White Dogs."

"Oh, how disgusting! Who would do such a thing?"

Angers flares again in Felix's eyes.

"Whites, madam!"

"Oh, my god. I am so sorry, Felix. We didn't know. Honestly, we had no idea. She'll have to go, of course. We'll have to get rid of her. She wouldn't be safe with the children, with your children, I mean. I could never forgive myself if something happened to them." Her voice breaks. She is almost in tears.

"It's OK." Felix squares his shoulders. "I will train her."

Lady is coming to. Felix grabs the lead and begins to lead her away toward his compound. Lady growls slightly. Felix pulls her around, staring directly into her eyes. She sees the rake still in his left hand. She looks away. It is settled. Felix will deal with it.

The company lays on a grand party. We are all, around seventeen thousand of us, gathered in New Orleans in summer. Only a mad person or a multinational with more money than sense would bring thousands of partying employees to New Orleans in the middle of summer.

We don't care. It is hot, hotter than hot actually, but we have air-con during the day while attending the conference, and we have alcohol, plenty of alcohol, at night.

The party is set in the gorgeous, extensive gardens of some French colonial mansion. There are several blues bands there, pumping out intoxicating music and rhythms. The stars are brightly visible across the sky and everywhere. Scattered across the lovely gardens are small food stalls serving gumbo, catfish, or jambalaya or, for the more conservative, burgers, and of course, given that this is a multinational, an array of Asian noodle dishes.

I am wandering around with a friend, visiting the food stalls, listening for a little while to the different bands, and just hanging out.

I find one stall serving crayfish and salad. A lovely Latino woman stands in the centre of a circular table, her skirt billowing out around her to form the tablecloth upon which the various dishes are served. She must stand there the whole evening, serving crayfish and salad from her skirt. There is something disturbing and unwholesome about the tableau. She seems to be feeding the partygoers from herself. Her skirt connects her to the food in a way that makes it seem as though we are eating her.

My friend wanders off, but I am unable to walk away. I am frozen in a kind of weird, fascinated horror. She has a lovely smile. She has dignity and poise.

"Do you not feel a little weird being stuck in the middle of a table, feeding people off your skirt?"

"Yeah. It's freaky, huh?" I nod.

After a while, she asks if I am enjoying the party. I say I am, but that all these corporate parties, no matter how different, are all exactly the same.

She asks me if I have had my fortune told. Apparently, there is an area off to one side where most of New Orleans' palm readers and fortune tellers and voodoo clairvoyants have been hired to perform. She assures me New Orleans fortune tellers are the real deal. She points me in the right direction, and I wander off. She's probably fed up with me gawking at her.

The fortune tellers are set up in a kind of tunnel cut through swathes of wild, multi-coloured bougainvillea and other creepers.

Little tables are set out in small nooks cut out of the overhang. In each one, flamboyant black and Hispanic women are plying their trade. It's all paid for by the company, of course, and the most 'authentic' looking performers have long queues of drunken people awaiting their services.

I can't be bothered lining up. I've never believed in fortune telling or palm reading or anything else. I wander off towards the edge of the group, away from the crowds.

I come upon a very old black man, beautifully dressed in very smart clothes worn smooth and shiny by extensive use. There is no queue for his services.

On a whim, I stroll over and ask how he's going.

"I'm good." He stretches for a moment, "A little tired maybe. I don't usually work this late. Most of my customers are regulars."

I sit down, and he takes my right hand. He begins to read my palm.

"You have travelled a lot." I nod.

"You have lived in many countries." I nod again.

"You are planning a major move." Nod.

"Overseas." Nod.

"You are planning to move your whole family." I nod again.

"You are planning to settle in another country far away from where you live now." I nod again. By this time, I am beginning to get a wee bit interested because, as chance would have it, everything he has said is true.

"What about the move?" I ask, "How will it go?"

He stares at my palm again for a while, then he looks up at me.

"Goes just fine – for a while."

"Just fine?" He nods.

"But only for a while?" He nods again.

"Then what?"

"Then pain. A lot of pain and heartache."

"Really?"

"I'm afraid so. More pain than you can imagine right now. More loss and more heartache."

"Oh"

"Well, I got to tell ya. I wouldn't go."

"You wouldn't?"

"No"

"Well, what do you see if I stay where I am?"

"Just of more of the same. If you happy now, you gonna stay happy."

"And if I'm not?"

"Well, then it don't get no worse."

"Does it ever get better if I go?"

He takes another look at my hand. He mumbles to himself, turning my palm this way and that. He looks up, right into my eyes.

"Yep, it does get better, but only after a long time."

"How long?"

"Years."

"And then?"

"And then, after a long time, it gets much better."

"Well, what would you do?"

"I wouldn't go." His tone is final.

"What if I have to? What if I have no choice?"

"You always got a choice."

"Well, what if I don't?" The old black palm reader in the shiny suit leans back in his chair and stares at me for quite a while.

"Well, if you got no choice, you got no choice."

We sit silently, staring at each other for a little while. There is a shared recognition between us. I have decided to go, to move my family across to the other side of the globe. I tell myself I have no choice, but we both know that is not true.

I am choosing. Actually, I have already chosen to move my family to Sydney from Dublin, even though, somewhere at the back of my mind, in some not-quite-conscious hideaway, I know I am walking into a world of pain. Some intuition tells me I already know this, he has told me nothing I didn't know, but now, for the first time, I have heard it.

WALKING OUT

Christmas is finally over. The bin men came round at five this morning, taking away the detritus of another year. Amelie and her kids have flown back to Ireland, and we are alone again after a whirlwind fortnight of entertaining. I have not yet mentioned to Miriam my 'fling' with Amelie back in July. I am not sure if it was a fling or not. I am not sure what it was, and neither is Amelie. I think that is, at least in part, why she came to Australia this Christmas. To find out.

Seeing Amelie again, spending some private time with her, even in the surreal and duplicitous circumstances of a family holiday, has confirmed to me, to us, that our feelings for each other are real and powerful and not to be ignored. This is not, after all, a mere fling. I think we were both half expecting whatever it was to have burnt itself out. No such luck.

I listen to the sounds of Miriam stamping around upstairs, banging things, sulking. Our Christmas truce, frayed and battered by the tensions of the holiday season, is under increasing strain. It is plainly not going to hold. I am trying to get Miriam to complete her university application form. She says she wants to complete her master's degree. I have been trying to get her to do this for three months. She absolutely refuses to do it. I just cannot understand why not. She has already done the hard part. She has been for the interview and has been offered the place. I have agreed, yet again, to cover her course fees. All she has to do now is fill out a single-sided A4 form, ninety per cent of which consists of name, address, qualifications etc. There is only one section that requires any thought at all. That is the section where you write why you want to do the course. All she has to say is that, per her recent successful interview, she is very keen to start in February as agreed. There is really nothing to it. The problem is that Miriam wants me to 'help her' fill it out, and for the last three months, I have been refusing to do so. It is *her* form, it is a simple form, and if she is remotely ready to finish her master's degree and finally qualify, *she* must take the responsibility to fill the damn form out herself. I see it as a little test, the simplest of tests. I am not going to do everything for her anymore. That era is over, and Miriam does not like it, not at all.

I take a deep breath and go upstairs. The kids are downstairs in the kitchen making disgusting-looking cold drinks with coke and orange juice, and ice. It is a searing hot day. She is in the bedroom.

"College starts in just over two weeks." I pause for a moment. "I can post the form today if you like or drop it in by hand."

"Why won't you help me? You've been a complete bastard since you got back from New Orleans."

"You know why. I've told you why over and over again. This is your course. You need to fill out the form. You don't need me to reel out your endless list of qualifications. You know them all better than me."

"Just HELP me." She is angry now. Desperation in her eyes. I find myself gazing at her dispassionately, like a scientist studying an interesting specimen. I do not know what she really wants. I am smart enough to know that this form-filling phobia is symptomatic of some deeper need, but I am not smart enough to know what that deeper need is. I am also fed up, sick of the endless demands, and exhausted by them.

"What do you want me to do? Hold your hand for you? Move your fingers over the paper? Help you do what exactly? What help could you possibly need?"

She throws herself down on the unmade bed, arms, and legs rigid, face contorted. She lets out a low, guttural animal cry, ending with a grotesque, unnatural, piercing scream.

"JUST HELP ME!"

I cannot. I have reached my limit. I have hit a wall. I cannot go on a moment longer.

"Look, we cannot go on like this. I can't stand it." Suddenly I know what I must do. "I need some time to think, some space. I am going away for a few days to think."

"Well, if that's how you feel, you may as well go then!"

"Alright, I will then!" I bellow back.

"GET OUT, GET OUT, GET OUT!"

I grab the big red nylon flight bag I bought in New Orleans and begin to throw random clothes and shoes and books, and documents into it until it is completely full to bursting.

The boys are sitting silently in the kitchen downstairs. They have heard everything. Matthew is still a little too young really to understand what's going on, but Peter gets it.

I grab my wallet and my keys off the hall stand, drop the flight bag, take a deep breath, and walk slowly into the kitchen. The boys look up as I walk in. They look scared. I smile or try to. It takes a couple of attempts before I manage something other than what I feel must be a terrifying grimace.

"I am going away for a little while", I say. "I will still see you every week, all the time, really. It's just that mummy, and I are arguing a lot recently. You probably heard the shouting just now. Well, we both need a bit of time and space to cool down." I give both boys a kiss and head towards the front door. Peter comes running out and grabs my hand. He is crying. I want to be sick. I can't believe I am causing him so much pain. I know there is more to come. I open the door, and he walks out with me. I sling the flight bag in the back of the pickup and make my way around to the driver's side. Peter runs after me.

"No, wait, stop!" he cries out. I stop. I wait. He comes running up and throws his arms around my waist. For a moment, I think I really am going to be sick. I consider going back inside. Trying again. Twenty-eight years has to mean something! No. It is too late. Already too late. Something has snapped inside. Something irrevocable has happened. I hold him to me. Hold him tight. I kiss him and tell him I love him very, very much and I will always be there for him. I wipe away his tears. I get into the driver's seat and start the engine. I roll down the windows to say goodbye again as I begin to move off. Peter runs alongside the pickup for a few yards. In the rearview mirror, I can see Matthew peering through the open front door. I give him a wave. He sees it and waves back. I gun the engine. The rear wheels spin for a moment before catching on the hot tarmac. It is eleven a.m., almost to the second. I race out of the polite little Close of respectable middle-class houses, race out of my marriage, race away from Miriam. As the snap of an elastic band pulled too far, I fling myself into a terrifying new world.

I have been driving for perhaps half an hour before I realise I have nowhere to go. I stop the car and get out. I lean on the bonnet and smoke a cigarette, thinking, trying to think. An odd thought occurs to me. Something that really should have occurred to me earlier. A thought that could perhaps have made itself known at any point in the last two decades. Miriam is not the fragile, helpless creature she pretends to be. She is strong. Stronger than me perhaps. She uses her apparent fragility as a weapon. She uses it to dominate and control. I have been engaged in an endless power struggle with Miriam, and so far, she has won every round. I have no idea what to do next.

In the end, I go through the list of contacts on my mobile phone. I get to Connor's number. Connor and Colleen are mates. They will know what to do. I call the number. After a couple of rings, Connor answers.

"I left Miriam," I tell him. He is at a party. It is noisy. He can't hear what I am saying.

"You what?"

"I have left Miriam!" I shout down the phone. This time he hears.

"Where?"

"Where what?"

"Where have you left her?"

I pause for a minute, not sure what to say. I want to giggle, but that doesn't seem quite right.

"At home", I say, then realising this is not going to help, "I am not living with her anymore."

"Oh. Sorry to hear that." The background noise of the party returns louder for a moment. "Pat's left Miriam." I hear him explaining to Colleen. There follows a brief confab between them before Colleen comes on the phone.

"Hi Pat. When did this happen?"

I look at my watch.

"About half an hour ago."

"Where are you going to stay?"

"I don't know. I hoped you could recommend somewhere."

"Come to our place right now. We'll meet you there."

"Are you sure?"

"You can stay for a few weeks while you sort yourself out."

"Look, I don't want to impose or cut short your party. I can meet you back there later."

"We'll see you at our place in half an hour, or I'll come looking!"

"Ok, thanks, Colleen, and thanks to Connor too."

Easy as that. Not what I was expecting. Amazing who turns out to be a real friend when the chips are down.

I get back in the car and head down the escarpment from the hills towards the city. I light another cigarette. I have no idea what my future holds, no idea what I have left behind, and no way to calculate the balance of my life. A pickup truck, a flight bag full of more or less random stuff and a temporary place of safety. I switch on the car radio, preset to some indie station. You never know what they will play. The announcer introduces a recent song by Jagged Edge, which is very popular in nightclubs, apparently. It's called 'Walked Outta Heaven.' The singer bawls. "Feel like I just walked right out of heaven. Feel like I have damn near thrown my life away." Well, that's one thing I know for certain. I realise it definitely wasn't heaven. As to whether or not I have thrown my life away, I have no idea.

MADRID

I have just flown into London from Singapore. I am jetlagged, of course. We are meeting at Heathrow and flying to Madrid together – it's cheaper than flying direct from Dublin, and there's less chance of being seen together. Madrid is freezing in March. Too high and too central for the warming coast to have much effect. I have a shave and change into a suit beforehand, so I will look the way she likes when we meet again.

I am so excited. I can hardly stop shaking. It has been nearly three months since Christmas in Sydney when we were last together, and before that, four months since we first consummated our hidden love in the Wicklow Hills above Dublin. I have been longing for her every second of every day.

We have arranged to meet at check-in. I head for the desk craning this way and that to see her, hoping I will see her first. Then suddenly, she is there, right in front of me. My heart sings with joy. I walk towards her, drinking her in. She is lovely. She is my soul mate. We have been apart too long. At the last moment, we are both a little shy. We reach out to each other and hold hands, confirming reality. Her hand is warm in mine, her skin soft and smooth. We come together. A gentle embrace, so full of love, of tenderness and the suffering of separation. I bury my face in her hair, inhaling her warm scent.

I hold her in my arms again. I am complete. We are so good together, so perfect. It is the best thing just to touch her hand, to know she is there. We gaze into each other's eyes. I stroke her cheek. She kisses my hand.

On the flight to Madrid, we curl up together in the narrow seats, intertwined. There are few other passengers on the flight, and we have a row of seats to ourselves. Two young women across the aisle cast furtive glances at us. They are amused to see an older couple so deeply in love, so apparently oblivious of their surroundings.

We take a taxi to the conference hotel and check-in. We lie together on the bed, just cuddling. We make plans. First, we will visit the Prado and see the Goyas. She loves Goya, and I love to see the world through her eyes. I treasure her appreciation and her discernment. We will visit the old parts of the city and eat in a small, family-owned 'Meson'.

We lie close together, craving closeness, making up for a lost time, filling up on it. We make love late in the evening. We take it slow. No rush. She wears the clothes I have brought her. She is the most beautiful woman I have ever seen. In her deep brown eyes, I see the most beautiful person I have ever known. We will only be together for a few days this time. We are staving off the thought of departure. We are fully present for each other, fully in the moment. We have an eternity in that moment. Our lovemaking is good. We fit. Our bodies know each other.

In the morning, we set out for the Prado. We are like school kids on an outing. The weather is unaccountably mild for the time of year. There is occasional liquid sunshine – just for us. We practically skip. The museum is massive. She shows me the Goya rooms. We talk about the pictures. We inspire each other. Each picture comes alive to me through her eyes. The Nude Maja seduces us.

It is a whirlwind day. We stroll in the gardens next to the museum, so happy to be alive, to be together. We wander down meandering backstreets and lanes until we find a lovely, ancient, higgledy-piggledy Bodega. The place smells of centuries of wine and smoked ham. We order tapas, more tapas than we can possibly eat. Wonderful cheeses and jamón. The woman who runs the Bodega is so charming, helping us to understand the menu and warning us that we are ordering too much. We gorge on cheese, dried ham and olives. We drink Mahou beer. We are happy and at peace.

After a long lunch, we wander back to the main road to hail a cab. Not too far off, we can see the central railway station bombed a few days before. So many innocents were killed. Flowers flow over and around the building, emphasising impermanence and death. There is a chill wind. We can't wait to jump into a taxi.

In the evening, we find a Meson in the old town. It is very Spanish, very Castillian. We have more tapas. Albondigas and patatas bravas, tortilla, artichokes and jamon. The food is good. The waiter takes a couple of photos for us.

After dinner, we head off to find a bar, which is not all that hard in Spain. It is freezing outside. Icy sleet falls gently. We settle on a bar at the edge of an old square. We sit at the bar on high stools and drink brandy. We talk, and we share ourselves. We merge.

As the evening wears on, our stools move closer together. She has her coat over her lap. I stroke her calf as we talk. We smoke too much – Fortuna, red pack. We drink more brandy. We sidle closer. We are practically one organism. My hand caresses her knee as we talk, her thigh. Here, in this bar, in Madrid, we are whole.

All too soon, the weekend is over. We sit in the taxi together, holding each other, grabbing every last second of closeness. We drink coffee in the airport from cups emblazoned with the word 'Bonka'. This is amusing in English.

As always, when the time comes to part, we part quickly, never looking back. I go back to the hotel alone. There is no moment of peace. I am immediately overwhelmed with loss. It is snowing.

COMING CLEAN

It is time to tell Miriam the truth. It is way past time. I glance at the phone. I should call her now. There's no point putting it off. I feel sick to my stomach. I summon up a bit of gumption. I must call her now while I have the courage. I reach for the phone. I lift the handset, hearing the 'brrrrr' of the ringtone. I set it down. I am paralysed by indecision and fear. If I tell her now, she may take the boys back to Ireland. Now is not the time. Let her settle into Australia a bit more first. Let the boys settle down. I glare at the phone. I resent its mute accusation. I must call her! I am resolved. I reach for the phone. There is a sudden ringing tone coming from somewhere. I am startled and confused. 'Ring-ring, ring-ring, ring-ring. I realise that the phone is ringing. I stare at it in horror. I dare not answer. I dare not leave it ringing. I know who it is. I don't know how, but I know it is Miriam. I lift the receiver.

"Hello."

"I don't understand you. Nothing you are saying makes sense." It is Miriam, "My counsellor says there may be someone else that you're not telling me about." I feel sick. I taste bile in my mouth. I say nothing. I am unable to speak.

"Pat, are you there?"

"Yes"

"Is there someone else? Have you found someone else?"

"Well, sort of."

"Sort of! What the hell is that supposed to mean? What do you mean, *sort of*? Is there or isn't there? Have you or haven't you?"

"Well, yes, in a way."

"IN A WAY?"

"Let me explain."

"Bloody right, you should explain. You've got a lot of explaining to do and not just to me, to the boys too. You dragged us here, away from our family and friends, and then deserted us, dumped us!" I remain silent. From experience, I assume it will be a while before Miriam has vented sufficiently to let me speak. Not that I can blame her, really. She stops suddenly.

"WELL, WHO THE FUCK IS IT? DO I KNOW HER?"

"It's Amelie."

"Amelie?"

"Yes."

"Oh, my God! I knew it. I thought something was going on between you two when she came over at Christmas."

"I'm sorry."

"Sorry! SORRY!"

"Yes. I don't know how it happen…"

"Amelie! My best friend! You've taken everything from me now. My country, my family and now my best friend. You've stolen her from me! Oh my God. I only spoke to Amelie a couple of days ago. I poured my heart out, and all the time, that lying little bitch was trying to steal my husband!"

"I'm sorry."

"Stop saying that! Stop saying you're sorry! What good does that do, you fucker!? You absolute fucker! You shit! You pathetic, useless, crippled piece of SHIT!"

"Sorry."

"I'm taking the boys back to Ireland! You'll never see them again, you fucking bastard!" The phone goes dead. She has hung up. Again.

ANGER MANAGEMENT

Miriam's behaviour is becoming ever more extreme. It was difficult enough to manage when we were living together, her obsessive-compulsive telephone calls to my office, "Have you called the estate agent?" "Have you called the plumber?" "Have you called the pool guy?" Sometimes, nine calls in a single day drove me mad, but now that I have left, she has become truly savage.

Her little attacks – that's how I've come to think of any communication with her – increase in frequency and eccentricity.

She calls me at work. Says we must talk. I call round after work. She is in the front garden weeding when I arrive. The boys are out back in the pool.

"I must have more money!" she is practically snarling. I am taken aback. I have only just arrived.

"What's the problem exactly? What do you need more money for?" Miriam has always spent money like water, and since I moved out, she seems to have gotten worse.

"None of your bloody business, you bastard. You brought me and the kids out here. We only came here because of you. You only brought me because you needed my points!" This is one of her obsessions. She has somehow decided that she contributed towards the Australian Immigration points test. It is pure fantasy, but I cannot seem to shift the notion. It is part of her litany.

"You know that's not so."

"You dragged me here away from my family and friends. You planned it with that common little tart of yours!" The litany continues.

"I already give you every cent I can."

"It's not enough. The least you could do after all you've put us through is give us enough to live on."

"I simply don't have any more to give. Look, after I pay child support to you, I only have…"

"Crap! Crap! Crap! You fucking bastard." Before I know it, she has me by the throat and is banging my head repeatedly against the wall of the house.

"Give – me – some - money! Give - me - some - money! Give - me - some - money!" with every syllable. My head goes crack, crack, crack against the brickwork. Her voice has changed. The sound has become a high-pitched wail, repeating. I reach into my pocket. I have a hundred dollars, I think. I am stronger than her. I could break away. Instead, I wave the notes in front of her face until she notices them. She lets go of my throat and grabs the cash. The boys are standing in the doorway watching.

"Mummy needed some money." I smile. Their eyes are wide. They slip back into the dark of the house.

"I'd better go." I practically run to my car. I give the boys a wave as I pull away. They wave back. No time to talk to them, to give them a hug. Shit!

A day or two passes, and I get another call. She says we need to talk again. I suggest a neutral public venue where I hope she will not go berserk. We go to a little coffee shop in a mall a couple of miles away from her place.

We order latte and baked ricotta cheesecake. I pay upfront, just in case. She wants to go back to Ireland for Christmas. She wants me to pay.

"Look, Miriam, I have no more money. I can't do it. Why don't you get a job?"

"None of your fucking business if I get a job or not! It's your responsibility to support us, and you're bloody well going to!"

"I bloody well am, though, aren't I? I give you every penny I can, don't I?"

"Don't you DARE speak to me like that, you little shit! How dare you! After all, you've done to us." People are stopping their own conversations now. They are beginning to look over at us. She throws the remains of her latte over me and then the cup itself, which I catch. Then the saucer. Which I also catch. Then the spoon, which falls to the floor. The waitress begins to come over but thinks better of it.

"You have to support me and the kids!" she screams, clouting me hard with her handbag as she runs out of the café, tables and chairs flying, "You fucking bastard!"

All eyes are fixed on me.

"That didn't go as well as I'd hoped", I say, stumbling out with as much dignity as I can muster. I can feel disapproving eyes boring into the back of my head.

I see Miriam a few hundred yards up the road. I slow to offer her a lift, but she sees me and stoops to pick up a rock or whatever she can find.

I drive back to her place and explain to the kids that mummy will be a while. I make them a sandwich and a cold drink. We have a little while to cuddle and chat. I am close to tears. Half an hour later, it's getting dark. I drive back along the route Miriam will most likely take and find her after about a mile. This time she accepts the lift in stony silence.

A week or two later, my phone rings. It's reception. My wife is downstairs demanding to speak to Human Resources. She is extremely distressed. Will I come down? I start down the corridor towards the lift. The HR manager runs up beside me.

"It's alright, Pat. We'll handle this. Better that way."

"I'm so sorry."

"Pat, please don't worry. These things happen sometimes. Best you leave it to us to handle – it's no reflection on you, mate. Ok?"

"Ok. And thanks."

"No worries."

It's Sunday morning, 7:00 am. She is screaming as I pick up the phone.

"Listen to me, you shit! You fucking, fucking shit!"

"What's up? What's happened?"

"What's up? What's up? You dare to ask me what's up? I've been dragged halfway around the world and abandoned without friends or family, thousands of miles from home, without enough money to live on and no way of getting home! That's what's fucking up!"

"Why did you call?"

"I'm simply not prepared to put up with your abusive behaviour any longer." That's one of her recent obsessions. Everything I do or say is either 'threatening' or 'abusive'.

"I will not put up with you insulting and abusing me."

"I see."

"I think you should do a course in anger management."

"You think *I* should do a course in anger management?"

"Yes, you need to get control of your anger."

"But I'm not angry."

"You need to learn how to speak to people respectfully."

"But you're the one who is angry."

"Damn right, I'm angry, and haven't I every right to be?!"

"Is that all you called to say?" The phone goes dead. She has hung up.

Monday morning, 9:00 am. It's reception again. She's down there again, demanding that the company repatriate her and the children. Saying they have stranded her in a foreign country. Repatriating her is surely the least they can do.

Not for me to worry, they've called HR. Perhaps if I need to leave the building in the next little while it would be better to go through the car park?

It's Easter Sunday. I drop round some Easter eggs for Miriam and the boys.

"You're never coming home, are you?" she sounds resigned. I no longer think of the place she lives as 'home'. I realise I have absolutely no intention of ever going back.

"No", I say, "I don't think so."

"You fucker! You absolute fucker! Get out! Get out! Get out!" The boys look up from their Easter eggs, flecks of chocolate around their mouths. I walk towards the door. Suddenly something crashes against my back. It's the Easter egg I just gave her. I look around just as she is swinging the broom at the back of my head. I grab it with one hand, fending her off. The boys are staring. Not knowing what to do. I make it to the door and race to the car. Miriam comes tearing out after me screaming in that animal wail of hers.

"Get out! Get out! Get out!" Various neighbours turn and look. Not sure what to do. I get in the car and drive off. Something heavy bounces off the rear window.

She's downstairs again. Same story. HR are firm but polite.

I am in the city working. I get a call on my mobile.

"Peter has a congenital birth defect in his spine and could be crippled for life with one wrong move, and Matthew has two missing ribs and curvature of the spine!"

"What?" I am shaken, unable to breathe, unable to take it in.

"Peter could be crippled simply by standing up awkwardly, and Matthew has spinal problems that could cripple him in later life."

"How do you know?"

"I had a chiropractor appointment, and I took Peter and Matthew along. He found out."

"What prompted him to look?"

"He said he might as well take a look while they were there. He took X-rays. He showed me."

"What did he show you exactly?"

"X-rays! I already told you."

"Yes, but what exactly did they show?"

"Congenital birth defects!"

"Perhaps you should take them to a specialist for a second opinion."

"Anyway, I just thought you should know." The phone goes dead. I stand looking at it, uncomprehending. My babies could be crippled at any minute. I call Colleen. She is a physio. Maybe she'll know what to do.

"Miriam says the boys have congenital birth defects. Peter could be crippled at any moment if his lower back gives out and Matthew is missing two ribs and has curvature of the spine."

"Crap"

"Pardon?"

"That's just crap. Bring them in Monday, and I'll have a sports doctor take a look at them. Listen, Pat, I know your boys. I've seen them run around and play. It is extremely unlikely that they have any significant issue at all."

"You're sure?"

"I'm sure it's extremely unlikely. Try not to worry, Pat. See you Monday."

I awake to the sound of the phone. It is Sunday morning, of course. I am groggy from a little too much grog the night before.

"Matthew has Oppositional Defiance Disorder."

"He has what?"

"Oppositional Defiance Disorder, and it's all your fault."

"Thought you said he had Attention Deficit Disorder?"

"Hyper-Activity Attention Deficit Disorder."

"OK, that then."

"Yes, we thought he had that, but now we think it's ODD."

"ODD?"

"Oppositional Defiance Disorder."

"How did he get it? When?"

"Since you walked out, you bastard."

"So, he doesn't have the hyper one, then?"

"No. I told you. We thought he had that, but now we think he has ODD."

"Who are 'we'?"

"What?"

"Who else thinks he has ODD?"

"The doctor, of course."

"The same one who thought he had ADD and then HAADD?"

"You always dismiss everything I say. You don't treat me with respect. It's bad for the children to see you treating me so badly."

"What makes you think he has ODD and not HAADD or just plain ADD, or autism, or Asperger Syndrome or dyspraxia or dyslexia or whatever else they come up with?"

"Don't talk to me like that!"

"OK, but why do you think he has ODD?"

"He argues with me all the time, and he refuses to do what I say."

"How is that different from just plain naughtiness, or self-assertion for that matter?"

"You're just afraid to accept what you've done to the kids. Our kids that you brought here and then abandoned for your tart."

"Maybe they have Munchausen's Syndrome By-Proxy." The phone goes dead - again.

MUSHROOMS AND CONDENSED MILK

I am six years old, and I am in Zambia. I have stolen the charcoal money (again) and bought a large tin of condensed milk to share with Sawa, his brother Jeffrey and his sister Constance. It is a feast. We sit happily atop one of the giant prehistoric anthills that dot the landscape taking turns to dip a finger deep into the goo, slurping it down.

The tin is scraped clean, and I begin to realise that I will probably get into trouble when the theft is discovered. We discuss the problem. Jeffrey comes up with a solution. We can perhaps replace the charcoal money. The rainy season is just about over. Why don't we go deep into the forest and collect some of the oversize mushrooms that people sell by the side of the road? Each mushroom can be as big as a frying pan, and they fetch a good price, as much as a tiki each for the really big ones.

This is an excellent plan. We set off into the forest and spend a happy hour or two collecting piles of mushrooms. We have about ten good ones. We head for the main Lusaka Road and plonk ourselves down, our wares piled up on my shirt, like pizzas, in the orange gravel at the side of the road.

Pretty much the very next truck to come along stops a couple of hundred metres beyond where we are sitting. The driver gets out and walks slowly back, a curious look on his face. We watch him approach. We can see he is an Afrikaner and prepare to bargain hard.

He nonchalantly examines the pile of mushrooms, asking if they are fresh. We show him the damp earth still attached to the short stubby bases. He is at something of a loss. We pick up on this and begin to fidget somewhat. He selects two medium-sized mushrooms and asks how much.

"A tiki each", I tell him. I have a firm but fair look on my face. I am not to be trifled with. He hands over the money without a word and walks away. A couple of times, he stops and looks back. He clambers back up into the cab and drives off.

A little while later, a car stops. A white family out for the day. This time the mother gets out. She, too, has a look of mild confusion on her face. She goes through the same rigmarole as the truck driver. She buys four mushrooms without attempting to bargain, and then, as she turns to leave, she stops. She gives me an odd, searching look and asks.

"Are you alright, dear?"

I am surprised. I don't know what she means. We are shifting mushrooms like nobody's business.

"Fine", I say.

"Does your mummy know where you are?"

"Oh yes", I lie, "she'll be coming to pick us up later". The white lady does not appear entirely satisfied with this but walks doubtfully back to the car, nevertheless. We can see her talking with her husband in the car. There is a good deal of looking back. Even the two kids in the back seat are staring at us. Eventually, they drive off.

There is a reasonably long wait until the next truck appears. We talk, Sawa, Jeffrey and Constance and me. There is obviously something odd going on. We have sold six mushrooms at a tiki a piece in a little over half an hour. It's just too good to be true. At this rate, we will soon have enough to replace the charcoal money.

In the distance, clouds of orange dust appear, visible long before the truck itself. We remove the broad flat leaves that have been protecting the mushrooms from the sun. We wait. Four little humans in a row. Constance begins to laugh quietly to herself. She is a little older than the rest of us, maybe eleven.

"I see what it is."

"What, what is it?" We are curious to know what Constance has realised.

"It is because you are white."

We all think about this for a while. For me, it is something of a revelation. Of course, I have always known I was white, but it has never occurred to me before that it *meant* anything. We all play together. We are just kids. I know I have a big house and they have a small hut. I know we have TV occasionally, and they don't, but until that moment, it has never occurred to me to wonder why. It has never occurred to me that there could be a reason so simple, so obvious, once voiced. I look at my friends, and they look back at me. There is no resentment, we are still firm friends, but there is realisation.

Being practical kids, we decide to put this newfound knowledge to good use. The truck stops. The driver gets out. Before he can say anything, I tell him, "Ten cents each, bwana. Top quality. Freshly picked." He pays. We have two left. They go with the next car.

We have enough to replace the stolen charcoal money. We consider this option with all seriousness for some time, perhaps five minutes.

We buy more condensed milk. It is a lovely afternoon.

BEEF-IN-GUINNESS PIE

For a long time, I have been unable to write about Miriam. This bothered me a great deal before, and, either as a compensatory mechanism or simply for distraction, I found myself constructing complex, clever, and ludicrous reasons for the mental block. I decided it was all due to crushing feelings of guilt that I was pushing aside, tossing her memory out with the bath water. Or else it was all due to volcanic and barely suppressed rage from which my subconscious mind was steadfastly protecting me.

I now think that I could not write about her simply because I could not *see* her, not any longer. No image of her would coalesce in my mind. She was gone.

Unsettlingly, after many years of peace, in the last few days, I have had occasional glimpses of her, tiny and distant but perfectly formed as though seen far, far off, through the wrong end of a telescope. I feel that with a little effort if I could bestir myself sufficiently, I would smell the old, much-fingered, occasionally polished brass barrel of the instrument. That if, even for an instant, I were to break through the veil and really smell the verdigris and dried-in Brasso, it would all come rushing back. She would be real and present, and I would once again be engulfed by confusion and self-doubt and an uncanny dread that she might be right. That the world might really be as incomprehensible, malevolent, and capricious as she believed it to be.

"That's what she was like!" my mind cries out, unexpectedly connecting the teeny image with a memory, confirming this miniature being's identity. "Oh my God, that's exactly what she was like!"

Unforeseen memories slam into my waking thoughts, welcome as brittle shards of glass from an improvised explosive device. I taste bitter pomegranate juice mixed with sweat on my lip. I don't believe it is real. I don't know if it is. Tiny terroristic memes, without coherence, incomplete, stolidly refusing to suggest a whole from which they may have been sundered, invade my puerile reverie. I smell diesel. I feel sick.

In my mind's eye, she is standing by the Thames in spring, smiling, bathed in milky sunlight, wearing a green cotton pinafore dress, sporting a large red parrot stitched across the right shoulder – very fetching. Within the memory, I catch the bilious stench of Thames water slapping against the embankment at high tide.

On another occasion, I see her in a tiny blue bikini, lying on a 'hamaca' on the Costa del Sol, drinking a tequila sunrise and reading 'Romancing the Shadow'. She smells of Ambre Solaire sun tan oil. Her body is lithe and slippery and almost orange due to the oil. My feet are beginning to burn. Five or six books, all in a similar vein, rest in a scorched pile on the sweltering sand. Top most is 'Man's Search for Meaning' by Victor E Frankl. The sickly scent of garlic and the sound of some old Gypsy Kings hit mingle in the searing heat. Someone's 'corazon' is broken or breaking or at the very least at considerable risk of same.

She is gazing into the full-length, mahogany-framed mirror, absentmindedly brushing her short, spiky black hair. She is distracted, her look far away. Static electricity crackles as she draws the antique silver bound brush through her short black hair. It flies up alarmingly. She looks like a cross between a hedgehog and a startled meerkat. She is wearing a simple white cotton nightie covered in a pattern of tiny Embroidery Anglais clover leaves. We are staying in a posh hotel, I think. It's someone's wedding. The place smells of antique wax and boiled cabbage. She is unaware of my presence. Her mind is wandering where it will. I am her excess baggage, not wanted on voyage.

I do not experience extended recollection. I see prospects and panoramas, vistas and tableaux inhabited by this shy, almost mythic creature who was once my wife. I still cannot recall her as a real woman, complete and whole, with a history and an enduring present.

Perhaps that will come. When I see her at all, as I do now in my mind's eye, sometimes, it is as a reclusive spirit, like a fallow deer, half hidden in shadows, withdrawn and timid. Not the raging, betrayed animistic force of our later encounters.

These memories are no longer as painful as they once were. I no longer feel the pressing need to shoo them away. You will not see me now, on some street corner, wild-haired and preoccupied, swatting away invisible demons. Not that you would have before, of course, it's all tragic exaggeration, hyperbole, and farce.

Perhaps her return marks the end of some important psychological stage or the beginning of one. It would be nice to remember without rancour.

There are some tastes and smells that always bring her back, though, such as excessive turmeric in place of the subtlety of saffron or the flavour-scent of Beef-in-Guinness pie – not that I can recall her ever making it.

DESOLATION

Shadows fall like rain, sweet as angel's tears. I am bathed in delicious guilt. It starts with the taste of blood on the tongue. I am asleep. I am dreaming. I wake up. I have that crawling feeling at the back of my mind again, that feeling of imminence and dread. It has been growing for weeks in the blackness beneath my thoughts. I am a dot on the edge of a black hole being drawn inexorably in. It's coming. I can feel it, horrible intuition. She has gone silent. Her occasional text messages are full of doubt, sadness, and regret. Fausto has made a reappearance. I can sense it. There is nowhere to hide. I am being circled by sharks. I am on the edge of a cliffhanging by my fingertips. I fall.

There it is, in black and white, the text message on my mobile phone.

[We must talk]

I have been expecting this for weeks. I know what is coming. "We must talk". My heart and soul are about to be ripped out of me. I am about to be gutted. I must be brave. Strong. I must be supportive. I must say I understand, tell her we will always have the wonderful memories of our time together, say "Keep in touch".

I text her back.

[I would love to hear your voice. Can you manage five minutes?]

My finger hovers over the Send button. Maybe, if we don't talk now, she will change her mind. She will pass through her moment of doubt, and we will be ok. I hit the button.

[Message Sent]

[Ok, can you call me now on my mobile?]

I call. We talk about the inconsequentialities. I know she is trying to find a 'good' moment to say it. I feel an almost overwhelming urge to shout, "Don't say it!" down the phone. I am terrified of the magical independence of words. If she says the words, they will become real, independent, a magic spell or curse with a life of its own. I help her out.

"I could fly to Dublin to see you at Easter". That is the trigger. I knew it would be. I hear her sigh.

"I can't continue with this".

There, the words are said, the spell is cast. My world ends. Right there, right then. I am stripped to the bones.

A thousand years pass before I can find the words. Inevitably, knowing what was coming, I have made notes. I scrabble for my wallet. I find the crumpled-up phone bill envelope on which I have prepared my thoughts while I was rational, while I could. I begin.

"That must have been an agonising decision for you".

"It was. I really do love you, but I can't bear it anymore."

"It must have taken great courage to make your decision. If we must draw our love affair to a close, please let us do so beautifully, with tenderness". She agrees.

I continue, from my notes, "Please don't ever regret our love, our time together." She agrees.

"Please know that you are deeply and sincerely loved." I have lost control of my voice. The sound is tremulous and weak. I clear my throat. I break down for a moment.

"Oh please, don't do this to me". Her tone is desperate. This is hard for her too. I collect myself immediately, afraid of losing her respect, of becoming an object of pity, not the strong, capable man she loves or loved. I cannot bear to be unworthy of her. I realise what I have always known, though she is a Goddess, she is also a fragile woman, struggling alone with an almost impossible burden. She must set something down. She has decided it must be me.

I return to my notes, a fossil record of an earlier age when I could think rationally.

I ask if she has decided to give her relationship with Fausto another go. She says she has been thinking about it. I am hollow. My guts spill out across the floor. I cannot think. I do not know what to say. I tell her I love her with all my heart and soul and that I will try not to make things worse for her. I break. I want to plead with her, to grovel, to wash her feet with salty tears and cry, "Don't leave me! Please don't leave me!"

I say, "Please don't see your decision to end our relationship as the same as your decision to go back to Fausto. They are two different decisions, not one."

I say, "Right now, it's as though you are juggling a hundred balls at once and spinning a hundred plates. It's too much. Give yourself time. Once you have me and our relationship out of your mind a bit, you may find the emotional space to think about Fausto and decide then what you want to do." I am talking like an automaton. Somewhere, at the back of my mind, I am ashamed. Somewhere I know that the advice I am giving, un-asked for, is double-edged. Yes, she would be wise not to make any decision about giving Fausto a second go while still in turmoil about ending our relationship, but at the same time, somewhere, I know that I am playing for time. If she lets Fausto back in immediately, all is lost, but if I can keep her from making the decision until she is feeling more centred, I have a chance of putting my suit again. I am a manipulative shit.

I suggest that it is best to wait until she is sure before getting Fausto and the children's hopes up. I suggest that she give Fausto a reasonable time, say three months, to sort himself out, after which, if he manages it, she will consider giving him a second chance.

I am torn between wanting to protect the woman I love from an awful, doomed second attempt at a failed relationship and the crushing fear that Fausto may pull it off. I am crushed by empathy for

Fausto. We are both in love with the same woman, and we both understand the loss. I am ashamed of putting my happiness before his. I am afraid that if the second attempt doesn't work, it will be even more painful for everyone. I am afraid that it will work. I know it is none of my business. I can't help it. I am desperate. I am terrified.

I say, "If you do, give Fausto a second go, and if it doesn't work out, please call me."

I say, "I am not saying that we would end up getting back together again, but you are a very important part of my life, and I will always want to know how you are and that you are ok." She agrees.

She tells me that I have been a very important part of her life and that she will always want to keep in touch with me. I think we both know that she will not keep in touch. If she gives Fausto a second go, she must cut all contact with me. It is obvious. She is saying whatever she can to make my pain a little less. I know it. She knows it.

I have left Miriam. I am alone in a small apartment above my landlord's house. I have nothing. I have no one. I continue, from my notes, "I will not mope around waiting for you. I may not be able even to think about another relationship for a long time, but I want you to know I will be fine."

I say, "I will always be there for you". I have come to the end of my notes. I am on my own. I realise that I have been doing almost all of the talking.

She says more things to me, more words. She is explaining, trying to let me down gently. Trying to help me see that our relationship cannot work. It is too complicated. Impossible.

Eventually, sometime later, I say. "You were going to take the children out today. Please, go out with the kids, have a lovely day. I will be fine. Goodbye, Amelie." We hang up.

I am alone. It is one in the morning. I am in shock. I simply cannot take it in. I cannot believe it. We were so in love, so perfect together, like two halves of the same person. She completed me, and I her. We were the special two, the unique, perfect couple. I make a cup of strong sweet tea – a cure-all remedy of my Irish mother's. I wander out onto the deck and stand there smoking and drinking tea.

My mind is racing with possibilities and options. I am desperately seeking a solution. What if this? What if that? Shall I rush to the airport right now, this minute and catch the first plane to Dublin? I can be there within twenty-four hours. Should I rush to her, sweep her up in my arms and swear I'll never leave her side again? Does she want me? Does she not? At some point, I wander back inside and fall asleep on the sofa, still in my clothes.

The alarm goes off. I have a meeting at eight. It is five – my annual performance review with my boss. I am meeting Miriam at the Family Court this afternoon in a last-ditch effort to avoid going to court for a settlement. I have had perhaps an hour and a half's sleep. I jump up, shower and dress. I am collecting my things as the uneasy feeling steels over me again. I have the unnerving sense that I have woken up in a parallel universe.

Yesterday I lived in a universe in which she loved me with all her heart and soul. She wanted to give herself to me completely. She had no doubt. Today I have woken in this alien universe, this opposite universe. I am in hell. I hear a strange animal sound nearby, loud, wailing. I am astonished to discover it is coming from me. I am holding the banister rail with white fingers and howling into an infinite abyss of pain and loss. I am a ghost.

I manage to get to work and have the meeting with my boss. It seems to go all right. How can I tell? There are two further meetings with customers, and then I am rushing to the court in Parramatta. A speed camera flashes as I pass. I get there early and sit watching the sad, slow procession of husbands and wives unravelling their lives. I cannot bear Miriam's pain. I know that our relationship had to end, have known it for years, perhaps. I think about turning the clock back – would I want to if I could? What would I have done differently? I force myself to face these questions, to look on my own behaviour in judgement. I try to figure things out. I am certain that my relationship with Miriam is not retrievable. I think about Amelie. Was it a mistake? Is she right? I wish I had told Miriam sooner. I wish I had told her more, made a clean breast of it. Do I regret my love for Amelie, our times together? No! Never! Our love is good and pure and wonderful, the most wonderful thing that has ever happened to me. I cannot imagine life without her. It is a place my mind simply will not go.

BASTARD

Miriam walks into the court waiting area. I see her before she sees me. I am assailed by a kaleidoscope of images, memories of happy times together. We *had* happy times, but there was always a shadow. I remember the holiday we had in the Pyrenees Mountains of Spain just before we left Dublin for Sydney. The boys are involved most days in all kinds of fantastic, organised activities. Matthew tells me so proudly, so excited about catching his first fish – admittedly in a fish farm full of fish, but he did it! Peter goes mountain biking, and Miriam and I walk together through the mountains, ride the ski lifts, and have lunch in pretty alpine restaurants here and there. It is lovely, but Miriam and I never once make love. We are like brother and sister, such close companions. I fully acknowledge that I have come to love her as a kind of sister, not as a woman.

I remember the boys being born, Peter in a Dublin hospital, and Matthew at home. Peter's birth is traumatic. Miriam is in labour for hours and hours. The midwife keeps trying to fix a little clip to his head so she can monitor his vital signs, but it keeps falling off. Each time it falls off, she looks worried and tuts at her monitor, believing that something is wrong with him. Each time she attaches the clip, his signs come back up to normal. I point out this pattern to her and suggest that the change in the baby's vital signs is due to the clip not being securely attached. The midwife does not take kindly to advice from a prospective father, thinking perhaps that I am criticising her clip-attaching abilities.

After a couple of hours of this, she calls in an obstetrician. He arrives fairly quickly with a pretty trainee woman doctor in tow. More or less, without warning or discussion, he pulls out a pair of forceps and declares that he is going to deliver the baby immediately. I know that Miriam does not want that and raise an objection. We try to discuss next steps with him, but he ignores us. He is too busy flirting with the midwife and the trainee.

We do finally manage to break through the bastard's veil of indifference and state our preferences. Miriam is given a quick injection for the pain, but long before it can take effect, and while chatting idly with his harem, he lifts a scalpel off a nearby trolley, makes two quick incisions and pulls Peter out. Miriam lets out a deep guttural scream from the centre of her being and all but passes out. "Episiotomy." The smug bastard smiles patronisingly and marches smartly out of the delivery room.

I am left holding my new son, my firstborn child, in my arms. My perfect boy, tiny fingers and toes, thick mop of black hair. It is one of the most magical, moving moments of my life. He is perfect, utterly gorgeous. I look over at Miriam, white as a sheet, completely wrung out, like a rag doll, with specks of blood all over her. I wonder for a moment if she is dead. I am in shock, momentarily disoriented. It's all too big to take in.

The midwife smiles unctuously at the obstetrician's receding back. I imagine he is dragging the pretty trainee off for a fuck, or at the very least, a blow job. Bastard!

Miriam is too weak to look after Peter on her own for several weeks. I take on the job of bottle-feeding him through the night so she can sleep. Peter and I sleep on the sofa in the sitting room so as not to wake Miriam. This, had I but known it, is perhaps the beginning of the end of our relationship. Miriam and I begin to sleep separately, at first because she is so ill, but later out of habit. She is always a very light sleeper. By the time we try to get back into a normal pattern, she is unable to stand my snoring. I am banished from her bed. I sleep on the sofa or wherever.

Matthew's birth is completely different. Matthew is born at home in the sitting room with two lovely lesbian midwives and a woman doctor. They catch sight of a row of Minnie's books in the bookcase next to the sofa. I explain that she is my sister. They are most impressed. They do not share the radicalism of her earlier works but agree that it was a stage the movement had to go through. All I can recall of the lesbian separatist philosophy is a kind of Neo-Nazi apartheid world in which women ruled, and there were either no men or men who lived as re-educated slaves.

We chat and listen to music and generally have a bit of a party until the contractions are coming too close to allow it. The midwives retreat to the dining room, only popping back from time to time to check on Miriam and the baby. The labour is very long. Eventually, they, too, become concerned. I hear muttered mention of the word ambulance.

We all gather around Miriam, encouraging her to push and breathe. It is a Herculean effort, but at last, Matthew's head begins to appear. "I can see his head!" I shout enthusiastically. "Just pull him out!" snarls Miriam with a mad gleam in her eye. One of the midwives shows me what to do, and I take up my position, ready to help him out once his whole head appears. There are one or two more mammoth contractions before I can take his head gently and help him out. He is delivered normally. It is an absolute triumph for Miriam.

Matthew has even more dark hair than Peter. The midwives, one of whom is Asian, glance questioning looks at each other. We notice this and ask why? There is some embarrassment before. Eventually, they ask if we (two obviously Caucasian English people) have any Asian ancestry. The blue patterning on Matthew's skin and his thick dark hair are, it seems, typical of Asian babies. I remember my mother talking about her Burmese great-great-grandmother and ask if that could be it. Evidence, albeit sparse, of an actual Burmese forebear. Years later, I have my DNA sequenced. Sure enough, there is a tiny trace of Burmese ancestry. My mum would have been pleased.

Whatever the case, Matthew is utterly gorgeous and wonderful, just like Peter. There are several years between them, though, so there is going to be friction.

There are other memories, many, many holidays in Spain, Austria, France, Croatia, and Germany. And there are happy times at home, too, with family and friends, parties, casual evenings chatting and laughing, and wonderful moments bringing up our children together. But there is always the shadow. We are not lovers, but we do love each other, I think.

CONFIRMATION

I hear through my mum that Minnie's longstanding relationship has ended too. She is having trouble getting access to her kids. Acrimony, intense, like smoke from burning diesel, pollutes the atmosphere obscuring fact and fiction alike. Poor Little Min, I send her an email offering banal consolation and filial support. To my surprise, she writes back almost immediately, a nice note, reasonably bright, reasonably optimistic. She has good friends. Many people are providing direct material support. She is reasonably happy amid the tears. I pick up the phone to call her. It would be nice to hear her voice. Haven't seen her since we met at Mum's in Western Australia a few Christmases ago. I hesitate. I bet she still hides in the wardrobe whenever the phone rings or rolls out that pedantic alter ego of hers. What does she call her? Molly! That's it, Molly, the tedious know-it-all. Such a quirky person.

I remember Minnie, at the age of eight, wearing a white dress with a veil and studying the Catholic rites of confirmation, determined to join Mum (who had recently converted) in a life of pious purity. She gets quite het up about it if she feels doubt is being cast.

"It's a blessed sacrament!"

"What's that mean?" I am not really interested unless there's going to be cake.

"It's a sacrament, and it's blessed!"

"What's a sacrament?"

"It's like a sign or a promise."

"To do what?"

"Be good, I suppose."

"You suppose? Shouldn't you know what it is if you're going to do it?"

"You don't *do* a sacrament. It's done to you."

"Who does it?"

"The priest."

"What does he do?"

"Puts oil on your head."

"What on earth for?"

"Dunno."

"Will there be cake?"

"Better be!"

Mum comes out and makes Minnie go back inside and change.

"Minnie says there's going to be cake."

"Yes."

"What sort?"

"Sponge."

That's more like it. I run indoors.

"Sponge! Mum says there's going to be sponge cake!"

Minnie has changed back into shorts and a t-shirt. She is crucifying one of her dolls on a little wooden cross made out of a fruit packing case. There's a blue and orange paper label on the top saying 'Del Monte!'

"Are you going to bury it?"

"No. I'm going to put her under the wardrobe with the others."

LOSS

Miriam is thin and drawn. Too much pain. Too much suffering. I know that I have played a large part in that. I have not been honest with her. I have not been straight. Oh, what a tangled web. I know that our married relationship is over. I want her to be happy, to find happiness and peace. I understand regret. I wish I had been open and honest with her. I wish I had known what I wanted, how I felt, and known how to express it. But at first, I really did not know. I did not know how I felt or what I wanted, or even really, what was wrong. At some point in the last five years, I slipped into a long dark depression without ever recognising it. Miriam saw it eventually and told me to get help, but I didn't. I did not feel depressed. I couldn't see how I *could* be depressed without feeling depressed. I tried to solve the problem myself. I told myself that if we could just get to Australia, things would be alright. We would be happy. We would stand a chance.

There is too much on my mind. The mortgage company in Dublin is threatening to re-possess the house due to mounting arrears, which we cannot pay. The second prospective buyer has suddenly pulled out after several months. I have just picked up another speeding ticket which I will struggle to pay. Amelie has ended our relationship. Miriam is in despair, and my boys won't talk to me. I am again at absolute rock bottom. I can't see how things could possibly get worse.

The meeting at the court goes on and on for over three hours. I am exhausted, emotionally and physically, at the end of my strength. It is one year since I left Miriam. Yet somehow, against all the odds, we manage in principle to agree on a settlement. There is still a chance it could all unravel, but neither of us really wants to go to court. My lawyer will send me the divorce papers in the morning.

I drive over to a friend's house for dinner with him and his family. He has invited me because he is a close friend, a deeply good and caring man and because I broke down in tears in his office this morning.

I arrive at his place at the same time he does. He has headphones on as he is in the middle of a conference call to Singapore. It is seven in the evening. We go inside. The scene is one of simple domestic happiness, alien to me, unrecognisable. We go for a walk through the bush with his two sweet kids and visit the water dragons down by the creek. It is deeply tranquil. I smoke furiously the whole time.

The evening is very quiet, without vexation. I feel acutely aware that I will never have this. My family is broken. I am on my own.

I drive home and fall asleep on the sofa in front of the TV.

I wake at four in the morning. My mind is racing. I am filled with utter despair over Amelie. I pace around the deck smoking and drinking sweet black tea. I have run out of milk. I think of all the things I want to say to Amelie, all the things I should have said.

Kookaburras begin to laugh in the gum trees at the side of the house. It is not yet light. I remember the extravagant, foolish, triumphal last line of the sonnet I wrote for Amelie.

"And she shall hear the Kookaburra's song". The birds gather and continue the chorus. They are laughing at me. I know it. The song "The whole town's laughing at me, silly fool" goes round and round in my head. I begin to write her a text message. I am determined not to send it, but I need to get my feelings out in black and white. I write.

[Amelie, it has just hit me – i may never see you again, i may never hear your voice, i may never hold you in my arms, ever ever again. i am completely alone. i cannot believe it, i keep hoping that it is an administrative mistake, a glitch, that you will call me and say it was all a mistake, that you do love me. i am sorry, i am in too much pain. the knowledge that you wanted me was all that kept me going. is your decision final, is that it? i am stripped to the bones. i have nothing and no one in the world. i must not send this text. i must not send this text. i must not send this text. please god dont let me send thi...]

Too late, the treacherous thumb descends.

[Message Sent]

I curse myself for a bloody, weak fool. Why, oh, why, did I send it? I wait. An agony of expectation and dread. What will she say? How will she react? She will say, "It's over, don't contact me again". She will say, "I cannot take any more of this. Please be strong. I have my children and their happiness to think about." She will be disappointed that I was not stronger for her, that I didn't have it in me. She will feel contempt for me. Worse, she will feel pity. I want to bang my head against the wall. To knock myself unconscious. To grab the bottle of whiskey from the cupboard and drink myself insensible. I want to die.

Hours pass, or more likely, minutes. And then Beep-beep, Beep-beep. I stare at the phone in horror. What have I done? I dare not read the message. I dare not leave it unread. I walk around the phone, staring at it, trying to fathom the contents. Accusing it of my own crime. Blaming it for my own stupidity. Of course, I pick the phone up and read the message.

[I cant bear that you feel so much pain i have the kids here and their friends here. Talk tomorrow x]

I break down. She is determined, her mind made up. I cry jagged sobs from the depths of my soul. All self-respect gone, desperate, abject, I reply.

[So sorry so sorry oh Amelie oh my love i wish i were stronger]
There is nowhere anything but pain.

It's time to call Mum and give her another update. She is remarkably tolerant of my anguished updates, given that she is such a magnificently remorseless old lady.

"Hi, Mum"

"Oh, hello, it's you, good."

"How are you?"

"OK, I have been doing some gardening, and it is forty degrees outside." A brief pause, then, "How are you, dear?"

I give her the latest update full of extravagant emotion, nobility, fortitude and courage.

"Amelie has dumped me. She has decided to give Fausto another go. I told her I supported her in her decision and wished her every happiness with Fausto and the kids. And I told her that I realised that I had to let her go now."

"Oh, that was very good, 'you had to let her go now', excellent!"

"Mother! I am trying to pour out my heart, you know!"

"Oh yes, sorry dear, do go on."

"I said that we must end our love affair beautifully and gently, with tenderness and love."

"Poor lamb, it must be hard for you."

"It's awful, Mum. I feel as though I have been gutted. For the first time in my life, I am completely and utterly alone in all the world."

She is beginning to tire of the update.

"You just have to move on, darling lamb, find yourself an ordinary woman, a nice chubby blonde."

"I don't want a nice chubby blonde. I want Amelie!"

"Yes, dear."

"I miss her so much, Mum. I can't believe it's over!"

"Well, don't go doing anything rash, will you dear?"

"What do you mean? I'm not going to kill myself."

"You need to keep your job, dear otherwise, it will all go to hell in a handbasket, and you've got the boys to think of."

"I was thinking of flying to Dublin to see her. Maybe if she sees me face to face, she'll change her mind."

"Darling, you can't carry on a relationship from opposite sides of the world."

"I know, Mum. Maybe if I moved back to Dublin?"

"You don't want to be one of those jilted lovers who hang around the corner of the street moping and making whining phone calls after the pub shuts, do you?"

She is right. I don't want to be one of those.

"Anyway, have I told you my news? I haven't, have I?"

"Don't think so. What's your news, Mum?"

"I buried the fridge today."

"You buried the fridge?"

"Yes"

"Where?"

"Well, in the back garden, of course."

"Mum, burial is more usually reserved for people and the occasional animal."

"It was making dirty puddles of brown water on the floor during the night."

"Are you sure it was the fridge?"

"I'm not that old!"

"No, I mean, mightn't it have been the cat?"

"It wasn't the cat. It was the fridge, and I've buried it!"

"How did you do it?" She *is* in her seventies.

"I dragged it out of the house with a rope. Then I rolled it down the garden to the end. It took about an hour!"

"And then you buried it?"

"Yes. I dug an enormous hole."

"How long did that take?"

"About another hour, I think."

I finally realise I haven't asked the most obvious question.

"Why, Mum, why did you bury it?"

"Well, it was dead, you know, it had died."

"Well, did you put a cross on top of it?"

"No, dear, that would be ridiculous. Why would I want to do that? It was only a fridge."

There is a pause, slowly lengthening into silence. Then suddenly, as if on cue, we both burst into fits of giggles.

"I am a good and dutiful son, Mother, but I feel bound to say you are stark staring mad!"

"Yes, dear, it's in the genes."

As I hang up the telephone, I am almost certain I hear her mutter, "And it's not the first time either!"

I sit down to think things over *rationally*. Amelie, my goddess, the meaning of my life, has dumped me. I love her with every atom of my body, every fibre of my being, every beat of my heart, every thought and every deed, with everything I am, have been or ever shall be. I am hers utterly and completely and without hope.

She doesn't want me. She has realised, finally, that she wants Fausto. She loves him. They have been to hell and back together. I must respect her wishes. If this absolute love means anything at all, I must be true to it. "If I love her, I must set her free" - even in this wretched and distraught state, the phrase forces an ironic smile. I sound like I'm releasing a recovered racoon back into the wild. In my desperation, I find myself living in the script of a Disney movie.

I doubt I have the strength to do it. I cannot walk away without a backwards glance. I am seeking the strength to do nothing.

I dare to question her decision. Fausto cannot possibly love her as deeply as I. She cannot possibly love him as much, no, *more than* me! She has made a mistake, out of empathy, out of pity. She will come to her senses. She will see. I will help her to see.

So sly the ego, so insidious. I will *not* do it. I will not give in. I will love for love's sake. I will remain pure and true. I note that this is all becoming a little histrionic.

And then suddenly, quite suddenly, I have it. I know the answer. I see the wellspring of strength that will carry me safely home. I will redirect, repurpose, this overpowering love, this compulsion. I will draw sustenance from it even as I eradicate it. I must stop being in love.

(I am dimly aware, even as I wallow in these extravagant emotions, that another, colder, cynical me, loitering in some cloistered corner of my mind, is stifling the urge to throw up.)

That is the simplest solution. I must fall out of love. I must strangle love with love. This is something I can appreciate, this cruel dialectic. I have known love as pleasure, now I recognise it as pain.

How does one end a love, particularly a love that one doesn't really wish to end? Can it be done consciously, with malice of forethought? The traditional method is to find solace in the arms of another, but what if you don't really want the arms of another? What if you don't really want anyone but 'her'? What if every ounce of you screams out to be with her, just one last time, just for a moment, to touch her skin, to see her smile, just one more time? What then?

I don't know. I have no idea, but I know now that I must find out. I have a clear course of action. I have an honourable path. I can keep the faith. I can do what she asks. This is all very good in principle, but I have no idea how to execute. Where do I find the willing arms of another?

Colleen comes to the rescue.

"RSVP."

"RSVP to what? Have I been invited to something?" She raises her eyebrows to the heavens.

"RSVP is an online dating agency."

"Online", I repeat, "on the internet. I don't think I like the sound of that."

Colleen tuts at me. I hate it when she tuts at me. I have come to realise that Colleen only tuts when she knows she is in the right. Whereas Connor will say, "Pat, you're an idiot", Colleen tuts.

I do not give in easily, however, so Colleen subtly reverts to the time-honoured technique of inviting her single female friends around for dinner or to the pub, wherever I happen to be. They are very nice young women, attractive even. I like them, but they are too young. There is a gulf of experience that is just too hard to cross. I get Colleen to show me how RSVP works. RSVP is not, it transpires, the only online dating agency, but according to Colleen, it is, by some silent conspiracy, some unspoken compact, the one people use who are actually looking for a new partner. The other one is used where all you are after is meaningless sex. I suggest that perhaps I should start with the other one. Colleen snorts (equivalent to tutting).

"Trust me. In this context, you are an RSVP sort of bloke".

I shift rebelliously in my seat. I have learned not to argue.

"Pat, you are quite unable to understand the concept of meaningless sex, or meaningless anything else for that matter."

RSVP is something of a revelation. In a way, it is much better than the traditional drunken meeting in a pub or at a party. While completely sober, you get to read the lady's profile, where she has written what is important to her. This can be very telling, but as I begin to realise, not quite telling enough. The profile contains the age, hair colour, and body type (sadly no category for 'lissom', which I feel is an oversight) and then her long blurb about how important meaningful communication and deep understanding is. Followed by a "no time wasters" warning. There is also a photograph. The photographs, I soon realise, may bear, at best, only an approximate relationship to the woman. The profile also serves to cull non-smokers, athletes, religious nuts, and, so far, axe murderers. The downside, of course, is that you have to upload your own profile too and photograph, leaving yourself horribly exposed and naked to the gaze of the entire universe.

Having reviewed dozens of profiles, both female and male (just judging the competition), I decide to set up my own account on RSVP. I have gleaned some basic rules, the first and most basic of which is that what you say about yourself, your history, and your hopes and dreams should be, at the very least, ballpark accurate. This is simply polite.

The next rule is to find ways to filter out undesirables (see above). I carefully craft a message intended to appeal to the one, or at most two, women in Sydney whom I imagine might put a bizarre mind ahead of a buff body. I do not say I am a non-smoker. I say instead that I am giving up! I think this is brilliant until Colleen mentions that that is what all smokers say. On the pre-set categories page, I select 'medium build', 'brown hair' and 'no particular religion'. I want to put off the God-botherers without startling any sexy agnostics who might be out there. I mention the places I have lived to show that I am a bit of a global citizen and a couple of other more or less irrelevant things I like or aspire to. I show it to Colleen, who just shakes her head.

"Whatever". I think it's a work of genius!

My Profile.

I like writing. Terrible poetry, the odd song (lyrics only), not altogether awful prose, and improbable, unedifying philosophy.

I was born in Dublin but emigrated to Zambia when I was about four and to Swaziland when I was seven or eight. Moved to London when I was eleven, back to Dublin when I was twenty-two and to Sydney a few years ago.

I love strange words and bizarre names. For instance, I think the word 'epiphenomenology' is altogether a good thing and the fact that there is a road near Shark Bay in WA called 'Useless Loop', which is indeed both useless and a loop, is, or should be a National Treasure.

I love to cook but am spiritually unable to follow a recipe except in broad outline. I look ok in a suit but otherwise like a sack of potatoes. I walk with a limp occasioned by a motorbike crash whilst misspending my youth.

I love life and try to enjoy every moment. I have no formal religious beliefs but might be described as Buddh*ish*. Can't quite manage the real thing.

Last, of all, I upload a recent photograph of myself smiling, taken at Circular Quay, wearing a nice blue serge suit. I hesitate a day or two before finally unlocking my profile and making it visible to the world.

The effect is near instantaneous. Within an hour, I receive half a dozen emails and two 'kisses'. I go to the help pages to find out what a 'kiss' is. They turn out to be a sort of cyber-space nudge to attract your attention. Cheaper than sending an email. I ignore the kisses.

I open the first of the emails. It is from Tatiana Danilova, from Minsk, which I discover is in Belarus. She has some English, good German and fluent Russian. I check her profile. She is 39 years old with one child, a son, Alexander. She has uploaded an old photograph of someone I vaguely recognize, an old movie star, I think, from the 1930s. Next to the photograph she has written "I look a bit like this". She is looking for a "respectful, hardworking husband who has a good steady job", and she is willing "to perform all wifely duties". There is something very brave and quite hopeless about the email. I am deeply touched by the photograph, not of her, but of someone like her or someone she would like to look like. Such a human thing to do. I decide to write back. A short, polite note. Thanks, but no thanks.

I open the remaining five emails. They are all in a similar vein. One from Poland, two more from Belarus, and two from Russia. I do not respond to these. It costs five dollars per email within the RSVP system. Besides, I am looking for someone a little closer to home.

I decide to go on the offensive if 'offensive' is quite the right word. I set a few parameters, such as age and body type, in the RSVP search screen, hit the button and wait to see what pops up. After a few moments, a list of 120 or so profiles is returned. I begin to flick through them, one by one. It starts to get boring. I resubmit the search removing any that have not supplied a photo. This reduces the list to 80. Still not sure I can be bothered to trawl through that many hits. I limit the distance from my new home to 20 kilometres. That's much better. Now down to 25 profiles.

I start to read these profiles in earnest, but after four or five, I tire of that too. I flick through the remaining photographs selecting the three most attractive images, and I read their profiles. They all seem very nice, reasonably attractive and within 20 kilometres of where I am living. I have run out of criteria for further selection. I write each of them a pleasant email suggesting we meet for coffee or a drink. Then I go out on the piss with Connor and Colleen until three in the morning. I am not used to this lifestyle. There will be hell to pay in the morning.

Saturday morning, and I feel like shit. Connor and Colleen are already up drinking coffee and playing Faithless at top volume downstairs. Connor made the sub-woofer himself, a massive thing capable of creating medium-sized seismic shocks and confusing sperm whales in the St Andreas Fault. Colleen sees me shuffling downstairs and lights a cigarette for me.

"Here you go. Fancy a cup of coffee?"

I nod and go and stand in the courtyard where the Duf-Duf of the subwoofer is less detrimental to my well-being.

"Pat, is it yourself?" Connor is in altogether too fine fettle for the hour. I attempt to rise to the occasion.

"It is not. It is another man of the same name."

Faithless ends, and Groove Armada kicks in.

"Cos I feel good", Duf-Duf-Duf, "Cos I feel high."

My head really, really hurts. For a moment, I think I might cry. Colleen appears with a coffee and two mega-strength paracetamol and codeine tablets. Fine girl she is – I find myself thinking in pseudo-Irish brogue. Connor's influence.

"Any luck on RSVP?" Colleen wants to vet any responses. If she could, I think she'd ask for references.

"Dunno"

"Shall we check?" Big smile, irresistible force.

"OK"

She leads me back upstairs to the study, where the computer is already on. RSVP is already loaded. Colleen has been doing some research on my behalf. She's a born matchmaker.

"Look. She looks nice, don't you think?" The image of a sad-eyed woman with a broad and hopeful smile appears.

"Yes," I am non-committal, "nice smile."

"Well, log in!" Colleen is eager now. She pretends to turn her head away as I type in my password. I make a mental note to change the password every time I log in. God knows what Connor would be capable of if let loose with my password and my profile. He'd have Tatiana on a plane by now.

I have one reply from the least attractive of the three women. She says she likes my sense of humour and would like to meet for a coffee. Colleen leans over and begins composing a reply.

"Oy, Oy, Oy!" I yell, pushing her to one side. "At least let's maintain the illusion that this has something to do with me!"

"Sorry." Colleen manages to appear contrite as she budges me off the chair and begins to type. Fuck it. It is nothing to do with me.

"Better leave her to it, mate." Connor drags me back downstairs and puts on 'Big Audio Dynamite'. He finds two tall narrow beakers and makes us both tequila sunrises. It is ten a.m. I am done for.

Twenty minutes later, Colleen appears, very pleased with herself.

"Oh, God. What have you done?" I am not sure I want to know.

"Trust me, Pat", she is smug, "I'll find you a nice one."

"Thanks", I mutter, "really appreciate it."

Connor and Colleen have decided that we are going grass bowling in Balmain. I am drunk again, and it's only eleven o'clock. How on earth can they keep up this ruinous pace?

Playing bowls, drinking lager and eating potato wedges with sweet chilli sauce and soured cream turns out to be an excellent way of spending Saturday afternoon. Their friend Paru turns up, and we play in teams, me and Paru, Connor and Colleen. This is serious competition, red in tooth and claw. No quarter asked or given. Paru plays with a deadly incompetence, time and again smashing their bowls all over the green. The result is never in doubt. Paru and I crush the opposition beneath our feet. We all go back to Connor and Colleen's for a nap before going out again later.

I am pole-axed and collapse into bed immediately. I awake to fits of giggles coming from the study upstairs. I have a deep sense of foreboding. I stick my head out the door, considering my next move.

"Have another one, mate", Connor is mixing drinks in the kitchen, "Trust me, you don't want to know."

A few minutes later, the girls appear, but upon seeing me, they are unable to stifle their guffaws. Then they get a fit of the giggles and cannot speak for about ten minutes. Then they explain that they have set me up with three dates during the coming week. Two lunch meetings over coffee and one early evening drink in a bar off Martins Place. I am resigned. It seems the decision is far too important to be left up to me. Saturday night is, if anything, even more, murderous than Friday night. We end up in Gilligans, a shocking little bar off Oxford Street, at six in the morning, talking to a tall gay man in a red leather jump-suit with a dwarf on a lead.

Losing myself in the arms of another is turning out to be quite a chore.

I am extremely nervous. I am wearing the blue suit from the photograph I posted. I am walking up Pitt Street towards the allotted rendezvous with the first of Colleen's chosen women. I have read and re-read her profile until I could answer questions on it. She has brown hair and is of medium height with an 'average' body type. She is thirty-five years old and of Italian extraction. Her photo, though professionally done, is worryingly soft focus. She likes music and singing. She has one eleven-year-old son. He is all-important to her. She is seeking meaningful communication and deep understanding. She wishes to dissuade 'time wasters'. She is Catholic.

I see her approaching the coffee house at more or less the same moment she sees me. Neither of us now has the opportunity of merely walking on by. She is at the generous end of the 'average' body type.

"Hi", I say, "You're right on time."

"So are you. I hate time wasters. You look like your photo too. That's got to count in your favour. Nice suit. Isn't that the one in the photo? I like blue. Good colour for a suit. I have a very similar coloured suit I wear on stage. I'm a singer, you know? Mostly jazz and blues, but also my own stuff. I'm a songwriter too, and a composer. Well, that's what I do in my spare time. During the day, I manage the mid-sized computers for a major credit union. Mostly back-office processing, general ledger, accounts payable and receivable, invoicing, and arrears management. You would be amazed how many people fall into arrears. They are so surprised when they are forced to sell their homes, but honestly, what can you expect if you don't keep up your payments on your mortgage or other loan secured against your property…"

I escape forty-five minutes later when Colleen calls to find out how it went. I have to take a walk beside the harbour to regain my equilibrium. I now know everything imaginable about a woman I sincerely pray I will never set eyes on again. I am exhausted. I need a nap. Colleen is contrite. She reassures me that the next one will be better. I get back to the office, still looking a little shell-shocked. People assume I've been for a job interview.

●●●

I am not so nervous. I am not wearing the blue suit in the photograph. I am walking up Pitt Street towards the allotted rendezvous with the second of Colleen's chosen women. I have read her profile, but I could not answer questions on it. She has brown hair and is of medium height with an 'average' body type. She is thirty-eight years old and Canadian. Her photo, taken on some social or family occasion, is crisp and clear but is cropped such that a man's hairy arm dangles insinuatingly down from her shoulder. She likes reading and cinema. She has one eleven-year-old daughter and a two-year-old son. They are the most important aspect of her life right now. She is seeking meaningful communication and deep understanding. She wishes to dissuade 'time wasters'. She is Christian.

This time I hang around for a few moments until I see her arrive. The photograph she used is not recent. She looks nice, though, good figure. I follow her a moment or two later and lead her to a table near the door.

She is very easy to talk to. She puts me at ease, asking if I found the place ok, confirming that I have about an hour before my next appointment, and ordering coffee for both of us. She has a very pleasant manner. She then begins to sound me out on a precise list of prepared topics.

What is my position on the war in the Middle East?

How central do I think oil is to the conflict?

Do I agree with Australia's stance?

Am I now, or have I ever been a member of a political party?

What is my favourite piece of music?

Why?

What is my favourite film?

What do I view as its most important shortcoming?

Which Latin-American author is my favourite?

What was my family doing in Africa?

What aspect of philosophy is currently exercising my mind?

What do I understand the word 'epiphenomenon' to mean?

I am able, in the intervals between one question and the next, to ascertain that she lives in Mosman and has a German Shepherd dog called Brutus. Her daughter starts secondary school next academic year, and her ex-husband lives and works in Switzerland. I also find out that she is the Director of HR for a major management consultancy.

"Well." It's ten minutes prior to the end of the allotted interview time. "You seem like a very nice, well-educated man, but I didn't notice any particular chemistry, did you?"

I acknowledge that, sadly, I do not seem to be her type.

She picks up the bill.

Colleen calls a few moments later. I tell her all about it. We laugh until we cannot breathe. She was a very nice, precise, considerate woman. And she was right. There was no chemistry.

●●●

I am not at all nervous. I am wearing jeans and a T-Shirt. I am walking up Pitt Street towards the allotted rendezvous with the third of Colleen's chosen women. I have flicked through her profile. She has brown hair and is of medium height with an 'average' body type. She is thirty-four years old and Australian. Her photo is a professionally done glamour shot. She likes bush walking and foreign travel. She has one fifteen-year-old daughter and one twelve-year-old son. She insists on keeping a balance between their needs are her own. She is seeking meaningful communication and deep understanding. She wishes to dissuade 'time wasters'. She is of no formal religion but has a deeply spiritual side. And from where I'm standing, she has a great arse

She is peering through the window of the coffee house, trying to see if I am already there. She sees my reflection approaching in the window and turns.

"Hi." Her tone is bright and breezy. "I could really do with a glass or two of wine if that works for you?"

We go to the cellar bar on the corner of Martin Place. She orders New Zealand Sauvignon Blanc and some snacks.

"I have the afternoon off," she ventures. "How long can you spare?"

"As long as you like." She really does have a very nice smile. I switch my phone off. Colleen can wait.

Her name is Marianna. She teaches art at a fairly exclusive boy's fee-paying secondary school in Sydney. We get on very well. There is chemistry, heaps of chemistry. We polish off two bottles in fairly quick succession before she suggests we go back to her place in Glebe. I pay the bill with almost indecent haste. Marianna goes outside to hail a cab. The trip to Glebe takes nine minutes and thirty-seven seconds. She has a cute little house with a tin roof and a bull-nosed veranda.

Marianna opens a dusty bottle of Shiraz from under the sofa while I select something from her CD collection. I find The Very Best of Marvin Gaye, Sexual Healing *and* Let's Get It On. She pours two generous glasses. We dance. She is the first actual Australian I have ever dated. She smells very good. She likes to dance close and slow. We kiss. Game on.

God Bless Australia and God bless Colleen!

LAUREN

After the fling with Marianna (I know what a fling is now), I stop using RSVP for a longish time, several months. Colleen is right. I am not really good at the meaningless sex thing. Marianna eventually gets that I am looking for meaningful communication and deep understanding. She is not. We agree, we actually do agree, in a grownup and non-fraught and mutually respectful manner, to end our approximately six-week relationship. This is a revelation for me. I phone my mum immediately to tell her.

"Hi, Mum!"

"Oh, it's you, good."

"How are you?"

"I'm fine, dear. I've been doing a little gardening out the front. The thorns on the cactuses are very long and very sharp." She is extremely pleased about that. While she wouldn't, well probably wouldn't, go to the lengths of actually misleading a caller into impaling themselves on one of her cactuses, she mightn't be too disappointed if one of them did, err, somehow.

"Marianna and I have split up!"

"Oh, I am sorry dear. Still, plenty more fish in the sea."

"No. It's great."

"Oh dear, I do get things the wrong way around sometimes. I thought you liked her."

"I did, I do, she's great. She's just not the one for me, is all."

"Well, as long as you're happy, dear."

"I am mum, but that's not it. Well, it is it, but in a different way."

"Mmmm?"

"We *agreed* to split up. We agreed on it together, like grownups. It was brilliant!"

"Oh, I see what you mean. Well, jolly good thing then."

"Just wanted you to know."

"Yes. Well, thank you, dear."

It is several months before I feel like trying again, but eventually, I publish my profile again on RSVP and take a look at who's out there. I set the criteria very narrowly this time. I get two hits. A very lovely-looking Catholic woman reclining in a chaise longue and an entrancing brunette with the most beautiful smile I have ever seen. I decide to email the beautiful smile first. It is Thursday night before a long weekend, so I ask her if she can meet at any point over the holiday.

The reply comes back sooner than expected. She would like to meet, but she cannot manage it over the long weekend due to family commitments. I write back, giving my personal email address and mobile phone number. I say I am happy to meet up whenever works for her.

On Saturday, I get a call.

"It's me, the lady from RSVP."

I thank God I haven't emailed the reclining catholic in the meantime.

"Hi. How nice to hear from you. Wasn't expecting you to call until next week."

"Well, here's the thing. I took my mother out for her birthday dinner tonight, but we got back earlier than I was expecting. Look, I know it's short notice, but can you manage a quick drink tonight?"

"Sure, I was only watching T.V. It'd be great to meet up."

"God, you sound so *English!*"

"Do I?"

"Yes. It's nice, though. I lived there when I was a girl."

"Where shall we meet?"

"You decide. I have rather sprung this on you."

We talk about possible venues for a few moments. She says she lives in Camperdown. I am in Ermington. Splitting the difference, I suggest we meet in Balmain, at the Monkey Bar on Darling Street. It is agreed. We will meet in an hour.

I jump in the shower and then scramble to find something casual but smart to wear. I get to the Monkey Bar a few minutes early. There is a parking space waiting for me down a side street.

I wander inside, but the joint is heaving, a band is playing in the corner, and it is quite impossible to hear yourself think. This will not do at all. I go outside and call her mobile phone. A woman two yards down from me answers. We laugh.

"Hi."

"Hi."

"Look, this place is just too crowded and noisy. Shall we try somewhere else?" I am desperately trying to think where might work.

"Sure. Where do you suggest?"

I suggest an Irish pub in Rozelle called The Welcome, which is down a quiet side street. It is only when she agrees that I realise I don't know how to get there exactly. Piss, poor start to a date. I call Connor, and he directs us through the maze of little back streets that give Balmain its charm. The Welcome is perfect, a traditional pub with great food. Finally, we get to talk.

We hit it off straight away. She keeps smiling at me. Each time she does, I am dazzled. I lose my train of thought. I must come across as a bumbling, tongue-tied idiot.

"How long did it take you from Camperdown?" I ask during a lull in the conversation.

"Camperdown?"

"Yes, weren't you coming from Camperdown?" She looks confused for a moment, then smiles at me again. I give her my best village idiot grin in return.

"Not Camperdown, Campbell Town."

"You drove all the way from Campbell Town?"

"Well, no. Ingleburn actually. But nobody's ever heard of it." I have never heard of it.

"You thought I said Camperdown?"

"Yes, that's why I suggested Balmain. It was sort of halfway between where we both lived." Pause. "But Campbell Town's halfway to Canberra, isn't it?" She smiles at me *again*.

She is lovely! Her name is Lauren.

There are few things as annoying as a phone ringing in your kitchen at 5.55 a.m. on a weekday morning. Whatever it is, it can't be good. My guess is that one of my seventeen-year-old son's mates is calling him to crow about pulling an all-nighter, or it's a wrong number, or it's a Mumbai-based telesales company getting their time zones mixed up again.   5.55 a.m. is just a bit too early to get up, even if, like me, you were already awake. The phone keeps on ringing. I stumble out of bed and grump through to the kitchen.

Once out of bed, it occurs to me that it might be my sister Minnie calling from Berkley, California. She always gets the time zone mixed up. I sent her the first presentable draft of my new novel to read. She's a linguistics professor at Berkley, in the French Department and has many published titles of her own. She said she would love to read my book for me. She said, "How exciting!"

A few days have passed. She could have read a bit by now and be calling in person to give me feedback. The old ego gets going, and since there's no one else inside my head at the moment, I briefly imagine her telling me, "It's brilliant, Pat, just brilliant! I couldn't put it down!" Of course, I know she is not going to say that. She will say, "Very promising, I liked it a lot", or "Great first draft, I have an idea or two on how you might refine it." But by this time, I have reached the phone. I am no longer feeling quite so wrathful. I shall not feel bound to give the caller a good piece of my mind.

I pick up the phone. I hear a woman say.

"Hello." The accent is American, I think.

"Hello." maybe Minnie is calling from a friend's, or someone is helping her to put the call through because she can't navigate around the leading zero in Sydney phone numbers. I don't want to give too much away. It could still be a telemarketer.

"Is that Pat... Paterson... brother to Minnie Debar?" The woman's voice quavers slightly, hesitantly, like a little girl. Tiny sharp teeth of foreboding begin gnawing at the back of my mind.

"Yes", I say, in a strong voice, a voice of certainty, "this is Paterson Curse."

"This is Lottie," the woman's voice breaks. "Minnie's partner". My stomach flip-flops. I don't want this. I want to start again. I want to hear an Indian accent explaining that I have been selected to receive a brand-new mobile telephone. I want someone to sell me a timeshare. I do not want to continue this conversation.

"Yes?"

"Something terrible has happened to your sister." The little girl's voice continues. "She died. She has died... she's dead". An American woman with the voice of a little girl is calling me to tell me my sister is dead. This is where a British middle-class upbringing can really come in handy, in a way. A good understanding of etiquette and the rules of polite conversation can carry you through almost any difficult social situation. I have been living in Sydney for five years, not long enough for the easier, more genuine Australian responses to kick in.

"I see. Thank you for letting me know. When did this happen?"

"We don't know. We think maybe over the weekend or Monday".

"Do you know how she died. What was the cause of death?"

"No, we don't. The medics ruled out all the kind of causes a layperson might think of intuitively." I grasp around mentally, trying to conceive what a layperson might intuitively imagine. At a time like this, I can be intuitive *or* British. Take your pick.

"Do you mean like heart attack, stroke, brain haemorrhage? That kind of thing?"

"Yes. The medics have ruled out all of those. There's going to be an autopsy."

"An autopsy."

"Yes. Apparently, it's normal when someone has died unexpectedly, and the cause of death is not evident."

"I see, thank you." Lottie gives me her contact details. The call ends. My sister Minnie is dead.

Sleepwalking, I put on the kettle to make tea and wander out into the yard. The sun is already up. It is warm. It is going to be a lovely day. I cannot assign the correct significance to the news. I know what has happened, I understand, but I cannot make it mean anything. I cannot pair the information with its appropriate emotional response.

Lauren is still asleep. I will let her sleep. I drink strong Irish Breakfast Tea in a big mug, sitting in the backyard in the early rays of a new day. A day Minnie will not see.

I am four years old. London. Earliest memory. I am in my parent's bedroom. It is early evening. I am amazing them with my feats of daring-do. I climb to the top of the wardrobe, and, with all due solemnity and seriousness, I leap from the top of the wardrobe down onto their double bed.

It is clear to me, after several turns, that they do not appreciate the finer points. I explain. There are, in fact, two quite different stunts being performed, entirely for their entertainment and at no small risk to life and limb. First is the Flaming Bonkdown, the more aesthetically pleasing of the two, being performed as it is with arms and legs akimbo. The second, and to my mind, more courageous manoeuvre, is the Flaming Margarita, in which no concession is made to personal safety. In this manoeuvre, I show not the slightest fear. Not so much as a flicker do I allow to pass across my stern countenance. I leap nonchalantly, from the very top of the wardrobe, with both arms straight and stiff by my sides. I disdain to break my fall. I laugh as the full weight of my four-year-old body slams, meteor-like, into the covers.

Having highlighted the nuances, I perform both stunts again, one after the other. First, the Flaming Bonkdown, then the Flaming Margarita. My parents educated now in the distinction, watch avidly, agape.

"Well?" I demand, after concluding the second performance (my face steely), which did you prefer?

"Oh, the Flaming Bonkdown", my father's voice is firm, his mind made up, "definitely".

"Oh, no." My mother gives him a look of withering disdain. "The Flaming Margarita, without a doubt!"

It is four in the morning. A dog is barking outside the window. The old weatherboard house creaks peacefully in the cold pre-dawn breeze. I have just taken a piss for the eighth time tonight. I am forty-eight years old, and I am staring down the barrel of prostate cancer.

"Shut up, Inigo", I half-shout, halfway between silencing the dog and waking the house. The manoeuvre half-works. The barking turns to whining. The other dog, Coby, joins in. We have two Australian Cattle-Dog/German Shepherd crosses. Big dogs, powerful and loyal. Not to be messed with.

"Shut up, Coby", I mutter.

It might not be cancer. I am only forty-eight, and there is no history of it in my family. There could be dozens of other explanations. I can't think of any of them, but logically, there must be dozens.

It's not such a problem these days anyway if caught early enough, just outpatient stuff. I vaguely remember watching a TV doco about it. I remember it said something like that, seek help early and get regular check-ups. I can't remember the symptoms except one, constant pissing at night, and one other thing. There are few noticeable symptoms. By the time most men get to the doctors', the disease is well advanced.

There is no blood in the urine. Is that good? I don't know. I slide open the screen door and shuffle out into the dark. The dawn is not far off. A few trucks can be heard in the distance, changing gears on Silverwater Road. Tradies out and about early, getting a head start on Sydney's horrendous morning rush-hour traffic, gunning their Ute's over the lights in anticipation of the motorway.

A breeze rustles the palm fronds, dry as death. The chill wind of mortality licks my ears, sending a shudder right through me. I stick my hands over the fence into the dogs' enclosure. Warm, soft noses snuffle my hand, dribbling gooey saliva down my arm. Hot wet tongues greet me. Sweet dogs.

"Good boys, "I say. "Go back to sleep now."

My own boys, my sons, are sleeping inside. It is my weekend. We have four kids this time, my two boys and Lauren's two girls. A full house.

I make another cup of tea and sit on the porch, sipping and watching the sunrise over the cemetery. Enjoying a few moments of peace. We live across the road from Rookwood Necropolis, the largest cemetery of its kind in the southern hemisphere. A suburb in its own right. A city of the dead indeed.

I hear stirrings indoors. The littlies are up, watching cartoons on the TV in the sitting room, wrapped in fleece blankets against the early chill. I make them each a bowl of cereal which they begin to eat without once taking their eyes from the screen. Automatons.

I know I must go to the doctor. Lauren has been pestering me to go for weeks. I have an appointment. I must go.

The doctor's surgery consists of a plain white waiting room with a very loud TV showing Middle Eastern soaps and a portable air-conditioning unit which is now turned off. I am the first patient, waiting alone on the doorstep. The doctor lets me in. His receptionist has not yet arrived. He invites me into his consulting room and takes down a few basic details. Name, address, phone number, date of birth and Medicare number. He is Turkish. This is a multi-cultural neighbourhood. He has eyes capable only of expressing sadness. His eyes are deep brown pools evolved by infinitesimal degrees over eons to express the sadness of war and death, and loss. He smiles.

"What can I do?" he asks.

I don't know. It feels like an imposition to add my trifling problems to his already impossible burden.

"I would like you to check me out for prostate cancer." My tone is smooth and controlled. He gazes at me through the prism of endless, bewildered desolation. His expression is doubtful. He sighs.

"Why?" he ventures after a protracted pause.

"I am forty-eight years old, and I spend all night pissing."

He shifts in his seat. He considers his next words very carefully.

"There are two ways to identify this condition," he pauses, "by a blood test or by inspection via the anus." He waits, expecting me to answer what does not appear to me to be a question.

"You want the inspection via the anus?" his tone expresses almost infinite melancholy.

"I'm not absolutely mad keen."

This is plainly not an answer as far as he is concerned. He hesitates.

"But I'm not stupid either. If I have to do it, then I will."

"We could do the blood tests first." He offers, dejection written across his face.

"Oh yes! Let's do that."

"Is a very good idea!" For the first time, a flicker of hope lights up his face.

He has many devices on his desk. He selects one of them, which immediately straps a tourniquet around my arm. He is pleased. He almost strokes its smooth black matt case.

"Is very good." He smiles. He takes the blood and squirts it into three small tubes.

"What shall we check for?" He asks.

"Well, what *can* we check for?" I counter, "I was rather hoping you could advise me."

Again the gloom descends across his face.

"Whatever you want. We can check for everything."

"OK, let's check for everything". The doctor unfolds a long-form, examines it carefully and proceeds to tick box after box after box.

"I had no idea there were so many things you can check for in blood."

"Is unbelievable." He agrees. He passes me an envelope with an address scrawled on it.

"Take it here." He taps the address on the form. "Go this morning, and they will let you have the results back today."

"Now", he smiles, "What about ultra-sound?"

I am completely nonplussed.

"Ultrasound?"

"Yes, like for pregnancy."

"I know what it is."

"You can have an ultrasound first. If they see anything unusual, then you can have the inspection via the anus." Sorrow beyond measure woven into every syllable.

"Is it a good idea?"

"Is a VERY good idea."

"OK".

He gives me another note.

"Go here this morning, and they will give you photographs for me today."

At that exact moment, an extremely fat lady bursts into the consulting room carrying a large cardboard cup of coffee. It's the receptionist.

"You see? You see how good my life is, how well she looks after me?"

I have a lot to get done if I am to know the truth today. I take my leave.

"Yes, Yes. I see you later." I half expect to see slow tears rolling down his nose, dripping into his coffee. I feel bloody marvellous in comparison.

I rage across southwest Sydney like a Dervish on a mission from God. First, the blood work. I deliver the phials and pay the fee, then race across three suburbs to the ultrasound place. Many pregnant women sit in rows in the gloomy waiting room. The scene is vaguely reminiscent of The Matrix. There is only one chair left, next to the reception desk, facing the serried ranks of expectant women. The air conditioning is turned up way too high. I am at first attentive, then fascinated, and finally spellbound as the air-con does its work. Slowly but slowly, I am presented with an unnerving vision. The nipples of a myriad fulsome breasts, hardening, provocatively, a Roman phalanx, proof against the barbarian.

My name is called. Thank God.

"Why are we doing this then?" a good-natured male radiographer enquires.

"I mean, what's this all about?"

"I piss all night, and I want you to check for prostate cancer."

"What prompted you to come?"

For a very brief moment, I consider explaining the misery in the eyes of my doctor.

"My girlfriend nagged me." I offer, defeated.

"Don't know where any of us blokes would be without our women, ay?" Ebullient Radiographers, who knew? He continues,

"I left it until I couldn't walk before my girlfriend dragged me into hospital. I had a septic ulcer the size of an extra-large pizza on my back. Another couple of hours and it would have worked its way to my heart." He seemed, on balance, delighted both by the experience and the absurdly close call.

"Umm". I offer. The ultra-sound gel is freezing against my skin.

He makes copious pictures of my innards. Pressing the ultra-sound wand deep into my bladder.

"Press any harder, and I'm gonna piss myself!" Do all those bullet-nippled women put up with this, I wonder? Hardly seems credible.

"Funny, never get that from my female patients."

The ordeal is over. I have just enough time to race back to the lab to get the results of the blood tests and then back to the ultra-sound place to pick up the pictures.

I get back to the doctor's surgery no more than three minutes before it closes. The fat receptionist gives me a withering look. I want to say something clever and nasty, but the image of three dozen women waiting in bovine resignation for the benefit of their unborn children cows me into respectful submission.

"I'd really like to see the doctor if possible", I say, "I have all the test results, and my girlfriend is waiting for me at home."

I am not sure what exactly I have said, which bit made the difference, but she puts a call through to the doctor to say I'm in the waiting room.

I watch a blue-bottle fly buzz against the glass above the air-conditioning outlet. Futile, inevitable. In a curious way, almost indomitable.

The doctor opens his consulting room door and beckons me in.

I hand over two large envelopes. One, some implausibly large format designed to defeat any storage system, containing the ultra-sound photographs, the other, a more reasonable size, containing the results of innumerable blood tests.

The doctor opens the big square ultra-sound envelope first. He studies the pictures attentively and reads the accompanying commentary. He spares me a long look over the rim of his glasses before opening the blood test results. I have no idea what the long look means. Is a long look from a Turkish doctor a good thing or a bad thing? This is not the kind of information I have ever before needed.

He settles down to read the test results, occasionally looking up at me in a non-committal sort of way. He sighs. I take this as an indication that he is about to speak.

He goes back to the beginning of the blood test report. Tracking down with his finger, he comes to a significant result.

He taps the paper and looks up at me.

"AIDS!" he pronounces. My heart jumps into my mouth, then, "No".

"Hepatitis B? No"

"Hepatitis C? No"

"Kidneys? No"

"Prostate! No"

He stops reading and folds the document with slow deliberation.

"Cholesterol". He pauses, "Is ridiculous".

"What?"

"Your cholesterol", he pauses again, "Is ridiculous".

"Stand up."

I stand. He indicates another of his gadgets.

"Stand on the scales." I stand as ordered.

The device hums its electronic hum as my height and weight are measured. He presses a button on another device, and a small square paper ticket pops out. He reads a single number printed on it, like a fortune cookie.

"Is ridiculous."

"What?"

"Body-mass index."

"What's that?"

"Is ridiculous"

"Yes, but what does it mean?"

"Either you too bloody short or you too bloody fat".

He indicates another machine.

"Put you arm here." I obey. Something snaps across my arm, and the thing begins to inflate alarmingly. After a few moments, the fortune cookie device spits out another slip of paper. The doctor picks it up and reads the numbers written on it.

"Is ridiculous."

"What?" I allow a hint of exasperation to enter my voice.

"Hypertension. Is ridiculous." I give him what I fondly hope is a searching look.

"Worst I ever seen."

"What does that mean?"

"Blood pressure. Is ok, I have samples". He begins to rummage through a large pine box of medical oddments, flinging random medicaments into the air. He pulls out a small cardboard box.

"Is eighty milligrams."

"Oh," I am utterly lost.

"Is ok, break in half. Lasts fourteen days."

"What about the prostate cancer?" I finally recollect my reason for being there.

"Nothing! You just piss a lot."

"You blood pressure is bloody disgrace, but." He holds up his hands, wriggling his fingers sadly.

"I have very short fingers. Take the tablets. Ccome see me in a week."

I stagger out to the car. I am ok. It finally sinks in. I am not about to die. Elation fills me.

My mobile phone rings. It's Lauren. She is shopping for dinner on her way home from work. She is all bright and breezy and full of optimism.

"How's your day been, darling?"

"Uneventful," I am not sure where to start.

"Oh, what did the doctor have to say? Is everything ok?"

"He says I'm too fat, and I piss a lot."

"Pithy! Anything else?"

"Yes, he has mercifully short fingers."

DYKES AND BELLY DANCERS

The memorial service for Minnie will be held in a month. There are still some arrangements that need to be made, and I am acting as next of kin. I fire off a series of "To Whom It May Concern" type letters authorising Lottie to act for the family. I scrabble around for the funds and book my flights. Just me. No one else from the family will be going. I am glad that Minnie and I were on good terms when she died, relieved that the long estrangement had come to an end.

The day arrives, and I pick up my tattered old red flight bag. There are a couple of purple Mardi Gras beads in the zip-up pocket, left over from a trip to New Orleans a few years ago. The bag smells musty and disused. I head to Sydney International Airport. I am hours early, obsessively early, always. I am reading Dostoyevsky, Notes From Underground. Cheering stuff. The trip is entirely uneventful. I hardly sleep. Instead, I watch four mindless action movies.

I land at Oakland at 10:15 a.m. local time, exactly five minutes before I left Sydney. I am going to have two Fridays this week. Crossing the International Date Line, the wrong way can do that kind of thing. I wait for Lottie, who shows up almost immediately in an old blue-green Lincoln Voyager. She has a friendly Portuguese Water Dog named Picnic. Lottie tells me Minnie chose the name.

The short journey to Berkley takes a few minutes, during which we chat about the trip. Am I exhausted? Did I get any sleep on the flight? Etc etc. Lottie takes me for a quick tour of Berkley. Road signs flash past College, Alcatraz, Sacramento, University, and Oxford – familiar and evocative. I am struck by how pretty Berkeley is, and there are pedestrians! I have visited many American cities over the years, and in most, there seem to be very few pedestrian areas. Berkeley, by contrast, appears to be a pedestrian-friendly town. This is a revelation to me. The next thing that strikes me is that the people seem relaxed and happy. The town itself is very low-key, demure.

There are many busy little coffee shops and restaurants. A well-kept secret.

Back at Lottie's, I unpack and hang up my new black suit and black tie. I am not sure what the etiquette is here, and I don't want to let Minnie down. Lottie's house is very charming and pleasant. It smells slightly of ground coffee and toast. The sounds of the street are muted, the sort of place you can relax and feel at home. She has hundreds and hundreds of books. I recognise many of Minnie's stuffed horizontally into bookshelves, every which way, recent additions.

Lottie explains what has happened so far. There has been an autopsy that proved to be inconclusive, so the actual cause of death is still unknown. There are no suspicious circumstances, Lottie is quick to emphasise that, but the exact cause remains a mystery. The medics are looking at toxicology, apparently. When all the necessary samples had been taken, the Oakland Coroner released Minnie's body, and, in accordance with the stated wishes of her family in Australia, Minnie's body was cremated.

I ask who had attended the cremation, but Lottie explains that no one attended. The crematorium takes delivery of the body, cremates it, and returns the person's ashes in a container. I am tired and confused, and a hollow feeling is opening up in my stomach – it seems that Minnie's death has not been marked! She has not even had a funeral! I am becoming a little upset. Lottie tries to explain how things were handled.

The day after Lottie discovered Minnie's body, all her friends and her children were invited round to Lottie's for a Jewish ritual called Sitting Shivah. Minnie was not Jewish. None of us are Jewish. I am finding it hard to get my mind around what has gone on. Lottie attempts to explain some of the rules of the ritual to me, but they are complex and seem arbitrary, and I cannot take it all in. It seems that though Minnie was not Jewish, most of her friends *are*, and in the absence of anything else, they Sat Shivah for her. I need to be able to tell my mum that Minnie's death was treated with respect and that the right thing was done by her. I have only English Christian traditions to fall back on. I am uneasy. On the one hand, it is preposterous to suppose that Lottie and Minnie's friends treated Minnie's death with anything other than great sadness and respect. On the other, I feel I am searching vainly for a missing funeral.

"Does Sitting Shivah count as a funeral?"

"Not really. We also have a funeral service when the person's body is buried."

"So, Minnie has not had a funeral at all then!?"

"There was the Sitting Shivah, but in the Jewish tradition, we do not cremate. We bury. If Minnie had been buried, she would have had a Jewish funeral service." I try another tack.

"What are you going to do with the ashes?"

"We thought we would place them under a bench either in the garden of the French department or along Minnie's favourite walk down by the marina."

"I guess that's ok. You knew Minnie better than me. Do you think she would have liked that?"

"Yes. I think she would. We will put a brass plaque on the bench commemorating her life. It will give her kids somewhere to go to remember their mom."

"And there's the memorial tomorrow."

"Yes. We are expecting over a hundred people to come, friends from Berkeley and all over the country, colleagues from the French department and other institutions that Minnie worked with." I am beginning to feel a bit better.

The day of the memorial service is organised chaos. The venue has to be prepared, the order of events finalised and printed, and the catered food set out. People begin to arrive. Women outnumber men by a ratio of about 7:1, predominantly lesbian. Women I don't know approach me with sombre faces and sympathise with my loss. They say how they knew Minnie, what a wonderful person she was, and how sorely she will be missed. I feel the loss of Minnie, too, intensely, particularly today, particularly now.

The service starts with a slideshow presentation of photographs of Minnie as a little girl in Africa, a young author in her early twenties, as an anthropologist and linguist in India, as a college professor and more recently, as a mother.

Minnie's children stand and say their piece about their mom and how much they miss her. Then I speak. A glib, artfully amusing recounting of her childhood foibles and childish scrapes. I move on to her life in apparent exile in Berkley, acknowledge her wonderful circle of friends and colleagues and conclude by thanking the gathered mourners for the love and support they showed Minnie during her life. The full sadness of the occasion hits me. I have lost my sister. I shall never see her again, never hear her voice. My voice cracks. I cannot complete my oration. I rush to my seat and the comfort of Minnie's friends.

Others stand up to speak. More people I have never met. They speak fondly of Minnie, eloquently, full of feeling. She is admired, loved, and appreciated as an accomplished author, a well-known linguist, and a brilliant and caring professor. I learn more about my sister in the following two hours than I have ever known before.

The memorial comes to an end. A group of Minnie's closest friends come back to Lottie's place. We eat, drink and chat and tell funny stories about her. We laugh. We are happy and sad. Someone suggests we go out to a bar. We have all had a few drinks by now. Seems like a brilliant idea.

Cars are ordered. We set off in convoy to the Stork Club in Oakland. The bar is full of dykes when we arrive. The venue is part of the annual 'Girlstock' lesbian festival. A troupe of very young women, barely out of school, are belly dancing on the small stage. I am amused by my own conflicted feelings – they are very sexy and very young. I can't help wondering if their mothers know what they are doing and worry that they will catch their death of cold.

The lesbians in the crowd have no such scruples. They hoot and catcall energetically. I am out of my depth.

The belly dancers are followed by an incongruous and woefully out-of-place heavy metal band screaming of death and blood and hell. After that comes the main band. A brilliant lesbian country music band, knocking out bluegrass and contemporary songs with gay abandon. I am having a great time. These women are a lot of fun to be with. We are all quite drunk. I miss Minnie. I wish she were here with us.

Next day I fly back to Australia. I have spent a total of three days in the United States. I have lots to tell the family. They can be reassured. They can be at peace. Minnie had many warm and loving friends. They did right by her.

Lauren will be waiting at the airport. I'm going home.

www.ingramcontent.com/pod-product-compliance
Lightning Source LLC
Chambersburg PA
CBHW021418110726
47901CB00008B/2213